Bound by Prophecy

Book three in the Bound Series

Stormy Smith

Cover design by Toni Sarcone
Editing by Monica Black of Word Nerd Editing
Formatted by Allyson Gottlieb of Athena Interior Book Design

For more information about this book and the author, visit
www.stormysmith.com

For every person who has chased their dreams,
this is proof you can catch them.

to leave this place. "I want to stay here forever," I murmured as he continued.

Abruptly, Aidan pulled back. His hair pointed in all directions and his breathing was ragged, but compassion filled his eyes. "You know we can't stay here forever, Amelia," he said softly as he touched his forehead to mine. "This is everything I've wanted, but there's more at stake here than just us."

I released my ankles and slid down his body. As I stepped back, Aidan grasped my hand, maintaining our connection. I felt stronger for having it, but I already missed his closeness.

"Amelia, talk to me," he said, pleading and demanding all at once in the way only Aidan could. I couldn't refuse him.

"I remember the last few days like they were a dream," I started. "More like a nightmare, really. A place I've been that seemed too real at the time but so far away now." I paused and looked out into the trees.

"Look at me." This time, it was a demand.

I turned and his blazing blue eyes caught me off guard. "I will protect you, Amelia. I will stop it from hurting you."

"But how, Aidan? Do you even know how? Right here, right now, I'm safe. I don't know what this place is or how we found it, but this is the only place she isn't torturing me trying to get to you. They were right, Aidan. We are the subjects of the prophecy. Something inside us is drawn to each other and the Keeper understands how to unlock the power we have. If she succeeds, if we can't stop her and figure out how to use whatever this is for good, I will lose myself to her. And you don't understand who I become when she is in control. I don't want you to ever see that," I finished, turning away from him. I took a few steps, but couldn't keep going.

Dropping to sit on the ground, I brought my legs into my chest and wrapped my arms around them. Since Cresthaven, I had been huddled in that same ball in one form or another, but Aidan wouldn't have it. He sat beside me and pulled me onto his lap, my back against his chest and his mouth next to my ear.

"What I have seen is you using her power for more good than anyone has ever known. You freed those women, Amelia. We got them out—all of them. And one was reunited with her son. Elias and Nell are together again. More families will be together as the rest of the pack gets here. The Keeper needs to be controlled, I agree, but you are stronger than you think. What Cole did for you…"

I had started to smile, his words the reassurance I needed, but when Aidan's voice gave out, fear tightened every muscle in my body.

"What? What is it?" I asked. I tried to turn, but I was lifted and set on my feet. It was one swift motion human Aidan could have never pulled off, but AniMage Aidan acted like I weighed nothing at all.

"That's it! Amelia, that's how we're going to do it!" Aidan paced, clearly still reasoning through his revelation while glancing at me excitedly every few seconds. "Yes. Cole is the key. He helped you handle her, right?" He gnawed on his bottom lip as he stared at me for confirmation.

I stood there, confused and clueless. "Yes, he did, but, Aidan, she's too much. And I got to a point where I couldn't control how much I took from him. I don't want to hurt my brother. He and my father are all I have left." The instant the words were out of my mouth, I felt dread whip through him and knew something was wrong. His elation dropped to a crushing pain I didn't want to feel, even secondhand. Aidan's mouth flattened into a thin line and his jaw tensed.

"Tell me," I demanded, steeling myself. The emotion around Aidan only grew darker.

He stepped in front of me and tried to take my hand, but I recoiled. "No, just tell me. You aren't my crutch, Aidan. I have to stand on my own and start handling my life."

His head jerked to the side in obvious disagreement and he gripped my hand anyway. "You don't need a crutch, but you do need to know you aren't alone."

He paused and the hesitation drove my anxiety higher. Then, he spoke quickly and calmly. "Your father was killed in a fight with Rhi at Cresthaven. We were trying to get you out after the Keeper took over. I was holding you in my arms when Rhi came for us and Nathaniel tried to talk to him, but Rhi was so angry. He came at us, so they fought. We thought your father killed him, but Rhi faked his injury to get Nathaniel closer and caught him off guard."

I closed my eyes as the scene Aidan described played behind my lids.

"Your father was protecting you, Amelia. He died a hero—saving you and the rest of us. If he hadn't injured Rhi, there was no way any of us would have gotten out."

His words sliced through me, but I remained standing, my body frozen in shock. My hand itched to rub the soreness in my chest, to comfort the ache building. I never got to tell him I was sorry, or that I understood why he made the choices he had. I never told him I knew he loved me and I loved him as well, now more than ever. I never heard his stories of my mother, or what their lives were like before Queen Julia took over and our world collapsed.

A vision of Rhi invaded my thoughts. His fiery eyes and twisted lips as he sneered at me, always gloating. First, he took my mother, and now, my father. Anger overtook my grief in one sweeping wave.

"We have to find Rhi. I want him. I want to end him in the longest, slowest, most painful way possible. I need out of here. We need to find him," I hissed out past my teeth, clenching my jaw tightly.

He tried to pull me to him, but I refused, too angry to be tamed. I paced back and forth in front of Aidan while he stood still, his eyes following my movements.

I couldn't connect the dots. I couldn't reconcile that my father was gone. I couldn't stop the pain exploding in my chest or the tears pouring steadily down my cheeks into the dirt beneath my feet. I only just got my father back and now he was gone. Just another person Julia and her desperate need for power took from me. Cole was all I had left.

"Where is Cole? I need to get to him. He can't go through this alone. He knew Dad wasn't who we thought he was before I did. He was reestablishing their relationship. You have to take me to him!" The words came out as one sob-wrecked mess as I balled Aidan's sweater in my fists, clutching his chest.

"He's at Derreck's, just like everyone else." Aidan pulled me into his chest as I continued to cry. His arms wrapped around me and his power layered over mine, an attempt to calm the inferno of emotions I couldn't contain.

"Tell me about them," I said into his chest. "Tell me about everything there and what's happening. I just...I just need you to talk to me." It was a plea. It was me begging for distraction, anything to focus on outside of my own pain. The father I had known was selfish, delusional, and devoid of love. But that wasn't him at all, and I never got to know the real man beneath Rhi's binds. Now, I would never know him. I needed a reason not to run back into the depths of my own head where I'd been hiding from the Keeper. I needed a reason to fight.

"Tell me about your idea. Tell me how you're going to get her out of me."

Chapter 2
Aidan

One hand slid under Amelia's hair to her neck, slowly massaging the base of her skull as I tried to get her to release her rigid stance. I made my breaths a little deeper and louder, encouraging her to breathe with me and slow the quick, sharp intakes that would lead her to a panic attack.

It was strange to feel her power alone. Previously, I always felt the taint of the Keeper inside and around Amelia. Now, the bright pulsing violet light emanating from her core and filling the space around her was breathtaking. Her signature purple smoke wafted in the air around us, heaviest near her palms but spiraling up like the trail of smoke from a cigar on a still night, billowing outward in patterns I couldn't describe.

Neither of us understood why the Keeper couldn't find us here, but I was still hesitant, and kept my power restrained. The air was charged around us, our power constantly reaching for each other. So I allowed the blue and violet smoke to intermingle, but not in the way my power wanted. My wolf howled in my mind, demanding dominance and a closeness between us I knew Amelia wasn't prepared for.

"Aidan?" My name, coming from those lips, said in a way only she could, drew me out of my own head. She tipped her head up as I looked down and I couldn't stop myself from brushing my lips over hers. It was only a quick kiss, but I needed it. She had come and gone from my life more times than I wanted to think about, but there were no more half-truths between us, not anymore.

"It isn't a perfect plan, it isn't even a full plan, but I do think I know where we need to start," I said. I slowly pulled away from Amelia and took stock. She wasn't crying anymore, and while I could feel her internal battle, she was calm. I pulled her toward a large log and we sat facing each other, both of us straddling the fallen tree.

I couldn't let go of her hands or miss a moment of contact. The electric current of power bounced between us and the pinpricks of heat I felt everywhere she touched were becoming necessities. The wolf continued to howl inside my mind and a growl built in the back of my throat. No one would take her from me again.

Amelia must have sensed my emotional spike. She gripped my fingers tighter, and said, "I'm not going anywhere. It's you and me, Aidan. We're in this together. Talk to me. Tell me how I can just be me again. I want to see my brother, Bethany, and the women. I want to make sure the people who matter to me are okay. I was wrong. We can't stay here. I have to get out." Her gaze was so focused, so intent, I couldn't look away.

"With Cole's help, I think you can temper the Keeper and Baleon can place binds in you to restrain her. We just have to keep her distracted for long enough." I paused, then leaned in, looking Amelia directly in her eyes.

"I need more time to handle the details, but once we have her bound, then we can find a way to fulfill the prophecy. I don't know what it is yet, and I won't lie to you, or sugar coat it. But, I know I can at least get you back to yourself so that we can figure it out." I stopped talking and waited for her reaction. She had always wanted instant action and I asked for patience.

But this Amelia was not the same girl who left me only a few weeks ago. She was less impulsive and more thoughtful. Her eyebrows pulled together and her conflicted emotions clouded my mind. Her shoulders suddenly lifted and dropped back down as she shook her head back and forth in a short snap, as if needing to clear her mind before she spoke.

"Yes, let's do it. I have to do something, and I believe, together, we can beat her," she said, nodding. "The only thing I'm worried about now is how long it will take. I don't know what she will do to me when I'm back, or if she even knows I'm gone. All I know is she is relentless in trying to get to you. You have to stay as far from all this as you can. Get Bale to do it. Make Micah help. I don't care. But you have to stay back."

Her grip on my hands increased. She smashed my fingers together and pulled me toward her. I felt her anxiety and her need to be close to me. She rose up off the log to meet me in the middle. She settled into my lap, her arms around my neck. We hadn't disconnected for even a moment.

I grasped her hips and realized again this wasn't a dream. She was actually here. We kissed, inhaling and exhaling the same air, recycling the heat between us as our tongues circled and we pulled each other closer. I needed her. Maybe this was part of the prophecy, but my soul called for hers. My wolf howled, a longing sound I'd never heard, and it was all for her.

I put my palms on Amelia's cheeks and pulled back a millimeter, pressing my forehead to hers. "We've made it this far. You can do it, doll. Give me a day and I'll be back for you. Okay?"

She nodded against me. "I'll be here. And I'll be ready. Do you have to go now? So soon?" she asked, but by her tone, she already knew the answer, and she knew it was the right one.

"If I don't go now, I might never go, and what use would either of us be?" I flashed a smile and for the first time, I saw a light in her eyes I hadn't known I'd missed. "There's a lot you need to be caught up on, but I think it would be better to do in person. I know B is dying to see you, and Charlie hasn't left your side since we've been home."

Her eyebrow rose. "B?" she asked.

"Long story. One you'll love when she tells you. But, yeah, she's B to me, too. You picked a good one." I stood and held out a hand, pulling Amelia up to full height.

"I should have known she would stick around for all this," she said, shaking her head and smiling as we walked across the clearing.

I pulled Amelia into my side. "It's good to see you smile," I said quietly. We walked for a few more feet, until we hit the tree line.

Amelia turned to face me, that smile still tugging at her lips as she said, "You give me a reason to smile, Montgomery. Just go while I can still let you, and bring the whole damn army back with you."

I yanked her quickly to me for a kiss that started out as smashed lips and ended in one last tango of breath. I felt her need and it matched my own. It was the reassurance I craved. I had to know whatever she stirred in me wasn't mine alone. Finally, I kissed her forehead and darted out into the trees.

Chapter 3
Amelia

The second Aidan left me and the forest faded, she was back. The Keeper stalked through my system, agitated I'd found a way to get to Aidan. I had learned there was nowhere I could hide, but my little ball of violet light looked for any nook or crevice to bury itself in.

Something had changed while I helped the women in Julia's breeding center. The Keeper and I had a tenuous relationship before that moment, one where I could sometimes control us, but most often she rose to the surface when I needed her most. Only for the brief stint of having my mother's cuff was I able to make some progress toward working with the Keeper. The cuff allowed me to keep the Elder entities separate and merge them into my own power. It was the first time I had felt the significance of the varying powers of our people and their specific uses.

But, as I had pulled at Cole's power to give the Keeper more freedom to help save the women, I knew I could never take that control back. The barriers that held her were gone, and I was trapped inside myself. I was shocked she hadn't found a way to force me awake to do her bidding, but so far, I was able to keep my body shut down as she howled at me.

The Keeper didn't speak to me, per se. Her words were wailing echoes, causing the constraints of my physical body to be a cramped closet. She raged and screamed, her anger and determination to get to Aidan radiating through and around me. I heard her intent as clearly as words spoken in my ear. She knew he was the key. She needed him. *We needed him.*

She used her power, *our power*, to poke and prod at me. She lashed out and the scalding burn where our magic collided was another scar no one would see. She knew he couldn't bear my pain, and she used it to bring him back.

My body was tired and my power depleted. Exhaustion beat on my door and I wasn't sure I had much to contribute to a binding of the Keeper. I knew it had to happen, though. I couldn't take much more.

I prayed the whimpers I bit back from the depths of my subconscious didn't manifest themselves audibly. Coming back from the forest, my mind was clearer and my will was stronger. Being with Aidan had given me the strength I needed to face her. I had to stop running from her. I had to stop running from the reality of who I was.

Chapter 4
Aidan

I woke up lying across the bed, one hand bunched in the dark brown comforter and the other on Amelia's hip. She was whimpering softly, and I suspected the Keeper was somehow punishing her for our tricks.

I sat up and stared down at Amelia. Her eyebrows were pulled together, her eyes tightly closed. I softly brushed my thumb over each brow and was relieved to see the muscles around her eyes relax.

I pushed her hair away from her face, tucking it behind her ear as I'd watched her do a hundred times. My quest to find Amelia had shown me the truth. She brought out the best in me. Simply the idea of her forced the good parts of me to the surface, dissolving my default defensive and untrusting behaviors.

The sun sliced through the window and I finally saw what should have been obvious. Her skin was pale and she was even smaller than I remembered. I ran my hands lightly over her ribs and too easily felt the bones. The dip of her waist was too pronounced and her hipbones jutted into the denim of her jeans.

"There is always a cost associated with the energy we expend. She needs to be replenished. She cannot recover from this alone." Baleon voiced the concerns running through my mind. I turned to find him filling the doorway. His mammoth build covered in black leather, head shaved, and tattoos inked black against his brown skin, it was intimidating to see him up close. On the floor at the end of the bed, never far from Amelia, Charlie scrambled to his feet. He didn't growl, but he eyed Baleon with what looked to be the same skepticism I had.

Baleon didn't look away from me. He stood still and waited for the invitation to enter. I hesitated, but Amelia let out a sharp cry as she turned onto her side and curled into the fetal position.

"Whatever she needs, please, give it to her," I said, her pain and my lack of attention to what her physical body endured gnawing at my insides. I was so focused on what the magic was doing to her spirit, I had missed the obvious.

Baleon didn't make a sound, even as his heavy leather boots trekked over the wood floors. He stopped on Amelia's side of the bed.

"You need to leave," he said, his eyes on her.

"Absolutely not," I argued. "I won't leave her here with you alone."

Baleon flicked his simmering orange eyes up at me, an inferno of color holding as much threat as promise. I didn't question their validity, but I would fight to the death before I left her vulnerable. I still wasn't entirely certain I could trust this Hunter. "I have betrayed my race and my queen. I have given up more than you can imagine, because I believe she is the one. I will not harm your mate. Leave him if you want security, but you cannot be here." Baleon gestured to Charlie and the Dane sat at attention.

"Why?" I challenged, putting one hand on Amelia's side, prepared to quickly pull her to me.

Baleon showed the smallest smirk before he spoke. "The power inside her is vast and unpredictable. I do not know how either of them will react to my presence, but once I begin, it is more dangerous for me to stop than continue. You cannot interfere; therefore, you cannot be here," he finished.

I kept my eyes locked on his as I leaned down and whispered in her ear. "I won't be far. I promised to get you out of there and I will. We will come for you soon, doll." I raised to my full height, my gaze moving from Baleon to Charlie.

"Stay, Charlie," I commanded. He sat facing Baleon, white and black ears pricked, clearly poised to move if necessary.

"How long?" I asked.

"As long as she needs. I must circumvent the Keeper, feed her soul, and replenish her body, all without being taken hold of. I will find you, and if I cannot, he will," he said, kneeling beside the bed and gently turning Amelia to her back. He placed one hand on her chest above her heart and the other across her brow. Then, Baleon turned to me, his impatience clear.

I clenched my fists against the howling wolf in my mind and left, pulling the door closed behind me. Striding down the hall and out the back door, I ignored the various people speaking to me. I knew exactly who I needed to find and what I needed to know.

Derreck's massive green barn had been converted into a makeshift dorm for the women freed from the terror experiments where Queen Julia tried to force magic back into the children being born to Immortals. The barn was meant for horses and the stalls were already in place, but, lucky for us, Derreck hadn't gotten around to buying the horses yet. So everything was clean and it was easy to give each woman a little privacy and their own bed.

In those first few days at Derreck's, I rarely left Amelia's side unless Bethany or Elias forced me to take a break. Rynna had taken charge of the women, along with Dillon's mom, Cora, and I had left it to them. One day, I came out to find a half dozen women standing in a row with piles of stuffing, sheets, and sewing supplies in front of them. Not one of them physically touched a thing, but they all stood, arms swirling while they spoke softly, and the mattresses stitched themselves together. It took me a minute to shut my gaping mouth and attempt to walk past looking unfazed. There were still women bound by the Queen's Hunters, which was something I needed to focus on soon, but I could only handle one thing at a time.

Now, as I cut across the yard toward the barn, the sight of various women and the smattering of AniMages that arrived after Cresthaven were comforting. We directed the AniMages in Brighton to leave in small packs, making their journey less conspicuous while gathering our people in one place. The last group would arrive any day, and while I wasn't looking forward to Melinda and Braxton rejoining the group, I wouldn't turn them away.

As I walked down the row of stalls, small groups of pregnant women stopped talking and smiled at me. I knew some were AniMage, made obvious by their small bows, a sign of respect that still made their King uncomfortable. I wanted to shake my head and tell them I was the last person they should be bowing to, but I had to be the person they thought I was.

"Fake it till you make it," Bethany had said to me during one of our conversations. Apparently, she'd been doing it for years, and she promised the confidence you pretended to have would finally show up at one point. So, I kept faking it, returning their gesture.

Walking down the corridor toward the last stall on the right side, where I knew I'd find Elias, I smiled at the flowers in the stalls and the small name plates on the doors. Colorful sheets were tucked around the mattresses and books were stacked in the corners. While the barn smelled of hay and dirt, it was clear the women were making it their own. After all they had been through, I was glad to see it.

When I reached Nell's stall, the door was closed. There was an opening I could have looked through, but a sheet hung over it, so I knocked. Elias cracked the door open and seeing me, stepped through. He looked terrible. His red hair was both matted down and sticking up in multiple directions. He looked like he hadn't showered in days, his button-down covered in dirt and sliced open in a few places. I gestured away from the stall and he nodded slowly, the movement taking him longer than it should have.

"How is she, Elias? Is it almost time?" I asked quietly, inquiring about his wife. Nell was still in her cheetah form, and would stay that way until her babies were born.

He rubbed a hand across his eyes, pinched the bridge of his nose, and then ran a hand through his hair. "By God, I hope so. She's hurting and it doesn't seem like things are progressing. I can't help her while I'm shifted, so I'm staying human, but that seems to agitate her. As you can see." He pulled at his shirt and shook his head.

"Can the other women help? Maybe you should let them be a part of this?" I had no clue if my advice bore weight, but it seemed logical.

He sighed. "I plan to. Cora is the only one Nell will let close, but she's also trying to help with all the other women, so I try not to bother her constantly." Elias paused, and I hurt for my friend. I knew how it felt when the person you loved was in pain while you remained helpless. It was absolutely debilitating. It was why I had come to him.

"I apologize for changing the subject, but I need your advice," I said. He opened his eyes wide and gave his cheeks a light smack. "Alright, I'm ready. What do you need?" We both chuckled a little.

"Do you trust Baleon, the Hunter who came with Micah?" I asked.

Elias leaned back against the wall and looked at me thoughtfully. "I'll need a little more than that to give you a good answer, Aidan."

"I just left Amelia alone with him. I was so focused on just getting to her and getting the Keeper out, I hadn't even thought to be worried that she wasn't eating, or what her body had been through at Cresthaven. And now, it sounds like I'm going to need him to bind the Keeper. I have to ask a Hunter to do the very same thing that was done to me, that was done to her father…" I trailed off, my eyes focused on nothing as I silently berated myself again.

"Hey," Elias said sharply, pulling me back to the present, "we all make choices. We make the best choices we can in the moments we're forced to make them. Right now, that Hunter is the only hope you have of getting her back completely, that's what you're saying, right?"

"It is," I responded.

"Then, it doesn't sound like there's a choice at all. You'll do what needs to be done because that is your duty to us and to her." Elias spoke with such authority, I instantly reacted, standing straighter and nodding as the words repeated in my mind.

I reached my hand out and when Elias took it, pulled him in for a half-hug. "If you need anything, come to me. I will do whatever I can for both of you."

"I know you will, Aidan," he said. "It's what makes you a good King. You've maintained yourself well through all of this. Your father would be proud."

His words stopped me and froze the smile on my face. No one had ever told me they were proud of me, except my caseworker when I told him I got into Brighton's community college. I pictured the balding man in his sweater vest as he shook my hand and told me he knew I was headed in the right direction. If only he knew where that decision had led me.

When I snapped back to reality, Elias was already slipping back into Nell's room.

Chapter 5
Aidan

I stepped out into the sunlight, squinting as my eyes re-adjusted. I hadn't seen Baleon or been overrun by Charlie, so I assumed things were going well. I looked toward the house and had to force myself to walk in the other direction. I didn't get more than a few feet before Bethany was at my side and then, in my face.

"What in the ever-loving-hell are you doing letting him stay here? I know that lumbering oaf with him is a Hunter and you let them both waltz in here and make themselves at freaking home. He is—" I put one hand up and narrowed my eyes. It had the intended effect. Bethany stopped talking, slamming her mouth closed and returning a glare of her own. I hadn't meant mine, but she surely meant hers.

"It's my fault because I haven't had a chance to talk to you." Her eyebrow raised but I ignored it and gestured to a picnic table in the yard. There were people everywhere, women in small clusters, Rynna and Derreck talking by the back door, and Dillon running around, burning off his endless supply of energy.

"I know you want to hate him, B, but just hear me out. He saved Amelia. He saved me. If he hadn't been there, none of us would have come out alive. He fought at our side and risked the wrath of one of the most demented people I have ever seen. His mother…he betrayed his own mother. Micah fights for us. And so does his Hunter." I may have added that last bit in as much for me as for her, but I had to believe it.

I stayed silent and watched her as the words sunk in. Her face gradually relaxed and the heartache I expected replaced her anger.

"You're sure?" she asked, leaning in and cocking her head.

"Absolutely," I answered. "I know this for a fact. He fought alongside us and stayed down in that death trap to get the women out. He stayed behind to make sure we could get away. I haven't even had time to thank him yet, or to find out the details. I've been too wrapped up in getting to Amelia and figuring out how to bind the Keeper. But I got to her, Bethany. She's coming back to us." I needed her to focus there and the light in her eyes confirmed I hit the mark.

"What did she say? How is she? How are you bringing her back?" The questions she rifled off were accompanied by excitement clear in her posture and the high pitch of her voice.

I considered how much to share with Bethany. The words weren't mine to give and Amelia deserved to tell her friend what she wanted to.

"She is as good as she can be and ready to get back to herself. But, I need help to bind the Keeper and I also need to get Cole out of his room. He hasn't spoken to me since we got here and I can't do this without him." I dropped my head into my right hand and pulled at the roots of my hair. Cole hadn't come out of his room and I knew he hadn't forgiven me for what happened to his father. It wasn't actually my fault, but he needed someone to blame and I wasn't going to take that from him.

"I can help, he'll listen to me," Bethany said.

I looked up at her, confused. "Since when are you and Cole buddies?" I asked.

She shrugged and shimmied a bit to sit taller in her seat. "There are too many of you here and I needed to get away from *him*, so I went to Cole's room and we've been talking. Mostly about nothing, because the poor guy's daddy just died and I'm surely not gonna push him on life plans or expect him to cry on my shoulder, but we talk. And I'm the only one he will let in his room besides Onyx."

I hadn't realized Charlie's brother hadn't been around much, but clearly Onyx had his role. He seemed to be as vigilant over Cole as Charlie was over Amelia, and I appreciated that.

"Thank you for the offer, but I don't have time for you to do your magic southern thing and convince him without him knowing you did," I said as she smirked.

I gestured Bethany toward me and spoke quietly. "To get Amelia back, we have to bind the Keeper in the same way the Hunters have bound so many of us. And to do that, we need the Keeper to be weaker—tamed, if you will. The only person I know who can do that is Cole. I can't even be a part of this because the Keeper can pull my power out of me. In Cresthaven, it took what I was trying to give Amelia and made itself stronger." I stopped talking, the idea that I was the reason Amelia was being held captive in her own mind and body becoming too much.

"Well, that must have been just a peachy experience." Bethany's sarcasm was actually welcome. I choked on the mixture of emotion and laughter. As I recovered, I looked up to find a half smile looking back at me and gave her a quick nod of thanks.

"I'll let you get to it, but I know Cole will come around, Aidan. Amelia is all he has left and she hasn't even had the chance to grieve. If he won't help her, then what was all this for?" Bethany stood up and turned, stilling when I spoke again.

"I think Micah may be here to stay, B. I know you don't love that, but we need him and his Hunter." I watched her back stiffen and then relax.

As she walked away, Bethany tossed over her shoulder, "Here or not, he's on my shit list and he's not coming off anytime soon."

Chapter 6
Amelia

He was gone. I knew Aidan had left the room because she disappeared, leaving me to go wreak havoc on some other part of my physical body. She painted my veins and arteries with her dark brush of power, a stain in my blood branding my body from the inside out. I'd grown used to the constant pain; it was a low burn that cramped my muscles but gave me time to breathe—to regroup and attempt patience.

The touch was light, a feather gently teasing my skin. I immediately assumed Aidan, but a light orange haze only broken by swirling eyes shimmered in front of me. He never fully took shape, but Baleon's soft voice was a whisper in my mind.

"Quiet now. Don't speak to me or react in any way. I am here to heal, to feed your body and soul. But this will be a game of cat and mouse, and I am not typically the mouse. I must keep moving and discreetly do what I can. I will stay as long as I can. I will give you what you need."

I barely moved my head in acknowledgement. Bale and I had slowly started to build a relationship at Cresthaven. I wouldn't call it a friendship, but he protected me from Rhi and made me feel less alone. Even now, his presence gave me even more hope that Aidan was right. We would bind her. I would come back to him and myself.

A slow trickle of warmth seeped through my system. Similar to a warm meal on a cold night, I felt replenished and comfortable. I stopped a sigh before it left my lips and huddled farther back in the corner where Baleon found me.

Nothing would look out of the ordinary, but I was preparing for a war.

Chapter 7
Aidan

My last stop was Cole. I approached his door with a certain mixture of unease and determination. Baleon was still with Amelia. I snuck a look in her window to find him in the same position I'd left him in, except now a bright orange glow took up the space between his hand and her skin. I forced myself to move along and allow him to do what was best for her, satisfied I was doing the same.

I stood outside Cole's door, shifting my weight from foot to foot. Bethany offered to come with me, to bridge the gap, so to speak, but I knew she wasn't what we needed. If Cole needed persuading, it wasn't going to be with a big smile and some southern catchphrase. It was time to man up and get the job done. The words bounced around inside my head and were just as much for me as they might need to be for him.

I knocked three sharp raps on the dark-stained wood. The deep *thunk* was satisfying. He must have expected Bethany, which was exactly as I'd hoped, because he opened the door and then turned away, walking back across the room. I stepped through and let it stay open behind me. I stared at his back. The man I'd trained with, who I had even feared for a brief time before he knew about Amelia and me, looked like a shell of himself.

All the shades were closed, preventing even a speck of sunlight from entering his room. One small bedside lamp cast a low yellow glow throughout the room, giving me small hints at the mess that accumulated over the past few days. My nose did the rest. I smelled the dirty laundry, his unwashed body, and the food-crusted plates he'd piled on the small desk in the corner. This Cole was nothing like the regimented, controlled man I'd met in the gym.

"What do you want, Montgomery?" he asked, keeping his back to me.

"You can't hide in here forever, Cole. She needs you." I cut straight to it.

Cole whirled around and in seconds, had me pinned against the wall by my throat. His hold wasn't too tight, but the pads of his fingers and his thumb pressed against my windpipe as he eyed me from inches away.

"*She* needs me? *She* did this! This is *her* fault! Don't you get it? He sacrificed himself for *her*. Mom sacrificed herself for *her*. They gave me this godforsaken power *JUST FOR HER*. All these years, I thought I was making up for the fact that I had time with Mom and Dad and she didn't. Instead, I enabled her to do whatever damn thing she wanted so she could blame the prophecy, or being the one who had to protect us, or the one the Queen was after. I gave up my life and my relationship with my father…*and now he's gone.*"

His emotions were everywhere. His magic spiked and eroded in the most erratic ways. I stood still, barely breathing as I watched his chest heave and heard his voice break. Cole had borne the brunt of Amelia's fate and she had no idea.

I wanted to empathize with him. To gently take him from here to where I needed him to be, but there wasn't time. Cole's grip on my throat loosened and his hand dropped to his side. He stumbled backwards and dropped onto the bed. I wondered if he'd been drinking, but I couldn't feel anything impaired about him outside of his spastic magic.

"Cole," I started quietly, "I hear what you're saying, man, and it isn't fair. What you saw, what you had to do, none of it was right. But, Amelia didn't choose this. She didn't ask your parents for this power, or this prophecy. She was a baby and she didn't have a choice. She needed you. She needs you now. I was able to get to her, to talk to her. I told her about your father and you were the first person she asked for. She begged me to take her to you, Cole."

I slowly took a step toward him and Cole's head shot up, wide, bloodshot eyes connecting with mine. "Me? Why would she want me?" I saw fear. Straight, unadulterated fear. And that wasn't something I expected.

"No, Cole, she wanted you because she was worried about you. She knew you and Nathaniel had been mending fences and she wanted to be there for you." I put my hands out and tried to inch closer. He pulled away and I stopped.

"Then where is she, huh? Why isn't she here? Why is she hiding from it all, from facing what she did?" His voice carried, the deep timbre getting louder with every word. I wondered briefly how Bethany dealt with this side of him, or if she'd seen it.

I squatted down to eye level. "She's stuck, Cole. The Keeper has taken control and the only way Amelia can keep it from forcing her into doing things she doesn't want to do is to shut down. But, I know how to get her back—a way we can take the Keeper power down, give ourselves the chance to fulfill this prophecy, and get the revenge you want. Rhi did this, Cole. The Queen, she controls Rhi. You've got to help me get Amelia back so we can stop them. That's what the prophecy says, we will stop them, but only with your help." I was pleading with someone who I thought might be insane. Everything Cole Bradbury was had been broken and I had no idea what would resonate within this fragmented person in front of me.

"You need me to do it again, don't you?" His voice was small this time. Defeated.

"I do. Exactly what you did before. Can you do that, Cole?" I asked cautiously.

"You don't understand what it did to me. Amelia pulled and she pulled and she took something she didn't give back. Don't you see, Aidan? She can do that, she can take parts of you and *never give them back*. I don't know if I can do that again." He scrubbed both hands over his face and through his hair, wrapping his massive hands around the back of his neck.

"Was it Amelia or was it the Keeper, Cole?" I knew from experience the Keeper had her own pull. She had taken my power in gulps and almost drained me in seconds. I'd had to ask Cole to give to me the way he'd been giving to Amelia so I could get her out of Cresthaven. Suddenly, my demands felt like too much, like I contributed to where he was now.

Cole leaned in and dropped his elbows to his knees. "It was Amelia, Aidan. She knew exactly what she was doing. I could feel her in there and with every piece of me she pulled in, she sighed like someone was giving her a massage, not like she was sucking the life out of her brother."

I wanted to argue. I wanted to yell and pound him against the wall until he broke and told me he'd do whatever I wanted him to do. But, that wasn't right. No part of that was right. So, instead, I pled.

"Cole, without you, we can't save her. Without you, she'll stay buried deep inside herself until the Keeper finds a way to force her into compliance and she starts ripping everything to shreds. None of us know what the Keeper is fully capable of and I don't think any of us want to know," I said. "But if we can't get Amelia back and find the answers we need, it isn't just her who suffers. The rest of us…we're going to die. The Queen will send her Hunters for us and maybe it will be all at once, or maybe it will be one by one, but they will come and we will all die. We did something at Cresthaven we can't take back, Cole, and you were a part of that. The best hope you have is getting her through this and her fixing whatever she broke when you come out on the other side."

His eyes hadn't left mine during my speech. It was my last ditch effort and nothing but the truth. He dropped his head down into his hands and shook it back and forth. "Do you think she can fix me? Because I know this isn't me, Aidan, and I don't want to be this guy. So, really, tell me if you think whatever my sister has inside her can fix me." Cole's voice shook as he looked up at me. This time, he was the one pleading.

"I think she can," I said. *At least, I hope she can*, I thought to myself.

"Fine. Tell me what I have to do." Cole stood on shaky legs and faced me, the determination I was used to seeing only a shadow in his features. But, it was there, and that was all I could ask for.

I paced the hallway outside Amelia's door. It had been a few hours and I was close to busting the damn thing down when finally, Baleon emerged. He stopped in front of me, and said, "I have done as much as I can. The Keeper did not find me, though she understood there was something happening and was not pleased. Amelia will be stronger now, but first, she must rest." His lingering stare made his request clear.

I barely got a "Thank you," out before he was out the back door. Knowing he wanted me to leave Amelia alone, I followed him, intending to ask about the binding and if he would help. I yanked open the door to find myself face to face with Rynna and Derreck.

They stepped back, and I did what I should have done long before now. I held my hand out to Derreck and he looked questioningly between Baleon's back and me as he shook it.

"I haven't stopped to thank you for opening your home and land to us, Derreck," I said, avoiding the question he didn't ask. "It's long overdue and I apologize for that. I don't know where we would have gone otherwise."

He nodded and squeezed my hand a little harder. "It's the least I could do. These women have been through too much and my shields should hold for a while, keeping us protected and giving us time to make a better plan." Rynna smiled at me as she nodded along with Derreck.

"These are our people, Aidan. They need us. We see ourselves as Immortals, not as Mage or AniMage," she said. Her words lit a spark inside me. I couldn't do anything for Amelia yet—Baleon said she needed rest— but there was an entire group of Immortals here who needed to know where we stood and what was happening.

"I have a plan to help free Amelia from the Keeper, but it has to wait until tomorrow," I said. "In the interim, can you help me rally everyone together? They need an explanation, to know where we are, what we're doing here, and what the plan is. I don't want them to worry unnecessarily. If the shields will hold until we can truly make a plan and some of the women who are farther along can give birth, then we can decide where to go and what to do."

"Of course we can, Aidan," Rynna responded. "Derreck and I have kept our distance, but we've waited to hear from you about Amelia and how we can best introduce Mikail and Baleon to the rest of the group."

"My hope is we can talk to everyone before the rest of the pack gets here. The people already here are our best advocates, and if we can convince them Micah and Baleon are needed and on our side, and Amelia is coming back to us, I think they can help the others integrate better. Or, at least, stop them from causing too much drama." I thought of Melinda and Braxton and felt a headache starting. At the same moment, my wolf made himself known for the first time in a while. He made it clear a shift was necessary—and soon.

"How about right after dinner? We'll have everyone gather behind the house and you can use the deck as a stage." Derreck's plan sounded good to me. We agreed and I turned to leave.

"Aidan," Rynna said quietly.

I turned back. "Yes?"

"How is she? I've tried to see her, but Charlie won't let me through the door. I can feel her, though…" There were many emotions mixed into the words Rynna didn't say.

"I'm going to bring her back," I said. Fierce determination made the words sound more defensive than I'd intended, so I softened my tone. "I was able to get to her and she's ready to fight the Keeper. I have a plan. There are just more pieces I need in place before it can happen. Soon, though, she'll be back soon."

Rynna stepped forward and put her hand on my shoulder. I looked down at the small woman with the huge heart and felt some peace come over me.

"It sounds like you need all your wits about you," she said with a small smile. Apparently, Rynna's calm personality extended into her abilities, much like Cole's used to.

"I appreciate that," I said. "Do you know where Baleon has been hiding with Micah? I told them to find a spot for themselves, but have no idea where they ended up. He's my last stop before I figure out what I'm going to say to everyone."

Derreck pointed to the back of the house. "There's a walk out basement under the deck. It's kind of hidden and acts as its own apartment. I pointed them that way knowing it was fairly self-sufficient and would keep them out of sight for a while."

I thanked him and walked around the house, ducking under the deck and knocking lightly on the glass door. Baleon recognized me and I heard the click of the lock before he slid the door open.

"Prince Mikail is resting. Now is not the time." He spoke softly, but firmly, acting as if we hadn't just spoken to each other.

"I'm sorry, but I need to see him. Things are happening and he needs to be part of the discussion." I tried to take a step forward and found myself with a giant palm planted in my chest. My wolf immediately responded and a growl released from the back of my throat.

"Will you two stop all the posturing? I am right here, and, Bale, contrary to your beliefs, I am not dying and am perfectly capable of speaking. I would simply prefer to do it sitting down." Micah's voice cut through the tension between us.

"Oh, good gravy, Bale, sit down. Aidan, come in." As Baleon moved out of my sight line, Micah leaning against a small island in the kitchen came into view.

"Good gravy? Is that the way royals talk these days?" I smirked and Micah responded with an eye roll.

"She may hate me, but that doesn't mean I hate her. That infuriating woman is stuck in my head." He looked like himself, but the moment Micah tried to take a step, he faltered and Baleon was there to support him. I could tell the Hunter wanted to pick him up and put him somewhere, but Micah glared and Baleon grimaced while offering an arm for Micah to use as a crutch while he hobbled a few more feet to the couch.

I sat down in a black leather chair, across from the matching couch. "You look like hell," I said as I sat back and looked around. The apartment was small, but it had the same class as the rest of Derreck's place — all dark wood, granite, and leather. The log cabin exterior was a front for a guy who liked nice things.

Micah snorted. "And I feel like it. Bale has done all he can to speed the healing process, but my mother has always fought to win. The pain she inflicted was meant to linger and teach me a lesson."

"Your *mother* did this to you? I assumed it was the Hunters." I was shocked, but Micah only shrugged. "I thought I'd had it bad growing up, but I think you win. At least the parents who hated me weren't actually mine."

"It won't make any sense to you, but she actually did it to protect me," Micah said as I stared, disbelief written all over my face. "If I had kept fighting the Hunters, she would have had to allow them to fight back. She controlled them for as long as she could and it took almost everything she had to keep them from hurting me. She finally realized she was losing control and it was easier to stop me from attacking than to stop them from hurting me. The lasting injuries are my lesson to learn.

"As I went down," he continued, "the women and AniMages were escaping while Joran and Bale fended off the Hunters. After my mother sent her last attack at me, she lost consciousness and Rhi caught her. Joran continued to fight, and Rhi called the other Hunters to him to protect my mother, giving us enough time to escape through the library and into the maze."

"Is she okay?" I asked, out of respect, even though I hoped he would tell me she was dead. It would make everything a hell of a lot easier.

"She is my mother, which means I can feel her life force," Micah said. "It is weak, but she is still with us. Rhi will not allow her death. It would ruin his plans to validate his race and bring the Hunters to power. He still holds a misguided notion that my mother will make him King." Micah yanked his long hair back into a ponytail and for the first time, his voice shook as he spoke. "You should be concerned about retaliation, Aidan. Once she can, she'll send Hunters for all of us. We need to move."

I leaned in, my elbows on my knees. "I know. That's part of why I'm here. I'm having a meeting tonight and I'm going to explain to everyone where things stand and what will be happening over the next few days. Derreck tells me we're shielded from the Hunters for now, which is great, but there's more we need to do and that means I need a favor."

"Anything that doesn't require movement," Micah responded drily as he shifted in his seat, grimacing.

"Actually, it's from your Hunter." I glanced toward Baleon, standing directly behind Micah, and his eyes narrowed.

"Was what he did for Amelia not enough?" Micah asked.

"No, as far as I know, she's fine. Charlie hasn't come for me, so I assume she's asleep," I said.

He nodded. "Good, that's good to hear. Then what do you need?"

"There are three things actually," I started, "both the AniMages and Mages need to be comfortable with you and Baleon being here. Tonight, at the end of the meeting, I'd like to announce that the two of you will help remove the binds from the women Amelia didn't get to and that you'll be cataloging all of the power from those already here. We need to know what we're working with when Julia sends the Hunters for us. I'd also like Baleon's help tomorrow when we bind the Keeper power."

The two of them spoke at once, then stopped simultaneously. Baleon gestured for Micah to go ahead, which I assumed was typical.

"As far as the first request, Bale, is that an issue?" We both looked to the Hunter.

"No, Prince Mikail, that should not be a problem. It will only take time," he responded, his mouth in a tight line.

"Very good. I'll also handle the documentation you need. I agree they need to see me as an ally and not a threat. As far as the last item, Aidan, is this a wise plan? Do you know what you're doing, or better said, asking to be done?" Micah sounded wary, but not skeptical, which I appreciated.

"My theory is a Hunter who can break binds, can make them, and given Baleon's confirmation, he can indeed break binds, it seems only logical he can bind the Keeper inside Amelia. Cole will do exactly as he did in Cresthaven. He will feed Amelia the power she needs to restrain the Keeper and control it so Baleon can place the binds. Given what Baleon did today, I'm assuming Amelia will be able to play her part. Did I miss something?" I looked up at Baleon as his nostrils flared, refusing to blink until he responded.

"And what exactly will you be doing while Cole and I put ourselves in danger?" he asked.

This time, it was my turn to react. I clenched and unclenched my fists, knowing my anger was misplaced. I kept making plans to save the girl I loved, yet couldn't do any of the saving myself. It was damn infuriating.

"I have to stay away from her," I forced out. "In Cresthaven, I tried to help her, to feed Amelia's power, but the Keeper latched onto me and almost drained me dry. It made the Keeper stronger and I can't put Amelia in that kind of danger. So, I need your help." The knot in my stomach grew as the silence lingered.

"You will have what you need from both of us, Aidan. We know what this means, for everyone." Micah spoke with quiet determination, and it was reassuring.

I blew out my next breath slowly, bringing my blood pressure back down before saying, "Thank you. Thank you very much, both of you. As far as tonight is concerned, I want to start by introducing the two of you and have Cora share the story of your help. I need her to begin convincing them you are on our side and aren't going to betray us, especially Baleon. Then we can discuss the unbinding. Is there any way to remove that collar?"

Baleon smirked, his teeth a white slash against his brown skin as he wrapped both hands around the collar and yanked it apart. "This has been merely decoration for years," he said as he tossed it onto the counter with a clanging bang.

"Perception is reality and all they need to know is she can't get to you," I said as I stood. "Come outside after dinner as you hear people starting to gather. The right people will know what to do and once it's over, you won't have to hide from anyone, except maybe Bethany."

Micah chuckled as he shook his head. "Touché."

Chapter 8
Aidan

"Right now we are in a situation with many unknowns," I said, speaking to the Mages and AniMages who sat and stood in the grass behind Derreck's deck. I leaned on the railing, my arms spread wide as my fingers pressed into the red varnished wood. Bethany stood off to the side near Rynna, the lone human in the group, but she stood tall and I appreciated the nod of encouragement she gave.

"We've come here to seek refuge from the Queen and her Hunters, to help Amelia fulfill the prophecy, and to set all of us free. There are many strong women here who have suffered a great deal through their years with the Queen. We also have AniMages who have been running, trying to save their race, since before I was born. It isn't easy for any of us to be stuck in one place without everything and everyone we'd like, but I believe we all realize what is at stake if we're found."

I stopped and looked out at the crowd. The women Julia had held captive stood with hands protectively covering their bellies. The AniMages sat haphazardly in a pack on the grass and looked antsy, a feeling I understood all too well.

"There are two people here we have not discussed yet. Micah and Baleon, please join me." I turned back toward the house as Baleon opened the door. After receiving a glare from Micah, he pulled his arm back, allowing the Prince to make his way to the chair we'd set out. Baleon took his place, standing directly behind Micah.

Murmurs erupted in the crowd and a mix of fear and anger replaced the peaceful resolve from moments ago. "Before you react, please, hear me out," I said as I raised my hands, trying to quiet them down. "I know you saw these two arrive a few days ago. This is Prince Mikail and his guard, the Hunter, Baleon. They are on our side. They fight with us. But, I realize my words are not enough for you. Not all of you have access to me in the way my pack does and you can't know I am telling the truth. So, I'd like to have one of you share a story. Cora, can you please come up here?" She made her way to the deck and Dillon walked with her, hand in hand, until she mounted the stairs and stood next to Micah.

She waited for the quiet, a patient smile on her face. "Many of you were there the night we escaped Cresthaven, but some weren't. Even if you were, what Amelia did to save us and the chaos of what happened makes it hard to know exactly what you did and did not see. I was the first to be freed. I was one of the first to jump into the fray once our reinforcements arrived, and I saw who stood beside me. It was the Prince and his Hunter. We fought the other Hunters back to back. There was no question and no hesitation. I am AniMage. For as long as I can remember, I have hated the Queen and her Hunters. A Hunter killed my husband and I thought, my child. But, I am here and so is he. I am reunited with my beloved Dillon because of these two."

Cora let her words sink in before she continued.

"After Aidan was able to get Amelia to safety, the Prince stayed behind. He faced multiple Hunters and showed mercy, even while they aimed to kill him. He did not shoot to kill. He did not use his abilities to their fullest. He deflected, he injured, and he held the line so each of us could be saved. He and his Hunter fought their families for us. Look," she demanded, pointing to Baleon, who stared straight ahead, "the Hunter does not wear the Queen's collar. He is not influenced by her or under her power as the others are. And the Prince, he cares for a human and allows his heart to ache versus bringing her any more pain. How could a man so compassionate be so terrible? And why would a man like that bring a spy into our midst?"

We hadn't talked about that particular detail and as Cora's words echoed through the group, heads turned to Bethany, who was as white as a sheet, a look of panic widening her eyes as she stood frozen. I turned to find Micah opening and closing his mouth, clearly working to find some sort of rebuttal but not finding the words.

Cora held a satisfied smile I didn't fully appreciate until I looked back out into the crowd. I thought the story of Micah and Baleon's heroics would be what they needed to hear, but it seemed a conflicted heart was something they all understood better. Everyone's eyes bounced between Micah and Bethany before exchanging looks of commiseration and understanding. I didn't miss the looks of judgement as well. Bethany was still the lone human in a camp of Immortals and I constantly worried about her.

"Um, thank you, Cora, for your honesty," I said, stumbling over my own words. She nodded, and with a pat to my arm, rejoined Dillon at the bottom of the stairs. They took their seats and I continued.

"I know there are a group of you still bound from your ordeal at Cresthaven, which is another reason I asked Micah and Baleon to come tonight. They can help you, if you'll allow it. I have to believe you'd rather be able to defend yourselves and start to feel whole again. Please, let them help you," I said, watching for reactions. A few women brightened and a few looked terrified.

"The last of the AniMages will join us in the coming days, and they may not understand everything we have been through together," I continued. "I need your help to share our stories and ensure they are ready to embrace this new world, because we will fight together—all of us— Mages, AniMages, and Hunters. You all know Amelia Bradbury is here and she is the one who holds the power of the Elders inside her. She will be visible and fighting alongside us again as soon as she recovers from her ordeal at Cresthaven. There are still so many decisions to make, but there are a few things I know for sure." I started flicking my fingers in the air one-by-one as I counted them off.

"First, if you have not felt them, there are shields here and we are protected — at least, for now. We may call upon some of you to help enhance those, so anyone with that particular skill set, please see Derreck.

"Second, the AniMages are allowed to shift and run, but only within a quarter mile radius from the house. I know it isn't much, but I understand the need to be free and I feel the pull as much as each of you. If you stay in that zone, you will be protected by the shields.

"Third, Rynna and Cora will continue to care for those who are pregnant. There are a few mothers expecting soon and we need to make sure they have safe deliveries before we move to another location.

"And last, we will fight. We will find more of our people, we will assemble, and we will fight. But, we have to be smart about it, or we will all die. So, please, be patient, and bring me both your ideas and your concerns. I don't know what each of you are capable of, but Micah will be in charge of logging who you are and which abilities you have so we can best form groups and determine how to move forward. We all know this war has been coming for a long time. It is only now that we have hope on our side."

I took a slow breath and steeled myself before finishing with, "So, I ask you, are you with me? Are you willing to be patient, to help each other and those who will be joining us, and give me the time I need to find the right path? Our people have fought and lost for years. If we want to win a war against the Queen and her Hunters, I need each and every one of you!"

I got louder as I went, punctuating the last sentence with multiple slaps to the deck railing. I was relieved to hear cheers and clapping when I finished, and couldn't help but smile.

"I am going to lead a pack of AniMages out to run, because I need one myself. Everyone else, please see Derreck and Micah so we can begin to build our plan. Thank you." I quickly hopped down the steps and stopped in front of Bethany while I gestured my restless pack to the trees. She was still pale, standing in the same position, but now biting her lip. I slowly reached out to her and put my hand on her shoulder, which made her jump.

"Hey, B. How you doing?" I asked, realizing instantly it was a dumb question. A moment of strained silence followed.

"Cheese and freaking rice," she finally breathed out in a rush. "I don't even know what I'm still doing here, Aidan. I'm human. I'm useless. My best friend is comatose and I can't help her. Some woman who turns into who-knows-what just told me the guy who broke my heart—whom I've made it my mission to hate—still cares about me and I spend all my time trying to convince a bunch of women I'm worth their time. This is worse than high school. At least back then I was the cool one, not the one begging to be included. What am I doing? Why am I here?" She looked at me helplessly, her eyes filled with tears and her posture slumped. Nothing about this girl was the Bethany I knew.

I pulled her into a hug, and said, "I know. Trust me, I know the feeling. But, I need you. I need you to help keep me sane, and I'm going to need you when Amelia wakes up, because she's going to need you, too. And I can't do any of this without Cole. You are the link with the Bradburys, B, whether you want it or not. That Micah stuff, I don't know where that came from, and we can pretend it never happened if that's what you need. But don't abandon me out here with all these crazies. I might shift into a damn Pegasus and disappear." A muffled laugh came from the face buried in my chest before she pulled back, wiping under her eyes and sighing.

"Fine, Montgomery. I'll stay. For you and Ame. But hear me now, I don't care how he feels or what some psychic woo-woo AniMage says, I want nothing to do with him. Give me any assignment you want, but keep me on the other side of the yard." She stood with her fist on her jutted-out hip, her feistiness returning. This was the Bethany I needed.

"All right, Blondie, done. Can you help Rynna make the rounds and check on the women? And make sure you guys get Cora to spend time with Elias. I know he's worried about Nell and it would be great if she could figure out what to do for her."

Bethany was already walking away, her hand waving back at me. "On it, boss," she threw out.

I shook my head and then dove toward the trees, unable to hold back my wolf any longer. We needed to run, and I needed to think and prepare for what was coming. I had no idea what to expect, but I wouldn't accept anything less than Amelia back in my arms, where she belonged.

Chapter 9
Micah

He left me in this damn chair and sent them to me. Aidan took off and the next thing I saw was him hugging Bethany. My Bethany. The Bethany who hated me, wouldn't look at me, and would likely use the tip of her favorite rhinestone-encrusted stiletto to punch a hole in my chest before she'd laugh with me the way she was laughing with him.

I sighed as the first woman approached me and Baleon handed me a notepad and pen. Her blond hair was long and loose, and it looked too much like another blonde I didn't want to think about. I could tell she was nervous by the way she twisted her hands together repeatedly.

"Hello, I'm…Micah. It's nice to meet you." I did not want to be Prince Mikail to these people. I wanted to be one of them, to belong somewhere. I lifted my eyes to meet hers and brought forth a smile.

"Hello. I'm Willow. I'm a Mage and a healer." Her voice was so low, I thought I might be the only one to hear her. *A healer?* My face must have given away my question because she laughed, a soft melody that brought a smile to my face before I could stop it.

"Yes, I'm here. The only one here, actually," she said as she looked around at the empty deck. "Not because I wanted you to write down my name, but because I could see you needed me. I was there. I saw what you did for us with my own eyes. I'm one of the few who were not pregnant at the time and I fought as well as I could. I only wish I'd seen Amelia's father go down. I might have been able to help him. As it is, I consider it my duty to help you, if you'll let me." Willow spoke quickly, the words coming out in a rush as she continued to fidget.

I was silent a moment. She stood there simply because she wanted to heal me. There were few times in my life where someone had done something for me out of personal choice.

"I don't know exactly what my mother did to me. All I know is I was hit multiple times and the pain is merciless. Each time Baleon finds a way to stop the pain in one place, it materializes in another. If you can stop it, please do." Part of me wanted to move inside, but staying out here was a political move. It showed the others I was willing to be real in front of them. No one but Willow had approached me to follow Aidan's order of logging their abilities. I needed help in more ways than one.

Bale tried to object, but I quickly silenced him and motioned for Willow to proceed.

She squatted down in front of me and took my hands. It was a closeness I hadn't had since Bethany and I wasn't prepared for the feeling of soft, warm skin touching my own. I saw Willow's healing energy. It was the same green as Cole's power, but a grassier shade. I watched the smoke gather around our joined hands and it reminded me of the leaves in the maze behind the library—the deepest, brightest green, promising life.

"I feel what she's done and it's going to take more than I expected, but I think I can rid you of the spell. Brace yourself. This won't be pleasant." Even while her words should have concerned me, the melodic tone of her voice had lulled me into complacency, making me wonder if this was part of the healing process. Then, pain ripped through me.

I cried out as I heard her yell, "Hold him!" and felt large hands on my shoulders. As the next jolt of pain flared through my core, my eyes popped open and I watched as tears streamed down Willow's face. She held onto me with one hand while a steady flow of red power came from the other. The fire that flared throughout my body, singeing my blood and scalding me from the inside out, was now bursting from her palm.

Seeing her in action forced me to hold myself together and stop fighting the process. Bale's grip released marginally and eventually, Willow let go of my hand. She dropped to her knees in front of me, her breaths shallow as she folded forward, her palms flat against the deck.

I gestured for Baleon to help her. He crouched down and spoke in low tones to verify she was okay. He helped her stand as another woman mounted the stairs, coming toward us.

"I'm sorry, Prince Mikail, this is what happens when she goes through an intense healing. She will be fine. She just needs rest." The young woman tried to help Willow off the deck, but I held out a hand to stop her.

"No, please, stop. Allow Baleon to carry her to her quarters and assist with her rejuvenation."

Only once I was standing did I realize I felt one hundred percent like myself. Better than myself. I stepped to Baleon as he lifted Willow into his arms. She was already asleep, likely passed out from the exertion, as Amelia had done many times before. There was only so much power a body could take before it shut down out of self-preservation—especially one whose power had been withheld for so long. The women from my mother's labs weren't much different than Amelia when we first met in Brighton. The Keeper power was too much to handle. Her outbursts, her sporadic emotions…it all lined up with what these women were also going through as they acclimated.

"Stay with her for as long as she needs, Bale," I directed as I looked over his shoulder at the dispersing crowd. At least a dozen Immortals had watched Willow do her work. "Make sure she's okay and then find me so we can begin our work breaking the binds." He nodded and followed the women toward the barn. As I watched their progress, I realized the area where Willow had allowed Mother's spell to release was now a charred hole in Derreck's deck. That was what she'd placed inside her son.

Only my mother would believe there was a lesson to be learned from that.

With Baleon busy and Aidan gone, I was free to roam the area. Since Amelia and I had been at Cresthaven, I hadn't had a free moment when I wasn't shadowed by Bale, Amelia, or my mother's Hunters. It was freeing to have my thoughts and actions to myself, even for just a few minutes.

I thought about heading into the house to check on Amelia, but was afraid I'd run into Bethany since I'd seen her going that way only minutes before. My pride still stung from Cora's admission, but she wasn't wrong. Bethany was the only person who had ever known me as simply me. I missed her strange southern language, her silly analogies, and her laugh. There was a light inside her nothing could put out and it shined so brightly, I was drawn to her in ways I knew I shouldn't be. But, what's done was done, and her feelings were clear.

I didn't need magic to feel the anger and hurt she felt while near me. What she would never understand was I was only trying to keep her off my mother's radar. Had my mother realized Bethany meant anything at all to me, she surely would have taken action against her. I couldn't handle the possibility.

Rather than coming up against the storm of fury that was Bethany, I walked toward the barn. Aidan had given me the job of collecting the abilities of those around us, and he was right. We needed to understand who and what we were working with. What he didn't understand was not everyone wanted to disclose their individual abilities. Those were often a best-kept secret until the battles were fought and the element of surprise was yours.

I stepped into the dimly lit barn and allowed my eyes to adjust. There were people loitering in various groups, but all their chatter stopped when I entered. Trying to stay casual, I approached the first group. A young man and two women stood together. I stretched out my hand and introduced myself, as if I hadn't just been made a spectacle of and they didn't obviously know my name and title.

"Hello, I'm Micah. It's nice to meet you all." I spoke as they shook my hand, each of them seeming intrigued, yet hesitant. I looked toward the women as I continued, "I want to apologize for all you've been through. I know simple words are not enough, but the actions of my mother are not mine, and I had no idea what was happening beneath the stones of my own home. The barriers in place kept me from feeling any of you or realizing what you were going through. Please know I will do everything in my power to right this wrong and you should never hesitate to come to me." The two women looked at each other and then back at me. A tingling in the air suggested they were discussing who would respond.

The first woman to speak identified herself as Sully. She pushed her long black hair back as she squared her shoulders. "Thank you, your highness."

I interrupted her, touching her arm to allow her to feel the genuine emotion behind my words. "I am just Micah, and I am here to help all of you however I can."

Her blue eyes widened in surprise and then her lips curved upward. Sully was a beautiful woman, and her belly swelled in a way that made it obvious she was one of those who would give birth soon. "Okay then, just Micah, you should know that even before we were bound, we were also unable to feel anything outside the walls of our room, so I believe you. And I appreciate your thoughtfulness to come see us. It is…unexpected."

The AniMage who helped with the rescue, Eric, interrupted. "Do you honestly think we're safe here? You understand the Queen and the power she holds over the Hunters, can't she find us?" He stood with his arms crossed and his feet wide, making himself appear as large as possible. His posture clearly communicated that though he knew he wasn't a Prince, he was someone who believed he should be feared. The smaller woman crossed her arms as well, her face pinched in a way that made her wariness obvious as she stepped closer to Eric.

I stood still, but relaxed my posture and clasped my hands behind my back. It made me vulnerable, but it allowed him to understand I was not there to challenge. "I do believe we are safe here, for the time being. There are many decisions to be made, but there are also lives at risk. We cannot take the chance of women like Sully giving birth on the run. There are too few children born to our races right now. Others will join us soon and we will begin to build our strategy. The time will come when we will need to leave this place, but not yet. And, as far as the Queen is concerned," I continued, refusing to acknowledge my blood ties, "she was weakened in the attack and the Hunters are not free to leave Cresthaven without her allowing it. Until she is of sound mind, or she dies, they are locked there."

I hadn't admitted that fact to anyone yet, not even Aidan, but this felt like the time to do it. The others in the barn were listening, and my voice carried across the stalls and into the rafters. I had just shared a very valuable secret, had committed treason, and could not have felt more relieved to betray my family and my crown.

Chapter 10
Amelia

I felt them all standing around me, and she felt them, too. An AniMage, a Mage, a Hunter, and Charlie, whatever he was—distinct, powerful entities that held my fate in their hands. I didn't understand the specifics of the plan—there was no easy way for them to tell me beforehand—so I prayed Aidan stayed away like he'd promised.

She stalked through my system, immediately seeking me out. She knew I played a part in their presence. She knew I could stop them, but I wouldn't. No matter what happened today, I would not stop them. And so, for the first time since Cresthaven, I pushed back. Aidan gave me courage and Baleon gave me strength, so I fought against her, pushing my violet flame higher and higher, lighting up the darkness I normally hid behind. I shined as brightly as I could to remind her I controlled us. This was *my* body and mind. I was coming to claim what was mine.

As she reared back, preparing to counter my small onslaught of power with her own, I felt him there. Cole was scared. His fear washed over me like the first swim of summer, the water like ice until you fully submerged. Once his emotion settled, he began to feed me his calming magic, and I allowed the deep green to swirl amidst my pulsing violet.

With one quick blast, the Keeper pulled away as she shrieked and howled. She remembered this. She knew what we'd done at Cresthaven and how I'd kept her sidelined, only pulling what I needed and could control from her. This time, though, she didn't understand what I wanted from her.

I forced my way toward her, the mix of my and Cole's powers becoming smoke, filling my veins and spreading through my system. Our only intent was to force her into a corner. Cole whispered in my ear, our sibling connection allowing only me to hear his hushed instructions. We had to contain her power in one place, to force her into a situation where the binding could contain all of her at once.

I could feel him holding back, keeping a tight grip on his power, giving me only what he felt I needed. I wanted to pull more, I knew he had it to give, but his apprehension was clear, so I kept myself controlled. When the Keeper retaliated, which she did with waves of nauseating emotion and blots of darkness that tried to envelope our light and force it away, he upped the ante, and I felt lightheaded with the rush of power. She ran from our collective brightness and moved through the dark shadows our light had yet to reclaim.

We chased her slowly, working methodically and filling my physical body one inch at a time with our combined power. It took effort to maintain the energy flowing through me while remaining strong enough to keep her from pushing back.

Cole had to help more and more. I struggled to maintain. I missed the boost the captive Keeper provided. I could have used a charge from any of those bright orbs of light right about now. But, finally, we cornered her, there was nowhere else for her to go. She hissed and wailed, throwing darts of power at us, slicing and tearing at the web we built around her. The closer we came, the harder she fought, seeming to realize what was coming next.

I didn't know what it would feel like, and Cole barely had time to warn me before Baleon blasted in, fully entering my mind, his orange inferno raging toward her. I couldn't avert my eyes. It was like staring down the center of a solar flare—orange, yellow, red, and black swirling together and away from each other in a force that radiated domination and promised pain. I fought to maintain my hold on the Keeper and screamed at Cole.

Stop holding back! You have to help me. We have one chance and Bale's power is too much for me to handle alone. He could rip me apart getting to her!

Cole hesitated one long second, and then I felt him fill me up. I almost sighed at the sense of completeness our combined energy gave me. He calmed the ragged edges and frayed pieces while bolstering my power and forcing the Keeper to recoil further. He was her kryptonite and my complement. I was stable, strong, and sure. The exhaustion disappeared and as Baleon's power burst through our barrier, surrounding the Keeper, I thought I was ready.

What I didn't expect was the searing pain. A white hot lance shattered my illusions of strength and dropped me to my knees. I screamed out as I heard him. *You must hold her! You must contain her or I will fail!*

The pain spiraled out from my core and with every bind he was able to make around her, I felt the same agony she did, like he stripped my flesh from my bones and replaced it with a spiked rope he twisted and tied. With every knot he completed, she shrank, but so did I. The idea that we were truly one being was never something I considered. This was torture.

Take it, Amelia! Take what you need. We're so close. I'm here, just do what you have to do!

Cole's voice broke through the haze. I felt him push more of himself toward me, giving me complete access. I grabbed at him and took. I quickly drew from the only power that could ease the pain, but it wasn't enough.

With every second of peace he brought me, Baleon's persecution by flame caused double the pain. The roped connection between Cole and I was strong. It was a connection I'd held my whole life and a constant I'd always counted on.

He told me to take what I needed and I stopped holding back. I drew from him without reservation, taking everything necessary for me to stand strong as Baleon continued to wrap his fiery tentacles around her to complete the binding.

I couldn't stop the screams, but with each lashing burn, I pulled from him again, and Cole's power soothed the pain just in time for another bind to wrap itself around me. As her shrieks and my screams died out, I heard Cole's anguished cry. The last bind still scalded my skin and instinctively, I pulled once more, only to feel nothing.

Chapter 11
Aidan

Her screams didn't end. She thrashed to the point where I called in Micah and Elias to hold her down, and all the while, I was completely helpless. I couldn't touch her, I couldn't help her, I couldn't give her anything to make it easier. Her cries were raw, guttural admissions of pain I not only heard, but saw. Each bind Baleon placed welted across her skin and slashed through her aura. I watched the violet and green smoke enveloping her glow bright, dim, and then brighten again as she pulled more from Cole. Tears streamed from her eyes and pooled in the curve of her neck, eventually spilling over to the pillowcase.

Cole gave her final permission and he slumped further and further over her, until he was draped across her chest. He gripped her hand in his as he paled and his breathing became more shallow. I wanted to pull him away, but knew they were close. Then Baleon shouted and Amelia's cries became more than I could take. I struggled to maintain human form as my wolf battled me to get to her, to protect what was ours, no matter the cost.

I took two steps toward the door when Cole bolted upright and roared, a bellowing scream that turned every head in the room. Charlie bayed uncontrollably and Cole tried to let go of Amelia's hand, to free himself, but Baleon latched his hand over theirs and forced him to stay the course. He fought and screamed and tried to make words as he whipped his head back and forth, only able to wail, "NOOOOOOO!"

The seconds dragged on until his eyes rolled into the back of his head. He fell over her body again and Baleon let go, sitting back in his chair. The room was too quiet. The terror of the last hour silently echoed as we all stood staring at each other without directly looking anyone in the eyes. Finally, Charlie whimpered as he tried to nudge Cole, and then licked Amelia's cheek.

"She has taken it all from him. I feel nothing." Baleon stood, picked up Cole's motionless body, and gently laid him next to Amelia. "He will recover, but he will never be the same. He gave all of himself to her, but it is done. The Keeper is contained. For how long, I do not know, but for now, she is whole."

Charlie leapt onto the bed and squeezed his massive frame between Amelia and Cole. He rubbed his head against each of their faces before settling, small whimpers still escaping. The sound of nails clicking and feet pounding down the hallway alerted us that Onyx would soon follow. He burst through, his black eyes wild and barrel-chest heaving. Sweat coated his fur. Without hesitation, he joined Charlie on the bed, bowing the mattress down as he stood next to Cole and leaned over to nudge his brother. He settled on Cole's right and laid his head on his shoulder.

"They will both sleep for some time," Baleon said, answering my question before I could ask.

"Th-thank you, Baleon," I managed to stutter. My voice came out a loud whisper, my throat tight and jaw still clenched. I cleared my throat and tried again. "Truly, thank you."

The giant Hunter dropped his head in a small bow and then turned to Micah. "We should go, Prince Mikail." Micah stood, still looking dumbstruck, as I'm sure I did. "Yes, of course, Bale. She needs to rest. And so do you, Aidan."

I shook my head more violently than intended. Elias found the words I could not.

"You need to run, Aidan. I can feel him prowling inside you. You need to free him. Let him feel her through your bond and know she's okay. The dogs won't react. You can shift here and I'll stay with her. The women are with Nell and I'll be able to tell you if she wakes." Elias maintained eye contact with me as Baleon and Micah left the room. Then he turned and released the window, pushing it wide open. "Shift now and use the window. She is your mate, Aidan. You cannot stop this part of you. Just give him the reassurance he needs—*you* need."

I didn't bother taking off anything but my shoes. In one explosion of cellular rearranging, I dropped from two legs to four and let out a deafening howl. The Danes chimed in with deep bays and Elias's eyes lit blue as he fought to maintain his human form against the natural instinct to respond to my call.

Howls erupted from all over the area as fellow AniMages confirmed they were there, they would protect her with their lives, and they were ready to run. I paced the perimeter of the bed and finally buried my nose in the crook of her neck, pushing under her hair so I could trace a path from her collarbone to her hairline. I could feel peace within her that hadn't been there in as long as we'd known each other. Her breaths were even, the heartbeat in her jugular was strong and steady, and her power was calm. She would be okay. We had succeeded.

"Go, Aidan," Elias growled. If my friend was going to be able to hold to his word and stay with Amelia, I had to get out of there.

Thank you, Elias. I won't be gone long.

He nodded stiffly and I leapt out the window, vaguely noticing Bethany standing in the doorway of the barn holding Rynna's hand. Both women cried silently as they stared at me, wanting answers I couldn't give them yet.

Chapter 12
Amelia

I opened my eyes and was struck by how warm I was, even though I could feel the breeze across my skin. A dry tongue scratched against my cheek and a whimper whined in my ear. I realized Charlie was the heater lying next to me. I reached across my body to scratch his head and just as I felt the coarseness of his short coat across my fingertips, it all came flooding back.

The Keeper. The binding. Something happened, but what? My mind couldn't find the information, but the gnawing in my gut told me it was bad.

I bolted upright, only to sway back and forth as dizziness took over. When my eyes focused, I found Aidan sitting in the chair in the corner. His posture was stiff, but he leaned slightly toward me, his lips parted and eyes questioning. He looked at me like he wasn't sure if I was real, like he needed permission to move.

"Hi," I said cautiously, the room still slightly swaying. Or maybe I was. In a second, he was next to me, on his knees as he wrapped his arms around me. Aidan still hadn't spoken, but I held his head against my chest and allowed those few seconds of silence. I was here. He was here. We were in the same place, together, for the first time since this had all started.

Finally, Aidan pulled away and my eyes traced up his arms, to the tattoos peeking out from his shirtsleeves, continuing up to his strong jaw, thin lips, and emotion-filled eyes. Eyes the color of a foggy mist. I was struck by how much I'd missed seeing his human eyes.

I put my hands on either side of his face and smiled, then I leaned down and kissed him. A brief touch of our lips ricocheted sensations through me and cemented the reality that this was not a dream. We were interrupted by a massive dog head-butting me in the back. As I turned to scold Charlie, I saw Cole lying between him and Onyx.

"Oh, God. What happened?" I asked as I took in my brother's limp form on the bed. Aidan quickly stood and helped me to my feet.

"He's okay, Amelia. He's still recovering," Aidan said as he steadied my wobbling limbs. I hadn't actually stood on my own volition since Cresthaven.

"Define okay," I demanded weakly as I pulled away from him and walked slowly around the bed. I looked down at Cole and the rational part of me knew this was my brother, but he felt wrong. Even sleeping, I should have felt his power—his calming, serene power. I should have seen his aura and been able to feel his health rebuilding. I felt nothing.

I looked up at Aidan. He tried to speak and then stopped. He lifted his arms and then dropped them again. "Aidan, you're scaring me. What is going on?" My voice wavered and I fought to search my memories for what had happened, but the binding was fuzzy. I couldn't pull a single clear memory from the haze.

"He told you to take what you needed," Aidan started quietly. "I heard him, and so did everyone else. And then you did. But…you took too much. You…Amelia, you took it all. You took his power. He's human." Aidan's mouth snapped closed as he said "human", like it was a bad word he wanted to take back.

"No," I argued. "No, Aidan, that isn't possible. I can't do that. No one can *do that.*" I turned back to Cole, his body lying so peacefully in front of me. The argument that this wasn't possible, that he would wake up just as he was before the binding, was stuck in my throat.

Hysteria gripped my lungs and my chest felt concave, leaving me no room to draw a breath. As quickly as it came, I felt my internal response. The slow build and spread of a power that wasn't mine, a power I'd always found comfort and calm in. Cole's power unfurled in my system and while my mind reeled, my breaths evened out and my heart rate slowed.

I stared down at my brother as the truth settled over me. A dark cloud of doubt cast over what was supposed to be a day of celebration. When I woke up today, I was supposed to be free. Instead, I found myself a thief of the most epic proportions. Cole's power acted like a sedative, lulling me back to simple contemplation and the realization that even the best laid plans have complications.

I turned to Aidan with tears in my eyes. They pooled there, filling me up with the same sadness enveloping my heart. He reached for me and pulled me to him. I wrapped my arms around his chest and tucked my head under his chin. We stood there, unmoving except for his hand gliding slowly up and down my back.

"Will he be okay?" I finally asked. Aidan pulled away and I looked up at him.

"He will," he reassured me. "Baleon said he will wake up and feel fine. He won't have magic, but he will otherwise be healthy." Aidan settled his hands at the small of my back and we continued to stare at each other. Our eyes moved up and down, scanning the other continuously.

I started with his hair. It was grown out—too long, actually. The dark locks were curling at the ends, covering the tips of his ears. The front dipped low onto his broad forehead and I brushed it off his brow so I could look deeper into his eyes. As I ran my fingertips down his cheek, Aidan smirked and his dimple appeared. I stared at his thin, pink lips and brushed my thumb over them. I pushed onto my toes and pulled him to me, unable to stop myself. I needed to feel his lips on mine. I needed confirmation that we were here, together, finally.

The kiss was a slow build. It started out tender and sweet, but as our power swirled together and our hands explored, it became urgent. Aidan was everywhere. His physical body wrapped around mine, his hands constantly shifting, gripping, trailing over my skin. His power was intricately laced with mine and I felt him in my mind and heart.

I leaned back, the closeness of him suddenly overwhelming. My breaths came in shallow bursts as I looked up at him. His eyes were bright, the blue of his AniMage side shining down at me. His hair pointed in multiple directions from my hands running through it.

Even now, his shirt was clenched in my fists. I couldn't decide whether I wanted to pull him to me or push him away.

Aidan didn't allow me to choose. Slowly, he drew his hands up my sides and trailed them over my arms, his gaze never wavering from mine. Gripping my hands, he looked at me with a mixture of passion and concern. He had to see the conflict brewing inside me, but he didn't address it.

Gently pulling my fingers apart one at a time, he locked our hands together, lowered them to my sides, and surprised me by tucking my hair behind my ears. "I want to see you. I want to make sure you're okay and prove to myself you're real." His words were gruff, heavy from our exchange, but filled with emotion. I nodded slowly, giving him permission, but for what, I didn't know.

Aidan gripped the hem of my tank top and slowly pulled it up, his eyes on mine, clearly watching for any hesitation. My arms rose willingly and the top fell to the floor. I was standing in front of Aidan in a bra and jeans. I thought he would kiss me. The darkening of his eyes and spike of power told me he wanted to, but instead, he leaned down and kissed my collarbone. Trailing his fingers down my ribs, he kissed that spot, too. It wasn't until he crouched, his fingers running directly over a welt from the binding, that I understood. He kissed each welt, each burn, and each place the binding had hurt me, sending his healing energy with it, easing the pain.

Aidan stood and circled me. He nuzzled into the space between my shoulder and neck, his breath warm, tickling my skin. I let my head drop and closed my eyes, relishing in this sweet and beautiful torture he put me through. For a brief moment, I had wanted space, but now, I couldn't imagine taking a breath that hadn't just been his. As Aidan kissed his way down my back, he dropped to his knees and wrapped his arms around me. I closed my hands around the ones now circling my hips.

"I love you, Amelia. You're finally here. You're whole. There's so much to come, but for right now, all that matters is you and me and this moment." His words both elated and gutted me. I felt so much when I was near him. I couldn't pull myself away from him. I couldn't imagine not being next to him. But, was that us or something else? I wasn't sure. There was so much wound around the prophecy, the mating and everything someone else had set into motion.

Until I was really sure, I could only reply with, "You and me and this, it is everything, Aidan."

Chapter 13
Micah

I paced the seven steps across the small parlor of Derreck's basement apartment for the tenth time. "This is bloody ridiculous, Baleon. She's been awake since last night. When is she coming out? We need to plan, make decisions, *do something*."

I kicked at a small ottoman and sent it flying across the room, using my power to stop it from hurtling through the window at the last second. I rarely allowed frustration to get the better of me, but there was too much at stake. Lives. Our future. My people needed action. I needed action and Amelia was integral.

Bale looked at me with one arched eyebrow as the ottoman floated back to its original position. "She cannot physically keep you out of the room, Prince Mikail. Just go speak with her." Of course, Baleon would completely disregard her personal preferences and simply use brute strength to do the job.

"That will not exactly grant me a welcome audience, Bale," I said with a sigh.

"You could use these as leverage," he said, pulling pages from his satchel. I stared open-mouthed at my guard.

"When did you get these? How did you get these? Why didn't you tell me?" The questions fell from my mouth as a grin developed, though I didn't actually care for answers.

Bale lifted one shoulder and with his normal cryptic sarcasm, said, "It is my job to know what you need and when you will need it."

"And you do a damn fine job of it," I said as I took the pages and dropped onto the couch. Amelia's mother's journal would surely win me at least a few minutes with her. I didn't allow myself to read the pages, as much as my curiosity tried to get the better of me. Instead, I went through and organized them once again. When all of the pages were in order, I stood and gave Bale a quick smack on the shoulder, thanking him once more. He nodded and shook his head at me as I strolled outside.

As I made my way up to the main house and let myself inside, I wondered how Tragar was doing. The old librarian was on a short list of people I cared for and he had been through too much.

I stayed focused on the mission at hand, but made sure to say hello and exchange a few words with the Mages and AniMages I'd been introducing myself to. With each group, my welcome seemed to increase. Some called out to me and asked how I was. Outside of my experience in Brighton, it was the first time I was treated like a normal person, and I quite enjoyed it.

Smiling to myself, I rounded the corner and found Bethany and Aidan arguing outside Amelia's door.

"Damn it, Ame," Bethany yelled over Aidan's shoulder at the closed door, "I'm sick to death of you acting like you aren't in there. I'm going to kick down that damn door and drag you out here by your damn hair. Do you know what I've been through for you? What we've all been through for you? You're being a selfish little—"

"Enough!" Aidan yelled. His voice echoed down the hall, causing Bethany to take a step back. That step only lasted half a second before she was right back in his face, her yelling directed at him this time. I pitied the poor guy, but I surely wasn't giving her another reason to hate me.

"Oh, no you don't, Aidan Montgomery. All you're doin' is makin' this worse. You're just makin' 'xcuses for her being A DAMN DRAMA QUEEN." Bethany's accent was as thick as her anger and wanting to kiss her should have been the last thing I thought, but it was what it was. I almost stepped in between them when the door opened and Amelia came into view.

The bags under her eyes were pronounced. Her face was gaunt and her clothes looked too big and too long worn. I made eye contact with Aidan and he looked at me with begging eyes. Amelia's solitude was clearly not his choice either. I jerked my head to the side and he wisely removed himself from between the two girls.

Amelia spoke quietly, the calm in her voice unnerving and unlike her. "You don't understand, Bethany. You can't. I took something. I took something that wasn't mine to take and I don't know how to give it back." Her voice cracked, despair slipping through. Amelia paused and shook her head. Her hands trembled slightly and she closed her eyes. After a brief second, she exhaled and the shaking stopped. The very power she spoke of helped to keep her hysteria at bay. "I don't even know how I did it in the first place. I'm dangerous. I am a danger to every Immortal."

"Then it's a damn good thing I'm not an Immortal, isn't it?" Bethany threw the rhetorical question out as she gave Amelia a caring, but impatient look.

"Honey, I know all of that and it doesn't matter," Bethany's voice softened. "Your brother is fine. He might not be happy, but he's alive and we're figuring it out. Everyone knows what happened, and no one wants you to hide in here. We want to see you, to help you. *I want to help you*. I miss you, Ame. I'm not one of you and until two days ago, I was the only human here and completely worthless. I just want my best friend back." Her last words were a hushed admission meant only for Amelia's ears. I felt like an intruder on the moment.

"Oh, B," Amelia choked out as she allowed a single tear to slide down her cheek. The girls fell into each other's arms, both talking simultaneously. They moved toward the room and I knew I could not lose my chance.

"Amelia?" I called out. She looked up at me in surprise as I came down the hall. Bethany glared daggers, but that was our normal exchange.

"I apologize for intruding, but I wanted you to know that I, too, have been waiting for you to emerge. I thought you might want these." I held out the pages and watched her eyes grow wide as she realized what they were.

"You brought them," she whispered.

"I will have to give Baleon the credit. He had the forethought to ask Tragar for them, but I am glad to put them in their rightful hands." I smiled as Amelia gingerly took the stack of pages. Bethany and Aidan looked at both of us curiously.

"It's my mother's journal. Something we found while I was at Cresthaven," Amelia explained. "Tragar, who you would love, B, is a little old man who hates Hunters and grumbles all the time in the most adorable way. He kept them and hid them, hoping to someday give them to me. I had only just begun reading them when I was taken downstairs. I thought I would never see them again." She looked back at me and the happiness brightening her expression was a relief. "Please thank Baleon, Micah." Her eyes shone with more tears, which was not what I wanted to see. I wanted strong Amelia to return.

"You tell him yourself," I said, shaking my head at her. "Bethany is right, you cannot hide any longer. You did what was necessary and now you have to be the woman you were meant to be. There are people here who need someone to fight for. They've already rallied around Aidan and they wait to rally around you. The fight is coming. We can't stop it. You are wasting time. You cannot outrun destiny, Amelia. And you will never find a set of people who believe in you more than the people you have here."

I hadn't expected to say so much, or be so personal, but it was the truth. And the way Bethany's eyes softened as I spoke, how she looked at me for the first time like she remembered what we were...I needed that as much as Amelia needed to hear me.

Amelia looked between the three of us, holding her mother's journal in one hand with her arm wrapped around her best friend and her mate standing feet from her, and said, "They're wrong. You're all wrong. I'm not part of some destiny, or prophecy. What I am is a curse."

Chapter 14
Amelia

"Oh, that is it," Bethany said with a huff. Grabbing me by the elbow, she pulled me back into the bedroom, slamming the door in Aidan and Micah's face. She shoved me toward the bed with one hand and shooed Charlie off with the other to make room for herself. He let out an indignant snort and settled on the rug on the floor.

Once she situated herself against the pillows, she said, "You know, I would just about kill someone for a latte," as if nothing were different and we were at home in our apartment, not in the middle of the woods fresh off a conversation about the fate of the Immortal races and my role in it.

"Yeah?" I responded drily.

She bent one leg and pulled it under her. Her nose wrinkled as she said, "Seriously, Ame, these people have no class. The AniMages run around here, shifting all the time, leaving their shreds of clothes everywhere and setting a terrible example for little Dillon. Though, his mamma is the sweetest and has been doing everything for

Nell." She stopped and tilted her head. "You remember her, right? Her babies are gonna come any minute and I cannot *wait* to play with them. Cora tells me they'll stay kittens for at least a few months, and if they have power, Nell can start teaching them how to switch back and forth. And the Mage women…bless their hearts. Don't get me wrong, that crazy psycho Queen put them through the ringer, but *all* they do is complain about their pregnancies. Their backs hurt, their feet are swollen, the baby is sitting on their bladder—their bladder! Have they no shame? Who talks about their bladder in public? Can you even believe it?"

She went on, her arms swirling as she punctuated her comments with grand gestures and the most ridiculous facial expressions. She raised and lowered her voice to mimic Elias's Irish lilt and a little boy named Dillon who seemed oddly formal for a ten-year-old. From her story, I suspected he was very much in love with one Bethany Jackson.

She mimicked the women's complaints and I couldn't stop the laughter from coming. Soon, tears leaked from my eyes. I wanted Bethany to keep making me laugh and telling me stories, but we both knew that wasn't why we were in here.

"I appreciate the distraction, B, and I needed to laugh more than I even realized, but this doesn't change anything," I said as I met her eyes, keeping my tone level. "I'm a danger to these people. Even without the Keeper, I don't know what I'm capable of. I can't be out there among them. It's reckless. And the women with babies…what if I hurt their kids? I'd never forgive myself." I was shaking my head as the "what if" thoughts swirled around and the worst of the worst ended up planted in my mind.

When I looked up at Bethany, I expected her to be nodding and giving me the appropriate amount of sympathy. Instead, I met one sculpted eyebrow and a scowl.

"What?" I asked, my tone a little more screechy than it should have been. I reached for Cole's power. It had become instinct over the past day to call on the pilfered magic now floating in my veins alongside my own.

"You actually believe what you're saying, don't you?" she asked as she shook her head.

"Yes, B, I do believe it," I said. I could see she didn't understand, so I continued, allowing the calm inside to stretch into my tone. "Okay, let's play this out. I go out there and start interacting with people. Someone touches me, or we're attacked, or I just get scared…I have never had my own power without the Keeper being a part of me. I don't know how I will react to any of those situations. I could hurt someone, don't you understand?" I paused, and added quietly, "I stole my brother's power. I changed him forever."

I was shocked when she leaned in and in the most patronizing tone, said, "No, you didn't. He gave it to you. He told you to take it. He told you it was yours and you needed it and it was the reason your mamma gave him all that power anyway."

My head shot up as she continued. "Do you know how I know that? I know because *he told me so*. And do you know what that means, Miss 'nobody likes me, I should go eat worms'? That means he doesn't hold this against you. And if he doesn't hold it against you, you *damn well can't hold it against yourself.*" With each of those last words, she tapped me in the middle of my chest and then sat back, crossed her arms, and silently dared me to argue.

I stared at her, opening and closing my mouth as I tried to find the right words, but nothing came. Finally, I snapped my mouth shut and Charlie snorted, an amused little grunt that came with a wave of emotion that said *I told you so.*

"Oh, shut up, dog. I don't need to be tag-teamed." I threw the words over my shoulder as I crossed my own arms and scowled at Bethany's growing grin.

"Just because Cole doesn't hate me doesn't invalidate the rest. I could hurt people. Those women and their babies. I still don't know what's inside me." My head bounced back and forth in time with my quiet retort, but she just rolled her eyes.

"You don't even understand what's out there, Ame. All those Mages and AniMages have crazy special abilities and *he* has been out there cataloging them all," she said, absently waving her hand toward the door Micah stood behind.

"We've also got Baleon here, and Elias, and even Aidan. Who knows what's locked up inside Mr. AniMage King out there? Everybody here is in the same boat. Nobody knows who's got what, what they are entirely capable of, or what's going to happen to them, but you know what they all do know?"

She waited for me to respond, her smug smirk making her impatience clear. "What?" I finally asked with a sigh.

"They know they've been hearing 'bout this 'prophecy' their whole lives and now the two people clearly called out in it are within fifty feet of them and *nothing is happening* because one of them is too chicken shit to do anything about it." I hadn't seen Bethany like this. Normally, she was so supportive, but right now, she was ripping me a new one. I didn't really know how to take it.

This time, I didn't attempt to calm myself down. "Where do you get off—"

"Oh, honey," she cut in, "you do *not* even wanna go there with me. This friendship is about truth, even when it's ugly, and right now, it's really freaking ugly. But nothing—*nothing, Ame*—can move forward for these poor people without you. They took on a crazy Queen and her passel of Hunters *for you*. They risked their lives and the lives of whatever family they have left because they believe *in you*. And do you know what they are? They're *freaking grateful*. So, why don't you just get over your damn self, go out there, and at least meet them? See if they can help you the way they hope you can help them. Give them a chance. Like it or not, these are your people."

My people. Damn it if she wasn't right. They were my people and right now, they were sitting ducks while I hid in here, afraid to face the unknown when the unknown was all they'd had for years.

"When did you get so smart about all this?" I asked, disbelief clouding what I thought was crystal clear vision.

She shrugged, her lips twisting into a facetious smirk. "I pay attention."

Charlie snorted again, and I had to laugh. "Well, I can see it's useless to argue anymore, but the first place I want to go is to see my brother."

She stood up and smacked her hands together. "I knew you'd listen to me eventually. And Cole needs you. Let's go."

Bethany flung open the door and both Micah and Aidan jumped. "Time to get this party started, boys. One kickass Elder reporting for duty."

Aidan grinned at me over her shoulder and I couldn't stop myself from doing the same.

Cole's room wasn't far from mine, maybe twenty feet. I was torn between wanting to hole myself in my room so I could read the journal Micah had given me and facing Cole, but my mother was still dead and I had to be certain my brother didn't hold my heinous act of magic thievery against me. So, I followed Bethany down the hall, my hand locked tightly in Aidan's. Micah gave me an encouraging smile as he stepped aside, falling in behind us.

Aidan squeezed my hand and the little jolt that came with it was filled with reassurance and positivity. I looked up at him and he was smiling down at me. "What?" I asked, unsure of how to take the blatant joy on his face.

"You're here, doll. For a while, I wasn't sure you ever would be, but you are. And we're doing this," he said as he held up our joined hands. "We'll deal with the rest of it, Ame, just always fall back on the fact that we are in this together."

His eyes were storm clouds at dusk, depths of unending gray. I wanted to fall into him. Thankfully, he was watching what was in front of us, and quickly yanked me into his chest before I walked right into Bethany's back.

"Sheesh, you two. We're on official business here. Wait until later to do all your lovey making up." Her sarcasm was light and her smile was big. B threw me a wink before rapping on Cole's door.

"Special delivery!" she called out.

"I don't want any of your damn cookies, Princess, how many times do I have to tell you—" Cole was scolding Bethany before he even opened the door. His voice dropped away when he saw me.

We stood there for a moment, just staring at each other. I still felt nothing from him. I had held out hope this was a short-term issue, but clearly, it wasn't.

I had no idea what my brother was thinking, which meant he could have lunged for my throat when he took a step toward me, but he didn't. In two steps, I was engulfed in Cole's arms and he was murmuring into my hair, "It worked. Oh, thank God, it worked."

He still felt like Cole. I still fit inside his giant bear hug like I always had. He was a little smaller than I remembered, but outside of the void where his power had been, everything else about him was the same.

I let the comfort of this familiar space settle in, but soon, the realities did as well. "I'm so sorry. I don't know what happened, Cole. I'm just so sorry." My shame choked me and I didn't allow myself to reach for his power. I had to deal with these emotions. They lodged in my throat and hollowed out my chest. I clung to Cole and the words were an incoherent stream.

"It just hurt so much," I whispered. "And he was just there and I couldn't do it. And everything he did to her, he did to me. Every bind, it was like he was ripping me apart. I just couldn't. I wouldn't have survived. But, I didn't realize. I didn't know. Why did you let me do this?" I asked.

I felt Aidan behind me, restraining himself.

Cole had been rubbing my back, letting me go on, but as I quieted down, he pulled back from me. He looked down at me with deep brown eyes that held no anger or hostility.

"It was the only way, Ame," he said. "Mom gave me that power for one reason, to help you when you needed it most. We always assumed it was your outbursts, but I think what we did was exactly what we had to do. And, yes, it hurt me, too. And yes, I miss my power, but I'm okay. Actually, I'm better than okay. I don't feel *everything*. My mind isn't a mess of everyone else's emotions and I don't have to build wall after wall to keep them out. My mind is quiet for the first time in more than twenty-five years, and that is okay with me."

"Really?" I squeaked out the question, hardly able to believe he was telling the truth.

"What do you feel?" he asked.

I stopped pushing his power away, stopped forcing it to the outskirts of my system, and focused on how I felt. I felt calm and for once, my thoughts weren't moving a hundred miles an hour. The hysteria that sat on the edge of my mind for months was finally a memory. His power layered over mine and I didn't stop it. It created a film, a barrier of sorts, as it encased the violet smoke that made me who I was. I watched it fade, watched the neon green light I had forever associated with my brother absorb into me, and I knew he was right.

This was how it was meant to go. I didn't feel everyone's emotions like he did. I didn't feel overwhelmed or even an intensified reaction to those around me. That power was never meant for him and his body knew it. It was meant for me.

I opened my eyes and looked up at him. "I feel right," I said.

Cole wore his big brother *I told you so* look and it was just as irritating as it had always been. I loved that I was irritated and that he was here. We had both made it.

"Good, that's how you should feel," he confirmed, but then he looked away, his eyes lingering over my shoulder. I turned to look at Aidan and felt a twinge of suspicion.

"What aren't you saying, Cole?" I asked.

"Aidan saw me after Cresthaven, and, Ame, I'll be honest, it was bad," he started, finally meeting my eyes again. "I don't know what we did or what we unlocked during that first run with the Keeper, but it left me pretty screwed up. I thought I was losing my mind.

"You were able to take some of my power that first time, but it was like my system was fried. My power fluctuated in spikes I couldn't control. I felt every emotion from every person here. I felt their deepest fears and their nightmares invaded my dreams. I didn't sleep for days. I...I just wasn't myself and I blamed you. But Bethany wouldn't let me run away like I wanted to, and Aidan helped me see that you needed me. Then it was all happening again, but this time, I knew exactly what needed to be done. I don't know how to explain it except to say something, or someone maybe, told me to just give it all to you, and that I would be okay. I heard it, as clear as you're talking to me now, so I did it. And they were right, I am really okay."

I pulled Cole in for another hug. I hated what he'd been through and what being there for me had done to him, but I was so glad to have my brother back.

I turned to face Aidan and Bethany. B fidgeted a little, giving away the awkwardness she felt at Cole's admission. "I couldn't very well let him just run off. I mean, really, Ame, you would have killed me," she said as she flipped her hair back over her shoulder and failed miserably at making light of things. I stepped forward and yanked her into a hug.

"I don't know what I did to deserve you, Bethany Jackson, but I swear, I will make all this up to you someday. I mean, how are you even doing this? How are you here? Where do people think you are?" I pulled back as the logic of my own questions hit home. Was her family worried?

Bethany's laugh filled the air. "Well, thanks to Derreck's computer and one of the AniMages being able to project images better than any green screen, my parents think I'm studying abroad in Italy." She paused and added air quotes, saying, "It's a very unique opportunity."

I could only shake my head while we all laughed. Of course she had thought to make sure no one worried.

"And I love you, too, girl," she said. "There was no frigging way I was leaving you with these buffoons. I knew you would need me eventually." Bethany squeezed my hand tightly and I did the same before stepping to Aidan.

"And you, I don't even know where to start with you." My smile only widened as his eyes darkened slightly.

I felt the spike in his aura and gave him a look that said, *down boy.*

Micah snorted, reminding me he was still standing off to the side. "What are you doing hiding back there? You had just as much to do with me making it out of there alive as anybody. And you brought my mother's journal. Micah, I can't thank you enough." Standing next to Aidan, the heat of his palm against mine and the strength of his power intermingling with my own, I knew I had been right all along. He was where I belonged. But Micah was a friend and an ally. I was equally as sure of that.

Micah flicked an unsure gaze toward Bethany. "Oh. Ohhhhh." I turned between them. "So, that's still there. Have you two even talked, because seriously, B. Just talk to him. None of what you are thinking is real. None of it makes sense. Just hear the poor guy out."

"I'll thank you to let me do my own groveling, Amelia," Micah piped in. He walked slowly toward Bethany, as cautious as a zookeeper approaching a big cat, and likely for good reason. She stood straight, her posture rigid as her toe tapped quickly on the floor, the only thing giving away her growing discomfort.

"All I ask is that you listen to me, Bethany. And ask your questions. I'll answer every one, no matter how long it takes. I'll tell you the complete truth. Every bit of it." He stood still and we all waited. I silently willed her to just say yes.

"Why does it matter, Micah?" she snapped. "Even if you answer every single question, this was never about me and you. You used me to get close to Amelia. You used me to learn about her and meet her family. *You used me.* And I don't give one single damn why." Bethany's words were sharp and Micah physically winced as she said them. And then she turned and walked away, the light *thud* of her cowboy boots the only thing breaking the silence.

Micah turned and gave me a sad smile. "I didn't expect it would be so simple, but thank you for your efforts."

"Don't give up, Micah. She'll understand. I know she will." I wanted her to, at least.

"Her stubbornness may actually surpass yours, Amelia," he responded, followed by a deep sigh. "But, we have a lot to talk about and you have many people to meet. We should gather those we need and get started, don't you agree, Aidan?"

Aidan squeezed my hand. "Micah's right. Unfortunately, we aren't safe here much longer and we have to figure out a plan. Are you ready for this?" His question hung in the air and I looked around at the three men who had stood by me through everything so far.

"Absolutely," I said. And I actually meant it.

Chapter 15
Aidan

In a perfect world, Amelia would have time to acclimate. She should have time to get back to full energy, to wrap her mind around what she did to Cole and what happened to her father. She still hadn't talked about it. I waited during her conversation with Cole. I expected her to say something, to ask all of us questions. We had been there. We were the ones who should answer for it. But, she didn't, and that scared me. Amelia had been compartmentalizing her feelings and fears for longer than she likely realized. I knew because we shared many of the same defense mechanisms.

But, there wasn't time and we needed to talk as a group. The last of the pack would arrive any minute and I knew Will, Melinda, and the other AniMages would not likely have the patience the rest had when it came to action.

So, we stationed ourselves in the living room while Micah gathered the people we needed. I sat back in one of

Derreck's leather chairs and watched Amelia from across the room. Her steps were cautious as she met Rynna halfway. She moved slower than normal, as if she didn't trust her limbs to obey her commands. I felt her internal battle when it came to touching people. Rynna reached for her and Amelia winced slightly before conquering the fear and wrapping her nanny in a hug. Rynna, ever the mother of the group, patted, squeezed, and looked Amelia up and down to make sure she was all right. Physically, she was.

I was used to my super-hearing and could easily dial it up and down now. I notched it up and caught the end of Rynna's conversation. "Are you sure you're ready for all this, dear? Don't you need time to figure out how to simply be yourself?" I appreciated Rynna's concern. After all, it mirrored my own.

"I can't, Ryn," Amelia responded. "I've used more than enough time already. I will figure it out as I go. Aidan is here and he gives me strength. Micah understands what we're up against. I have Bethany, you, Cole…all the people I care about are here and I won't leave them as sitting ducks. It will be fine."

"And we need to talk about—"

"No, we don't," Amelia cut Rynna off. "I know what you're going to say, Ryn, and I can't do that yet. I…just can't. I'm not ready." Amelia took a small step back and started to twist the ends of her hair.

While Cole's power helped her emotionally, we also established our nearness made a difference. My wolf was quiet and content when I could touch Amelia. She said I brought her peace, where Cole's power brought her calm.

I crossed the room in an instant, my hand wrapping around her bicep and down her forearm before I threaded my fingers between hers. She looked up and it was all I could do not to pull her to me. I hated the sadness in her eyes and the heaviness that surrounded her. She wasn't herself, but she was getting there.

"Let's sit," I suggested, pulling her back toward the chair I had vacated.

We only made it a few steps when I felt a familiar presence. I turned to see Cora and Dillon walk through the door. Dillon wasn't too proud of a ten-year-old to hold his mom's hand and he looked around the room, acknowledging everyone with a smile.

"Look who's here," I said as I nudged Amelia. She turned and looked just as happy to see Cora as I was to see Dillon. They approached us and I dropped to a squat. I liked to speak to Dillon on a level playing field, not treat him so much like a kid. He'd been through too much.

"How's it going, little man? Thanks for coming to the meeting," I said as Cora and Amelia hugged and started to chat. I put out my fist and Dillon bumped it with his own.

"You're welcome, Mr. Aidan. I was excited when Mamma said you asked for me, too." His pride at being included made his blue eyes even brighter and he stood taller. Then he looked sideways up at Amelia and leaned in to me. "How's she doing, Mr. Aidan?"

"She's doing very well. Thank you, Dillon. Has your owl told you anything new lately?" I trusted Dillon's visions, they hadn't led me astray yet.

He scrunched his face, his annoyance clear. "He's trying to, but I can't see it. The only thing I know is that there's gonna be more people here soon. And not all of them are nice."

"Don't you worry about them," I said as I started to worry for both of us. "I'll deal with them. Come find me if you see more, okay?" I held up a hand and he gave me a high five.

Standing, I projected my voice, "Everybody grab a seat, please. Let's get this going."

Cora did a quick introduction between Amelia and Dillon and his face turned bright red as she dropped down to hug him. As we took our seats, she said, "His little heart is so big. I can feel it so clearly. I just want to wrap that kid up and put him in my pocket."

Her smile was huge and she giggled when I responded, "You might have to fight Bethany for him," and nodded in their direction. Bethany sat next to Cora with her arm around Dillon, who beamed from his position between the two beautiful women.

I was still uncomfortable being in charge. I wanted to put air quotes around *in charge* because it seemed like such an insane prospect. Yet, these were my people. They were my responsibility. Well, now they were both of our responsibility.

"Everyone here knows Amelia now, so we don't need introductions," I started. "Now that she's back with us and the Keeper power is contained, we can make some decisions and figure out what to do next. To start, let's just go around and everyone give me a quick update on where we stand. Micah, go ahead."

I put my arm around Amelia and pulled her to me. I couldn't get her close enough lately. The way our power flowed in and around each other made it hard for me to focus. I felt her emotions very clearly, as real and raw as my own. I had no doubt that she meant what she'd said, that we were in this together, but I could also feel her hesitation and I wanted to know what caused it.

"I don't know what you're thinking about, but you're not hiding it well," she muttered under her breath. I realized then that I was staring down at her and looked up to find the room staring back at me. Dillon pulled the collar of his shirt over his mouth to hide his laughter.

"So, as I was *saying*…" Micah's sarcasm sent a snicker through the room.

"Sorry, sorry…go ahead," I said, laughing. "I promise I won't let the gorgeous girl sitting next to me distract my attention too much."

Amelia blushed and ducked her head into my shoulder.

Cole piped up, "Hey, man, that's my little sister you're talking about," and the room erupted in full blown laughter. It brought the tension in the room down and everyone visibly relaxed. I gestured for Micah to continue.

"*Ahem.*" He cleared his throat and the room settled once more. "I've collected information on the women and AniMages who are here. Once Baleon broke the binds on those who needed it, we realized there are a host of abilities between them. Some I think will be very useful— power redirection, shielding, projection. They continue to build back their strength and even though those with children are scared to try too much, the options are there once we're ready to explore them," Micah finished, sitting back and tipping his head to Derreck.

"As far as the shields I have in place now, that's part of who I am and what I can do," Derreck explained. "Baleon helped me reinforce them, along with another

AniMage who has a similar ability to mine. Between the three of us, we know we're safe and hidden for now."

I nodded and looked toward Rynna. "Nell will be giving birth any minute now," she started. "She finally allowed Cora and Willow in, and they've been able to help the process along. We have a few more who will also give birth soon. At this point, Lilith should be fine staying in her shifted form and the other AniMages are in human form.

"We still don't know what to expect from the children, but power or no power, they will stay with their mothers. Long-term, we need to decide where the women and their children should go if the time comes to fight. Or, if they stay here and we go. Some mothers are still very early in their pregnancies and the fear of the unknown from my sister's experiments haunts them."

"I trust your judgment, Rynna. And we will do everything we can for them and their children." I wouldn't allow another child to lose a parent because of Julia's insanity.

Amelia finally broke into the conversation, saying, "I don't understand why no one is concerned about them tracking us. I know you have shields, but they could be tracking the AniMages on their way here. Or, really, who knows which other ways they could get to us. The Hunters aren't going to give up. Rhi won't give up. Micah, you know Julia's insane. We can't just sit here and wait."

I opened my mouth to respond, but Micah beat me to it. "Perhaps I can explain that, Amelia," he said as I trailed my fingers lightly up and down her arm, a reminder that she didn't have to make decisions alone anymore.

"I've spoken with others about this, but you aren't aware of the connection I have with my mother. It is actually a common bond between parents and children, which allows them to essentially monitor each other. You wouldn't have felt it because of the binds." Micah stopped, realizing he'd referenced Nathaniel. Amelia's breath hitched, but she didn't acknowledge it any further, and Micah wisely continued.

"It isn't detailed, she cannot find me or see through my eyes. She can't read my emotions either, but she never could. She only knows if I am alive and I know the same of her. Right now, she continues to recuperate from the escape.

"The amount of power she used to control the Hunters drained her past a point she's ever been. The Hunters are doing what they can to heal her, but the process is slow and there are a select few Rhi will allow near her. The biggest boon for us is the fact that the Hunters cannot leave the premises of Cresthaven without my mother's permission. Right now, she is still unconscious and that means she is not able to grant the permission they need to come after us. If they attempt to leave Cresthaven now, the collars will activate and cause them excruciating pain. They know that."

Cora spoke up next, reaching down to grasp Dillon's small hand in hers. "I can confirm what he says, Amelia. Once my power was fully restored and we had escaped, I knew immediately that Dillon was still alive. I felt him inside me and only had to wait for him to arrive."

Amelia sat quietly, taking everything in. Dillon was next to break the silence. "Mr. Aidan, they're here." His small voice echoed through the room. The last AniMages had arrived.

I looked around at the people I trusted. "We don't know what will happen with everyone in the same place and I know the last AniMages joining us are the most likely to cause trouble. We don't know who we can trust outside of this circle, so what we discuss doesn't leave this room. We are all smart enough to know there will be people who don't like our plans, so keep your eyes and ears open, okay?"

I made eye contact with each one of them as they nodded. The tone in the room was a mixture of unease and determination, but I didn't mind that. Unease kept them alert. I'd always believed if you expected an attack, then you couldn't be taken by surprise. It had served me well in my various homes and schools throughout the years.

"I'll go out to meet them and try to set this off on the right foot. Ryn, please keep me updated on Nell, and tell Elias we are here for whatever he needs. Micah, can you get me that list and some of your recommendations? Cole, would you mind walking Amelia back to her room? We'll regroup tomorrow morning and talk more."

"I don't need help, Aidan," Amelia protested.

I gripped her chin lightly and swept a quick kiss over her pursed lips. "You don't need help, Amelia, but you do need to talk. Go with your brother and I'll be back soon."

I stood and strode out the door. I didn't wait for the argument I knew would come. She sent a wave of annoyance through our connection and slammed the door shut, dampening the constant flow of emotion between us.

It was good to know my girl was back.

Chapter 16
Amelia

I stood and glared at Aidan's back. I heard him chuckle as I slammed the door between us and was actually kind of pissed to realize I could still feel him. I couldn't completely shut him out. Go figure. When he turned the corner and I could no longer shoot daggers at his back, I turned to find Cole next to me, his eyebrows up and lips twisted into a stifled grin.

"Oh, don't start," I muttered as embarrassment flushed my cheeks.

Cole put up both hands, and said, "Hey, not my fight. You guys are something else, though. He totally gets you, Ame."

As I caught myself looking out the window wanting to see Aidan, I realized Cole was right. And, I kind of hated him for it.

"Oh, just shut it," I said as I shoved at my brother's chest playfully. "And I can make my own way back to my room. I'm not an invalid, you know." Cole brought out those little sister antics in me. I couldn't help but prod at him.

I started toward the door and Cole fell in step with me. He didn't speak the whole way to my room and I was content to let him do just that. When I got to the door, I reached out to open it, but Cole put his hand over mine on the knob.

"Dad's dead, Ame," he said, his voice low and soft. "He's dead and he died saving us—both of us. He loved you and he loved me and he did the best he could." I stood there frozen. Aidan had told me this. I knew my father was dead. I knew I would never see him again, could never tell him I was sorry, could never tell him I loved him, or that I knew who he really was. But, as my brother held my hand and spoke in my ear, I heard it for the first time.

One tear popped and trailed down from each eye. As the words spun in my head, the tears continued to fall faster and faster, until a cry tore from my chest and Cole pulled me into him. The sobs were ugly. I didn't try to speak, I didn't tell my brother all the reasons I was sorry my father had even been in that room in the first place, or how I would someday find a way to dismember Rhi one limb at a time. I struggled to breathe through a clogged nose and the vise grip in my chest. No amount of soothing power could calm the heartbreak I had finally acknowledged.

Footsteps thundered across the floor and I pulled away to see Aidan careening around the corner of the hallway. His eyes were wild, until they landed on me. He took in the situation—my red, swollen eyes, the snot dripping from my nose, and the giant wet spot on Cole's chest. He gave me a questioning look and I managed to shake my head. He looked over me at Cole and they nodded simultaneously. Then, he turned and walked away.

Aidan knew he wasn't the person I needed, although I could feel how much he wanted to be the one I was latched onto right now. Feeling his wolf, the AniMage part of him exuding even more alpha male than I'd ever thought possible, I was impressed he could fight it. That he did fight it, for me.

"Why don't we go into your room and talk, Ame?" Cole opened the door and gestured inside. I wiped my eyes and was thankful I hadn't asked Bethany for makeup yet. I could only imagine what mascara would have added to the mess that was my face.

"Leave the door open. Charlie will come back soon," I said before Cole could shut it all the way.

"Onyx has been glued to my side, too," Cole muttered as I dropped onto the bed and stared at the ceiling, the tears dripping a steady stream.

"I didn't get to say anything, Cole," I said, my voice wavering. "You got to talk to him. You made sure he knew you forgave him and that you understood. I never got to do that. I don't know what he thought of me, or what he thought I thought of him. The last time I hugged him and told him I loved him was the day I left home."

Cole reached across the bedspread and gripped my hand in his. He waited for me to look at him before he said, "He thought you were amazing, Ame. He said you were stubborn like Mom, and that you didn't think enough before you acted. That you were more than he had ever imagined. He hated what he had to be, but he never regretted a minute of it because he still got to watch you grow up. He got to see Mom in you. That's what he said, Ame. He saw *Mom in you.*"

I turned my head toward Cole, my cheek resting in a pool of my own tears. "He saw Mom in me?"

His dark eyes were filled and he swallowed down the same cries I imagined were choking me.

"More than once," Cole continued, his voice thick with emotion. "He believed in what we're doing, Ame. This was what he and Mom were doing all along. They ran because she saw it. She knew they had to get far away and that it wouldn't be easy. She knew it would hurt both of us—all of us—but we were the only ones who could change things. He looked at me, and said, 'Cole, there are times when you have to rip your own heart out to show it how to beat.' I thought he was crazy, but I get it now. We were his heart. And what he had to do to us tore him up, but we had to learn how to beat alone. We had to be able to take this on. He did his job the best he could."

I lay back on the bed and watched the ceiling fan slowly swirl around, the blades blurring through my continued tears. "I just wish I had something from him. I have Mom's journal, but there's no way for me to know who he really was."

"Journal?" Cole asked. I realized I hadn't had the chance to tell him about it. I pulled myself up, wiping my eyes and swallowing the pain. I reached into the bedside table, pulling the pages out carefully.

"These were Mom's," I said as I held them out for him. "I found them at Cresthaven. It's a long story, but Micah brought them to me. I only got to read a few pages before Julia took me down to where she was holding the women." It seemed like a lifetime ago. A nightmare, not our reality.

Cole held the pages gingerly. He didn't flip through them or try to read the words. He just stared at the top page, where our mother's looping script noted this was her journal. He stood and quickly put them back into my hands.

"I think these were meant for you, Amelia. You're right, I had time with Dad and I think you need this time with Mom. I got to know her, and this is your way. If you want to share them with me when you finish, that's your call." I took the pages and set them next to me as I stood.

Cole reached out and pulled me into a hug. "We're gonna make it, half-pint. I may not be able to help like I used to, but Bethany's proven you don't have to have power to make a difference. I'll be just down the hall, and if you need anything, you know where to find me, okay?"

I nodded into his chest. I wasn't ready to let him go. I wasn't ready to be alone with my thoughts. But I let Cole pull away, squeeze my shoulder, and quietly leave the room.

I sat on the bed and stared at the wall. Charlie nosed open my door and leapt onto the bed next to me, jarring me out of my thoughts. He whined as he dug his giant head under my hand and I gave in, scratching behind his ears and letting the normalcy of the act comfort me.

"Where's Onyx? I haven't seen him lately. Don't you two go everywhere together?" I spoke to Charlie as if he were another person in the room. I always had. We hadn't had an exchange like the one at Cole's apartment since I'd woken up, but I had a feeling the ability was still there. I just hadn't felt a need to use it, and neither had he.

Charlie grunted, a quick exhale through his nose, showing his annoyance for his little brother. "Pffft, been there, buddy. Brothers can be something else." Then, I leaned down, and whispered, "But mine's pretty great. Just don't tell him I said so."

Charlie's tail thumped a beat onto the bed and I couldn't help but smile. As I sat back up, my hand came down on the journal pages. Aidan was busy with the arriving pack, and maybe I should have been annoyed that he didn't even ask me if I wanted to join him, but I didn't want to and I wasn't.

I toed my shoes off and scooted back up against the headboard, piling pillows behind me. Charlie stood up and rocked the whole bed until he situated himself by my side with his giant head in my lap.

I laid the stack of pages on the other side of me and flipped them over one by one until I got to the last entry I'd read. A nervous ache twisted my stomach, but I knew this wasn't a choice. My mother wouldn't have kept a journal without reason and I knew I was meant to see this. There was something for me here, I just had to find it. I had to believe that.

Julia continues to seek me out. She hides in hallways and waits in corners for me to pass by so she can smile while she pelts me with questions she knows I will not, and usually cannot, answer. The problem is with every encounter we have, her questions only fuel more of my own. Our people have been here for hundreds of years and it is hard for me to believe that we have lived so long with no one requiring answers. But, I know what Julia is not saying. She believes

Mages are better than the other races. Instead of each race having their equal place among us as the Elders believe, she feels all others should be subservient, and I cannot fathom that outcome.

Tragar continues to assist me. He brings me books from his travels and we work together to try to understand. I worried he would question my loyalty, but he only laughed and told me any intelligent person should ask the questions in their heart. My heart wants to know why the Elders try to hold us all here. Why do they contain us within the lands surrounding the castle, and why do the Elders on the council hide from the people?

The council members should not be hidden. They should be respected and celebrated. I fear for Nathaniel. He shouldn't even know I am destined for the council. And I know Rynna has guessed. She looks at my brother the way that I look at Nathaniel. If only I'd been as smart as she was and kept my distance, then my heart would not be crumbling inside my chest.

I have been invited to my first meeting. Next week, I will stand before the council for the first test. With each test, I will understand more about what my life will be. I both fear and look forward to the coming days. It will stretch my power and my understanding, but perhaps it will all fall into place as it should.

She sounded so optimistic and hopeful, but I read between the lines. There were secrets and lies she was wading through to get to the truth. I turned the page to find a new entry.

Nothing is as it seems. Maybe Julia is right to question it all. My heart breaks a little more each day I'm away from Nathaniel and the visions grow darker. All I see is death. Our people. Their children. Our home. It will fall to ruin, and I've tried to tell them. I've tried to tell the council.

I've passed my first test, if you can even call it that, and I know who they are. I see how tired they are and I don't understand what they do in that chamber that taxes them to this point. But I can see they need me. They need someone with fresh magic, yet they continue to question my abilities, wanting to know each and every thing I'm capable of. I haven't told them, though. Not yet. Unless someone compels me, there are some secrets I must keep.

When I approached Lavignia after my test and I told her of my visions, she pushed me into a corner and told me to hush. She told me the time would come for the truth, but it was not now. That I still had too much to learn before I could understand what I saw.

One thing is certain, there is something in that chamber they don't want anyone to find, and I will know what it is before I am made to be married. They will not sell me off to the highest bidder. I will not have it. Since that moment, just days ago, I have slowly fallen apart, piece by shattered piece. Food has no taste. I see no humor in Derreck and Elias's antics like I used to. The only thing I know is I have a job to do and there is something wrong here. I just have to find it.

She was so strong. It was hard to believe I came from a woman who held so much strength. She gave up love. She did what she was told, sort of. For the hundredth time, I wished she were here so someone could point me in the right direction.

Chapter 17
Aidan

"You aren't alone," I said from the doorway I had been standing in for the last two minutes, watching Amelia read.

She gasped, her hands flying up to her mouth. "Ohmygod, Aidan, you scared the crap out of me!"

"You aren't alone, Amelia. We're going to do this together," I reiterated solemnly. I wouldn't allow her to forget I would be there for every single step.

I loved watching her pupils expand. Her eyes shined, a thin rim of violet around the darkness, like an eclipse from another planet.

"Are you a mind reader now?" she asked. "Do you just lurk around, Montgomery?"

I laughed out loud at the sassy look she threw me. It was a look I'd seen so many times before.

"You were projecting your emotions pretty strongly, doll. At first, I thought you were actually talking, but when I got to the door, I saw your lips weren't moving. Since then, I haven't stopped staring at your lips." That last part,

I didn't actually mean to verbalize, but I did and the creeping red blush sweeping from her neck to her hairline was worth it.

"Charlie. Out," I said. An ache inside me I had ignored since she woke up made my voice a little harsher than intended.

He hopped off the bed and didn't look up as he lumbered out the door. I kicked it shut behind him without taking my eyes off Amelia. The blush was still there. I watched as her eyes shone brighter and her breaths became shallow. I probably could have picked out her heartbeat, but it didn't matter. It matched the thundering of mine.

"I can't get you out of my head, doll. Every second we're doing what we should be, all I can think about is getting you alone." It was increasingly hard to keep myself still.

"Well, there, um, have been a lot of…um, things, we needed to take care of," she stuttered, rifling through the papers in her hand and shoving them toward the nightstand. They scattered onto the floor instead and she turned, but I couldn't let this moment go.

"Leave them. We'll get them later." I couldn't hold myself back anymore. I could smell her, could feel her power luring mine, drawing us both to her side. With each slow step I took toward the bed, I felt her wrap around me.

The air between us was thick with unspoken words, missed opportunities, and hope.

I wasn't afraid for her anymore. She was here, whole and herself. She was the girl I watched come down the stairs to the beach that night. The girl who flicked her sunglasses onto her head and told me she didn't need me, but she did. The girl who put on a tiny purple dress to seduce me back to her side.

She was sitting in the middle of the bed. There was no way for me to get to her without us being in bed together, and that hadn't happened with both of us awake. I briefly considered whether it was something she wanted. When Amelia sharply inhaled, my eyes jumped to hers and that was all I needed. I took one more step and lowered to my hands and knees on the mattress, crawling until my face hovered just above hers.

"Are you ready for this?" I asked her, my eyes trained on hers. I knew mine were glowing bright blue. We couldn't stop our power from taking hold when we were together. It had happened constantly since she woke up without the Keeper. Blue and violet swirled above us, dancing and twirling around each other.

"For what, exactly?" she whispered on an exhale. She licked her lips, just the tip of her tongue darting out and then disappearing. I wanted mine to be where it was.

"This is the moment of no return, Amelia," I warned. "This is the moment we don't come back from. There are no do or die situations. This is you. And me. And the truth of what we have. Are you ready for *this*." I struggled to get the words out. My wolf was howling in my mind, my power spinning a cyclone around hers. The pressure inside my head felt very similar to shifting, but I wasn't going to shift. This was something else entirely.

She nodded, a small jerk of her head.

"No. Say it, Amelia. Tell me you're ready, that you know this is you and me and nothing else." Every other declaration between us had been fueled by emotional desperation—life and death circumstances. She would choose me.

I didn't realize my eyes were closed until I felt her hands on my cheeks.

"Aidan, look at me," she whispered. I did, and it took my breath away. "I'm ready for us. For this." She didn't just look at me, she opened herself up. In a second, I was overwhelmed with everything she felt. It slammed into everything I was, and I couldn't stop myself any longer.

I wrapped my palm around the back of her neck and pulled her up to meet me. I kept her gaze until our mouths met, and only then, as I swirled my tongue with hers, did I truly let go. Her hands were in my hair and her leg wrapped around my waist as she pulled herself up to meet me. I let go of her neck and ran my hand down her side.

Those ballerina curves were just as I remembered— the dip into her slim waist, the flare of her hips. I grabbed her hip, yanked her to press against me, and then rolled onto my back, pulling Amelia on top of me. I needed my hands free. I shoved one into her hair and pulled her mouth back to mine. We explored each other, our rhythm needy and frantic. I felt her around me, above me, inside my soul. I couldn't separate the physical caress from the way her power seduced my own, drawing me in and completely encompassing me.

I let my hands wander, gripped her hips again, and then slid one up her back beneath her shirt. The feel of her skin, smooth under my fingertips, only made me want her more. At the same time, her knees gripped my sides and she held herself up with one hand while the other fisted my shirt. Amelia kissed me in waves; a fury of exploration and then slow, lingering kisses that branded me as hers.

I reached up, content to lose myself again, when banging started on the door.

"You guys need to get out here, now!" Cole's terrified voice sliced through the sexual tension. We scrambled to right our clothes and I yanked open the door. He was already halfway down the hall, and yelled back, "Come on, I can't get her to talk to me and she's covered in blood."

Like a rocket, we were both on his heels. We sprinted behind him and around the house. We careened around a corner, and there was Bethany. She sat on the ground, her back against the wall and knees pulled up, feet planted firmly. She held her hands out in front of her. The dark blood coating them matched the red of her flannel shirt. It was smeared on her jeans and had somehow ended up on her face.

Amelia motioned for us to stop as she slowly moved closer. "Bethany? Hey, B," she said gently. Bethany's eyes were unfocused as she continued to stare at her hands, turning them over and back. Amelia took another step and called her name a little louder. This time, her head shot up and I could see the anguish etched in her features. The shock and pain were plain as day in her stricken face.

"I…I just…I was there to keep watch, to help," she started to speak. She couldn't maintain eye contact and her voice held no emotion. "I wanted to help. But she passed out, and then the bleeding started. It was everywhere. Something went wrong. I yelled. I yelled for help. I screamed, but no one heard me. I tried to stop the blood, but she woke up and tried to hurt me. I couldn't do anything. It all happened so fast. All the blood. And her claws are so sharp. I had to leave her. I had to find Cora. I couldn't help her."

Amelia slowly knelt beside Bethany. "Did you get to Cora? How are Nell and the kittens?"

Bethany shook her head quickly, short snaps back and forth. "I…I don't know. They yelled at me. Not Cora, but the others. They told me to get out, that I shouldn't be there. That I could have killed her." She stilled. "She could have died because I don't have magic," she said, her words tortured and full of disbelief.

Chapter 18
Micah

I will kill them. That's all I could think as I came around the corner, hearing Bethany's story and taking in the disheveled, terrified girl hovering on the edge of a breakdown.

Cole and Aidan stood feet from her. They both looked unsure of what to do, but ready to unleash on someone. Amelia knelt on the ground next to Bethany, but each time she reached out, Bethany withdrew. She shook her head in jerky motions and I watched her hands tremble as she held them out in front of her.

Unable to allow her to get any worse, I quickly made my way to Bethany and gently put my hand on her shoulder. Bethany looked up at me, and I was shocked to see relief. That look was all the permission I needed to pull her into my arms, one around her and one under her knees. Without a word spoken, I walked away, and they didn't stop me.

It took two steps before her tears began to soak my shirt. Soft whimpers both shattered my heart and fueled my anger. They had broken her. After everything Bethany had done, and been put through, by Immortals, they had broken her spirit. I struggled to check my rage as Baleon opened the door to our apartment.

He took one look at me, and her, and disappeared into the back rooms. With as much grace as I could, I lowered both of us onto the couch. She didn't move, her bloodstained hands clutching my shirt as she continued to cry quietly. I reached up and brushed my thumb over her cheek. "It's okay," I murmured, over and over. Slowly, the tears stopped.

Bethany looked up at me, her eyes bloodshot and swollen, the tip of her nose red. For a brief moment, I saw trust. She trusted me to see her through this. That was enough for me.

I connected to Baleon and requested a bowl of water and a washcloth. In seconds, he was in and out of the room, moving quickly and quietly. So much so, Bethany didn't notice him coming up behind her and setting the bowl within my reach.

I shifted her slightly and was able to use one hand to wring out the cloth. I moved slowly, allowing her to see what was in my hand before I touched her again. I started with her face, gently wiping away the dried smear high on her cheekbone. She leaned into the cloth and my hand, her eyes closed. I held her there, with just that thin piece of fabric between us. It was the closest we'd been in months, and the ache of missing her subsided in the smallest way.

"I'm going to set you on the couch so I can clean your hands, okay?" I said, my voice wavering with unexpected emotion. She still didn't speak, but nodded warily.

I shifted her gingerly from my lap to the cushion and slid to my knees on the floor between her legs. We maintained eye contact throughout, hers widening marginally as I lightly spread her legs apart. I pulled the bowl of water closer and rewet the cloth, wringing it out before I unclasped her hands and brought one toward me. I wiped, rewet, wrung, and wiped again, until every speck of blood was gone from her hands.

"Do you want to talk about it?" I asked.

She finally spoke. "No. I don't want to talk about it. I don't want to think about it anymore."

She mashed her lips together in a tight line and her eyes darted around as she swallowed more tears. She was going to pull herself together soon. And then she would realize what she just allowed. She'd so diligently avoided me since I'd arrived. She made her disdain for me painfully clear. Too clear, actually. What was that quote? "The lady doth protest too much." I could only hope that was indeed the case.

She began to fidget and I knew the time had come. I stood and held a hand out to help her do the same. Surprisingly enough, she took it. She stood inches from me as she stared, gripping my hand tightly. I waited as she took me in, her eyes moving across my face, searching for what, I wasn't sure.

Her blue irises were vibrant against her bloodshot eyes and even as I told myself to stop, I couldn't. I lowered my head and captured her lips. At first, she responded, her tongue teasing my own. I held her face in my hands lightly, then moved one hand to the back of her neck, pulling her against me. I had no mate, I had no destiny, and I had been a joke to everyone but her.

Her hands gripped my shirt and I waited for her to pull me even closer. Instead, she shoved me back. A quick jolt of power stopped me from somersaulting over the table and into the wall. Bethany held her fingers to her mouth and her face gave away so much. I could feel the swirl of conflicting emotions and sighed as they landed right where I knew they would. She was angry.

"What was that?" she demanded.

"That was me kissing you," I responded.

"Where do you get off kissing me? We are done. We are nothing. We weren't ever anything. *I trusted you.*" She spit the words at me. Red flushed her cheeks and made me want to kiss her again, which would have required Baleon to save me from an untimely death.

She had just been through a traumatic ordeal and I didn't want to fight, but she clearly did. Since there may not have been another chance for me to fight for her, I went for it.

I took a step forward and while she winced, she didn't budge. "Were we nothing? Are you so sure? Because it was you kissing me back right then, wasn't it, Bethany? It was you who came willingly into my arms and sought solace."

I pulled at the button-down shirt I was wearing, and said, "Aren't these your tears on my shirt? Did I not clean the blood from your hands? When will you realize that we *were* something, that we *are something*? You cannot hate with such venom unless you have loved in some capacity. At least I am not afraid to admit my feelings for you.

"They have always been there," I continued, refusing to look away, refusing to miss one silent response. "From the moment I saw you, on every date we had, during every moment I tried to keep you safe and away from all of this. You didn't see the fights I had with my mother and her brood of Hunters so I could be the one who brought you your meals and made sure they did not treat you like a human toy. You turned me away and cursed my name while I convinced my mother a human could not interfere with her plans, all the while knowing if the day came when you set your mind to it, you would do just as much damage as anyone with power running through their veins. I see who you are. I see the person you hide."

Taking another step toward her, I breathed in deeply and lowered my voice. "I hide the same one—the one who has been used and spurned and done their best to make the right choices for the right reasons. I fight the battle to find myself and be myself while tuning out the constant judgment coming from all angles. My life is made of cleverly crafted lies I've been told since I could understand the words by someone who truly believes their intent is a justification for the decimation of a people they were sworn to protect. Take away the power and the royal title, and we are the same."

Bethany hadn't spoken. She hadn't moved. She stared at me, her face blank, giving away nothing. I tried to wait, to give her time to process all I had laid bare, but I couldn't.

"Say something, please." The words were choked, a hoarse whisper.

She closed her eyes and slowly reopened them, resignation settling across her features. "I can't do this right now, Micah. I can't process all of that, and all of this. I just…can't."

I nodded stiffly and stepped to the side. She moved past me, but stopped at the door.

"Thank you." Her words were barely there and as she walked away, they unraveled me further. Perhaps it had been easier to allow her to hate me, but the small fire of hope burning in my soul was enough to confirm I had made the right choice.

Chapter 19
Aidan

Amelia and I rushed to the barn, concerned for Nell and her kittens. I worried about Elias's reaction if anything had happened to either. With the rest of the pack here, devoted to the man who had been their leader for years, it could be mutiny in a second.

The barn doors were open and sunlight lit the path. Small groups of Immortals were huddled together, but went silent as Amelia and I approached. The AniMages bowed slightly and the pregnant Mages smiled sadly. I pulled Amelia around a corner, looked around to confirm no one was near us, then dropped the barriers Elias had taught me to put in place, allowing the emotions and thoughts of the other AniMages to flood my mind.

Amelia grasped my hand and pulled at the edges of my mind, wanting to know what I saw. I used our connection to show her as well.

We saw the situation unfold like a replay in someone's mind. They entered the barn as Bethany ran toward them, screaming for help. Just as we'd found her, Bethany was covered in blood, bordering on hysterical. The yowling screams from Nell pierced the background. The AniMage called for Cora and Elias. Elias was out hunting, trying to find something Nell would eat, but Cora was there in seconds.

Bethany tried to tell them what happened, but no one would listen. She was shoved aside, literally, as AniMages and Mages gathered to do what they could. It was Melinda who completely turned on Bethany, which wasn't shocking in the least. She hissed the words at Bethany, a venomous string of insults that had eventually broken our friend.

I came out of the memory filled with rage, ready to end Melinda once and for all. She had attacked Amelia and me against Elias's orders. She had taken Bethany and taunted her for hours when she was only supposed to watch over her until Amelia came. And then she had set Braxton against me. That woman was poison and had no business being part of my pack.

I took two steps before Amelia's hand wrapped around my wrist. I instantly felt the anger diminish slightly. "Aidan, no, not now. We need to focus on Elias and Nell. You have to show them that we don't lash out in retaliation. We lead. We take care of our people first."

She was right. Of course she was. But I wanted this made right. "She needs to understand that taking care of my people also means protecting them from each other. I won't allow this." A growl quickly followed my words and I felt the tightness inside me, a coiled spring ready to let my wolf loose.

Amelia gripped my arm with both hands now. Her power weaved in and around mine, trying to settle the fury building inside me.

"Bethany is with Micah, where she needs to be. We are here, where we need to be. We are not Julia and her Hunters. We don't attack without all the facts and a clear head. I appreciate that you love her as much as I do and want to protect her, but our decisions aren't ours alone anymore." As Amelia spoke, she continued to use the mixture of her and Cole's power to bring me down to a reasonable level.

The tension uncoiled and I audibly exhaled, rubbing my free hand over my face. "I haven't been that angry since…" I trailed off and she continued for me. "Since I left with Micah," Amelia finished.

I nodded. "I didn't mean to—"

She cut me off again. "I know, Aidan. It's hard to believe that was only weeks ago, but we are different people now. We're in this together and we have responsibilities."

I shook my head, once again awed by what the combination of Amelia's time at Cresthaven and the integration of Cole's power had done. She still had her impulsive tendencies, but she saw the bigger picture.

I leaned down and stole a quick kiss. The tingle of electricity that passed between us was expected and welcome. I wanted to linger, and I could tell she did, too, but I pulled back and quickly pecked a kiss to the tip of her nose, breaking the tension.

We walked back into the main aisle toward Nell's stall.

"Are they happy here?" Amelia asked me quietly, her voice coming over my shoulder. I turned to find her walking slowly, staring at each stall we passed. I forgot this was her first time in the barn and I could feel her conflicted emotions. I pulled her beside me and wrapped my arm around her waist so we walked together.

"They are, Ame," I assured her. "They're free and their children will be free. They're protected and they have their power. We aren't making them stay here, this is their choice."

We stepped up to Nell's stall and I knocked on the wood frame. The door was open, so we took it in simultaneously. Amelia's emotions spiked and I knew she was crying, but I made no move to stop her. I was just as taken by the scene.

Elias sat on the mattress spanning the width of the stall, his back against the wall. He looked exhausted, but absolutely enthralled by the woman in his lap. She was curled on her side, asleep. Her head was on his thigh and her arm came over that same leg, snaking up toward his waist where she held his hand. Her legs were pulled into a fetal position with just enough room to see three small kittens piled on top of each other, their tiny little bodies protected by both their parents.

"How is she?" I asked my friend.

"She's finally able to shift back and forth, and is resting now. I still don't completely understand what happened, but they worked together to stop the bleeding. My children are alive and healthy. We don't know yet if they have power, but it doesn't matter. She's healthy. And she's come back to me." Elias's words were choked as he looked up at Amelia. "You brought her back to me. She showed me how you healed her in Cresthaven. How you saved her life. Amelia, I can't ever repay this debt."

"There is no debt, Elias," she said, her own voice thick with emotion. "I did what was right. I did what I was supposed to do. I would do it again. These are my people."

Amelia stopped and looked up at me. Her eyes were full of unshed, happy tears, and for once, they weren't violet. They were the eyes I initially couldn't stop thinking about. The ones that looked more green than brown and belonged to the quiet girl I had to know.

"No," she corrected herself, still looking up at me, "these are *our people*."

"That we are, Amelia Bradbury," Elias confirmed as he stroked a hand over Nell's hair. He looked back up at us. His smile was gone and his blue eyes glowed softly as he continued. "You have done more than you realize. You have given us hope, and hope is a rare and fragile thing to people who have lost more than they've won in their lives. Know this to the depths of your soul: we will stand beside you and follow you anywhere."

"No, they won't." A small voice came from behind us. I turned to find Dillon standing in the row of stalls. He looked uncomfortable, shifting his weight from one bare foot to the other. I looked back at Elias and he waved me off, making a *shut the door* motion with his hand. So, we stepped back and I quietly slid the door in place.

"What do you mean, little man?" I asked. Amelia and I stepped toward him and Dillon shuffled forward, sticking out his hand.

"I know we already met, Miss Amelia, but I wanted to thank you for saving my mamma. Thank you for bringing her back to me." Amelia smiled tentatively and shook his hand. She stooped down, as I typically did, and kept ahold of his hand lightly.

"You are very welcome, Dillon. Miss Bethany and…uh, Mr. Aidan, have told me a lot about you." Amelia threw me a smirk over her shoulder. "Can you tell me what you were talking about just now? I know your mamma was able to know things. Do you know things, too?"

Dillon nodded quickly and pulled his hand from hers, shoving it into the pocket of his bright green hoodie. "Mr. Elias is only part right. He will follow you. Lots of these people will. But not all of them. Some of them don't want you. They want to hurt you."

I was beside Dillon in an instant, my hand gripping his arm. "Who, Dillon? Who wants to hurt us?"

"Aidan!" Amelia's sharp tone brought me clarity, and I saw Dillon's wide eyes and pale face. His freckles were like brown pebbles on a white sand beach. I immediately dropped his arm, apologizing.

Dillon backed up a few steps, but said, "It's okay, Mr. Aidan. I'm scared, too. But my owl isn't showing me who. I just know Miss Amelia isn't safe here. But she knows where to go, don't worry. Her mamma took care of her, too."

As he typically did, Dillon took off running once his message was delivered. He flew past AniMages and Mages, muttering "'scuse me," as he passed between them.

Amelia was staring at nothing, her eyes unfocused before she gasped.

"He said my mother took care of me, too. That means wherever I'm supposed to go, whatever I'm supposed to be doing, is in that journal."

Chapter 20
Amelia

I was so focused on getting to my mother's journal, on being able to make a real plan, I almost missed Bethany and Cole sitting in the living room. I immediately diverted in their direction, Aidan on my heels.

Bethany had clearly showered, her hair long and straight, and her clothes no longer stained. She was huddled in the corner of one of Derreck's massive black leather couches as she and Cole spoke quietly.

They saw us and beckoned us over. There were still shadows in her eyes, but Bethany forced a smile and tried to fake her normally bright attitude.

"Hey, Ame," she said. Her faked attempt fell flat and we both knew it.

"They are all fine, B. Nell, the kittens, and Elias are all fine. Because of you, they got to them in time," I said.

I watched the angst drain from Bethany in one deflating gush. Her shoulders collapsed, her eyes closed, and her head dropped back. "Oh, thank god," she whispered.

"If you hadn't been there, she may not have made it," Aidan said. We didn't actually know that for a fact, but I was okay with his white lie.

Bethany smiled and this time, it was genuine. It was relief and gratitude and I was thrilled to see it. I turned to find Cole wearing a similar grin and couldn't stop myself from reaching out, taking both of their hands, and squeezing.

"That's the good news, but the bad news is Dillon told us there are traitors in our midst and I'm not safe here. He alluded to the answers being in Mom's journal, so we were on our way to get them and really dig in." I tried to keep my tone light, but Cole was immediately scowling and concern flattened Bethany's smile.

"We can help," she said. "Let us help you go through them. It will be faster if we work together."

I started to protest, but Cole cut me off. "She's right, Ame. You said I should read them anyway."

I looked up to find Aidan wearing a look that asked why I was surprised. A small laugh escaped as I shook my head. "Fine. Fine! Four brains are better than two anyway."

"How about six, with two that understand a little more about our history?" Micah's voice carried from behind me and I turned to find him standing in the doorway. Bethany immediately stiffened next to me.

"Oh, you don't—"

"Oh, it's fine, Ame. There's no reason he can't help. The more the merrier, right?" Bethany cut in, her response obviously forced. Under no circumstances would she let him see that he bothered her.

I turned to her, ready to argue, but her eyes pled for me not to make it a big deal. "Um, yeah, of course. Of course you and Bale can help. But where should we go? We won't all fit in my room."

"Let's go down to my apartment. I have space," Micah suggested. He hadn't taken his eyes from the back of Bethany's head. His eyebrows pulled together and I watched him clench his teeth on one side, and then the other.

I looked up at Aidan to find him watching them as well. When our eyes connected, neither of us had to say anything. This was a terrible idea and we both knew it.

Aidan opened the door to Micah's apartment and allowed Charlie and Onyx to enter first. They had both been asleep on the bed when we retrieved the journal pages and wouldn't leave our sides now.

As we stepped inside, the tension in the room was obvious. Bethany sat perfectly straight with her hands in her lap while Micah stood awkwardly, trying to look anywhere but at her. Cole looked between the two of them from his chair, shaking his head.

"Is, uh, everything okay in here?" I had to ask.

Micah gave me a sad smile and Bethany at least met my eyes for a second. She and I needed ten solid minutes of girl time to get to the bottom of all this.

"We are fine. We should start reviewing the pages," Micah said as he held out his hand. I put a small stack of paper in it and continued around the room as everyone got settled, handing pages to Aidan, Cole, Bethany, and Bale.

I sat down on a small couch next to Aidan and felt a quick shiver as our arms brushed against each other. Warmth spread from our point of contact outward, easing some of the nervous energy I battled. The more often those moments occurred, the more I appreciated the strange balance we brought each other now that the Keeper was imprisoned. I still struggled to believe she was contained, but my connection to Aidan only grew every day she stayed bound.

Realizing I had drifted off into my own thoughts, I looked around at my friends, who sat silently, waiting for my direction.

"From what I understand so far," I started, "my mother knew something was going on that most of the Immortals didn't realize. She searched for answers and knew they were hiding things. She had begun testing to make her way onto the Elder council and had yet to find the entrance to the council chamber. I think that's where we need to focus. Why were there Elders? What were they hiding? But, if you read anything that seems amiss, just speak up. We don't have a ton of pages each, so this should go fast."

Everyone nodded and got to work.

I was quickly engrossed in the page I held. My mother's handwriting was more hurried here. What had been loops and swirls was now a tilted slant of letters, flowing together in what looked like a stream of consciousness from her mind to the page.

I worry for Julia. She has taken to spending too much time with Cane and I don't trust him. I see the looks she doesn't, I know what they are trying to hide, and I see where it will end. I hear the things he does not say, but there is no way for me to prove his true intent. That is for her to learn for herself, but her heart is already so fragile. She has fought the darkness of her father's polluted mind for so long, and I don't know how much longer she can hold strong. For now, she simply questions. How long will it be before her questions are demands and lives are lost? I only wish the visions were clearer.

I spent the day with Tragar and we poured over dozens of books, trying to find plans for the original castle. I have to find my own way into the chamber, but there is nothing. It's as if this castle materialized from nowhere. I have one last card up my sleeve, but I had hoped to keep my true ability a secret. No one, not even Nathaniel, understands what I am capable of. I cannot decide if this is truly a gift or a curse, but if my visions are correct, I will need to harness this power to save the ones I love.

"I think my mom really cared about your mom, Micah. It's strange to think about them at our age." My words broke the silence of the room, but Micah's gaze only flicked up to mine as he *mmmhmmmd* and went back to the pages.

"Got something good there?" I asked, intrigued by his lack of response.

"Not entirely certain," he mumbled without even looking up.

"I believe you will want to hear this, Amelia." Baleon's voice always surprised me. The calmness emanating from a man who oozed lethal force was such a conundrum.

"Please, go ahead, Baleon," I said.

He scanned the page again and flipped it over. "It appears your mother found her way to the council chamber, but she wasn't able to get in. Sentinels guarded the doors and refused her entry. However, she was able to gather some information.

"She notes a bright white light coming from the room that pulsed and brightened as she drew near. She felt the pull of it, drawing her in, and only the Sentinels themselves stopped her. They attempted to explain and then wipe her memories, but that particular power doesn't have the same effect on her. She was able to recall the memories, though not crisply. They said, 'Only those connected to the mother may enter this place. You do not carry her light.'"

I was mulling over his statement when Aidan spoke. "Hey," he sounded excited, but then stopped. I turned to find him scratching his jaw, his eyes unfocused as he stared at the ceiling. "I've heard the term Sentinel before…I just can't remember where."

"You have?" I was shocked, but then remembered there was a huge chunk of time we had spent apart. He had become such a part of me, it was hard to reconcile.

"Yeah, it just isn't coming to me. I'll remember, though. It'll come back." An intense look of concentration came over his face and I let him think.

Bethany spoke next. "I think you'll want to read these, but they aren't what we're looking for specifically. They talk a lot about your dad and her struggle with the betrothal. She really loved him, Ame. And he loved her."

I wanted to smile, to allow some of the joy of my parents' romance to settle on my heart, but the thought of my father was still hard to have without tears coming with it.

"What about you, Cole?" I asked, trying to redirect.

"A lot of these were visions," he said. "They weren't clear, but they were pretty gruesome. From what I know of how it all went down, Mom's visions were pretty accurate. She even called the Hunters' allegiance to the Queen."

"Trickery, you mean," Bale interrupted, his voice steeled. "There was no allegiance. She convinced us her lies were truth and used Cane's death to stir the spite and hate inside a few, which led to our enslavement."

Micah stood perfectly still and stared at Bale. I wondered if Baleon had ever been so forthcoming about his true feelings.

"Why did you stay?" I had wondered since I'd realized the power of compulsion didn't work on Bale.

"The one I loved was gone and Prince Mikail was only just born. It was easy to see where she would lead him and I wanted freedom for my people. For all of us. I knew of the prophecy, and took it as my duty to protect the future King. There was no way for me to know another King would fulfill it." The look exchanged between Baleon and Micah was one of quiet gratitude.

Micah tried to speak, but the sounds were choked. He pursed his lips and cleared his throat. "I believe I have something as well. Tragar traveled through the local regions, since no one ever strayed far from the castle in the old days, and talked to everyone. He listened to their stories, their rumors, their lore."

Micah skimmed the page as he continued. "He often scribed the stories while he was in the villages and brought them back to the castle. According to this, he heard a story from someone who claimed to have known one of the Elders. They knew the identity of the Elder and their mate, though they would not reveal it. They said once an Elder was claimed to the council, they could never be more than a short distance from the chamber without physical harm coming to them.

"This person talked about how the mates were just as important as the chamber. Mates were necessary to mix varying types of magic, which was not only a requirement for the marriage to be approved, but kept the Elders alive. This person, they didn't speak to share Elder secrets, they spoke out of fear. Your mother says here that her worst fears had come true. Even Tragar told her in order to become fully immersed in the council, to truly have her questions answered, she would have to give up your father."

"Okay," I said slowly, processing through everything. "So, we know my mother found the chamber, and was told she didn't carry the light, whatever that is. We know her visions were accurate and she cared about Julia, even though she knew who she would become. And she couldn't accept her position on the council without marrying the person they chose for her."

"Rhi." It was a quiet word that echoed off every surface and rattled inside my head.

I turned to look at Aidan. "Excuse me?" I said.

He sighed, giving Cole a look that my brother returned with an angry glare. "Your mother was supposed to marry Rhi. It's part of why he had it out for you, and why he enjoyed torturing your father. It's what they fought about."

Now it was my turn to glare. "And you're just telling me this now, because…?"

"It is irrelevant," Baleon responded. "It would never have happened. Your mother saw her destiny and it was with your father. She details her visions. She knew you and your brother would be a part of her life, and she knew what her sacrifices would be to get us to this place. She saw the need for the Elder power. She came back for it. She convinced them to give her what she wanted, whether they wanted to or not. She'd take the power she needed if she had to." Baleon's tone was clipped and a muscle ticked in his jaw.

"Wait." Dots connected in my mind. "That wasn't in the journal. It couldn't have been. Tragar said these were from before she left. How do you know what happened when she came back? What else do you know?"

I was on my feet and standing over him in an instant.

"Amelia, calm down." I barely heard Aidan's voice through the thundering in my ears. Had we been wrong to trust Baleon?

Baleon looked up at me passively, which only irked me further. My power was building and spreading, waves of energy pulsing through me. I hadn't been triggered like this since the Keeper was bound. Cole's power didn't calm me this time. The potential threat had every part of me on high alert.

"This is entirely unnecessary, Amelia. Bale, there is no reason not to be forthcoming," Micah cut in, and I whipped around.

"So, you know whatever he isn't saying?" I accused, and Micah held the same irritating passive look Bale had.

"Everyone accumulates knowledge, Amelia. And you never know when you'll need it. Baleon is the closest thing to a father I've ever had. I would not betray his trust unless absolutely necessary." Micah gestured to Bale, and he nodded grimly.

"My mate was one of the Council Elders," he said. "No one knew she was on the council; therefore, no one knew I was anything more than her husband." Baleon's words were more shocking than I'd anticipated.

"There were high hopes for your mother. My Lavignia spoke of her often. She also spoke of Liana's willfulness and that she would play a central role in what was to come. The others would not hear it. Lavignia was the seer, yet they disregarded her visions, so she confided in me."

Baleon's eyes never left mine, his voice flat until he mentioned Lavignia by name. Each time he spoke of her, his voice hitched. "When the time came and your mother found her way back into the castle, she went to each council Elder. Liana knew who they were and she knew where to find them outside the chamber. She started with Lavignia. The power your mother never disclosed was her ability to absorb others' powers, store it, and ultimately, transfer it to you.

"She refused to take no for an answer. Livvy gave to her willingly, she knew where we were heading, but she tried to warn your mother. Liana wouldn't listen. I wasn't allowed to be there, and I respected the fact that there were details Livvy could never share with me, but I felt it. I felt the drain on us both when she handed over pieces of her life source to save you. To save us all. When she came back to me, she had aged fifty years, no longer the young woman I'd married. Her power was a fraction of what it once was and she couldn't protect herself anymore." Baleon paused.

"Ultimately," he said, "her lack of power was what got her killed. My wife, my mate, died to save you. And, if I must, I will do the same."

The room erupted. Aidan, Cole, and even Bethany, were pelting Bale with questions. I sat down and let my mind spin. I ran through everything we'd learned, and the answer was clear.

"We have to go to the castle," I blurted. "She told me everything I need to know and we can't change anything unless we find that chamber and the answers she couldn't."

Chapter 21
Aidan

I paced the edge of the tree line and opened my mouth, only to swallow down the words. I was angry, there was no doubt about that, but I wouldn't resort to hurling insults. Amelia leaned back against a tree trunk, her hands in her hoodie pocket.

I walked past her for the umpteenth time and she waited silently while I figured out what to say. After she declared we should run off to a castle no one's been inside for almost three decades, the room filled with shouts and arguments.

Baleon was the only one to agree with her, while the rest of us took turns telling her how ridiculous her notion was. Finally, I couldn't take it anymore. I picked her up, threw her over my shoulder, and stormed out. The last thing I heard was Cole's laughter.

She pummeled my back until I set her down a few feet from where she now stood. Gripping her shoulders, I wanted to shake her. I wanted to shake her like a doll until she relented and told me she'd just do whatever I wanted so I could keep her safe.

A growl built in my throat and my wolf sat none-too-patiently in the back of my mind, telling me to force her into submission. Amelia finally looked up at me, and said, "I know none of this makes sense to you, Aidan. It barely makes sense to me. But I know I have to do this, and I know I can't do it without you."

It was the last thing I'd expected from her and the only thought I had was, "Of course you can't, because you are *mine*." My wolf howled in my mind as I crushed her to me. My fingers dug into her shoulders and she bent backwards with the force of my kiss. My tongue dove deep into her mouth. I claimed her. I made sure she knew I would be there even if I thought it was an insane idea. Because she was mine. Mine to kiss. Mine to care for. Mine to protect. *Mine*.

Just as abruptly as the kiss started, I stopped it. Her lips were the color of strawberries, the area around them pink from the prickly facial hair I hadn't taken the time to shave. Her eyes were violet and her power shimmered in the air around her, my bright blue smoke woven throughout the same space. She was beautiful, wearing my mark, her breath shallow from the exchange.

"You…I just…this is…" I couldn't find the rest of the words, just intermittent growls rumbling inside my chest. I clenched my fists and started to pace—again. As I spun on my heel, the truth settled in and I audibly exhaled my frustration. I looked up at Amelia and she must have sensed my resolution. She stepped away from the trees and into my path. I stepped to her, close enough that she was forced to look up at me.

"You're going to do this, whether I agree or not, aren't you?" I asked.

She nodded. "I have to. Everything has led me to it."

"In a minute, you're going to define everything, but for now, just listen to me," I said, tilting her chin up with one finger. Her eyes narrowed.

"You keep talking about this being us," I started, "you say we are in this together, but I don't think you actually mean it. There are things to deal with here and decisions to be made. Ones you don't get to make for both of us. You don't get to snap your fingers and expect me to come along for the ride. If we're really in this together, we make decisions like this *together*. Otherwise, I will resort to locking you in one of Derreck's stalls until you're willing to listen to reason."

We were nose to nose as the violet flared in her eyes, a starburst exploding from her pupil outward. I felt her intention and did nothing to stop her two hands from planting against my chest and shoving. I just didn't move.

Amelia shoved again and my only response was an arch of my eyebrow.

With the third shove came the anger I also expected, so before she could react, I spoke quickly. "Before you freak out, listen to what I'm saying, Amelia. You want to act. That's what you always want. But there are people here who are counting on us. We put all of these people in danger, just being with them. Earlier, you stopped me from going off the handle on a personal vendetta, and I'm trying to do the same now."

Her posture relaxed ever so slightly, but her power started gathering around her hands, so I continued.

"The thing is, we're all afraid. Bethany's afraid to stay here, but she's also afraid to go. Cole's afraid everyone will find out his power is gone. Micah's afraid his mother will wake up before we know what to do and how to stop her. Baleon's afraid his wife died in vain because you're so focused on what you do or don't know and finding the answer to some riddle we aren't even sure is still relevant, you can't see the big picture. And do you know what I'm afraid of? Do you, Amelia?" I asked.

"I'm afraid of you," I said, closing the distance between us faster than she could react. I snatched her hand in mine and felt the burn as her fire melded with my own. It slid from my hand to shoulder, singeing me, sending electric currents through my veins and arteries, which made me both want more and to pull away.

Instead, I pushed back, sending my own power back into her. "I'm afraid you will be so set on martyring yourself for this prophecy, you'll never give me the chance to love you, to be with you, to protect you," I gritted out as the flames licked down my chest, and swallowed a groan that was a combination of pain and pleasure.

I opened my eyes to find hers closed as she swayed on her feet, her head back. I pulled at her hand and her eyes fluttered opened.

"Do you feel that, do you feel what we are together?" I asked.

Her eyes were unfocused as she nodded. "I do," she said, breathless.

"Now, look around. *Look, Amelia*," I demanded. Her eyes snapped open.

The air around us was nothing but light—blue, orange, and violet light surrounding us, a glowing mist.

"Can you honestly tell me we shouldn't take a minute to figure out what this is and how we can use it?"

I pulled my hand from hers and took slow steps backwards as the light faded and our connection lessened. I wanted to do the opposite. I wanted to pull her to me and wrap my arms around her, but she wouldn't hear me if I did.

As Amelia's mind cleared, her hands came to her hips and a scowl twisted her lips. "You don't fight fair, Montgomery," she grumbled.

"But, I do make good points," I responded with an easy grin.

Her eyebrow arched and she rolled her eyes. As she opened her mouth to add something sure to be sarcastic, a twig snapped. I shoved her behind me, on the verge of shifting.

"Don't sound the alarms, it's just me." Micah's voice carried over the hill as he crested the top. I pulled up from a half-crouch and tried to calm my boiling blood.

"You're lucky you aren't in multiple pieces, man," I said, stepping toward him as Amelia smacked me from behind, saying, "And so are you. I can take care of myself, you know."

"Yes, I know. You're damn near invincible, Amelia," I muttered as I struggled to find calm between the emotions from our exchange and the residual fight or flight in my system.

"Bicker later," Micah snapped. "My mother is awake. That means time is short. We need a plan and you need to leave if you're going."

Chapter 22
Amelia

I didn't wait around for Aidan to say anything else. It was one thing to lose myself in his kiss, or for us to talk about our responsibilities to the Immortals, but he'd said it again. *He loved me.* I ached to believe it was true and that the emotion belonged solely to him. But, I also saw what just happened. I saw what we were capable of and that only made me question my emotional, and physical, response to him.

I made my way up the hill toward the house and as I got closer to the barn, found myself in front of a group of women, some pregnant, but all wearing huge smiles. I felt Aidan walk behind me, and thankfully, he kept going. I needed a moment of space from everything that we were.

Finally, Cora stepped out of the group and I sighed in relief at knowing at least one face. She reached out and pulled me into a hug. When she stepped back, her hands slid down my arms and she held my hands loosely in hers.

"It's so lovely to see you, Amelia. I told the ladies you were up and about, but that you'd need a few days before you had it in you to venture our way. From what we saw coming up over that hill, it looks like you and Aidan are finding your way." Her green eyes twinkled and I chuckled, imagining the light show we'd created. Cora wasted no time. Soon, I found myself formally meeting many of the women I'd only spoken to through the bars of my cell.

I had vague memories of a woman with black hair who introduced herself as Sully. One became clear as she took my hand. I remembered swaying over her, Cole screaming at me to pull back, to save myself.

I opened my eyes to find Sully rubbing her hand over her swollen belly, a small smile playing on her lips. "When?" I asked, the word stuck in my throat as emotion overtook me.

"Any day now," she responded. I held a bewildered smile as I looked around. Each woman here was a life I'd fought to save.

A girl who looked to be in her twenties stepped forward, her blonde hair falling down her back. As she pulled me in for a hug, she said, "I feel your pain, your conflict. Trust your heart to guide you and listen when it calls."

"Come now, Willow," Cora said. "No prophetic riddles tonight." Willow let me go and with a conspiratorial wink, rejoined the circle around me. As I went to speak, the ladies started talking over each other. They told me about their unborn babies, how Nell's kittens were doing, how every day their power grew and they felt more like themselves.

I was overwhelmed with their emotions. The gratitude, joy, and sheer happiness enveloping me from all sides were intoxicating. I was grinning from ear to ear when I heard one of them coo, "Prince Mikail, how are you?"

Micah chuckled from behind me. "Now, ladies, what have I told you? Please call me Micah. There are Kings and soon-to-be Queens that deserve your allegiance far more than me." I had to swallow down a snort of laughter as they oohed and awed like fangirling teenagers. *Micah had game.* That thought was hysterical to me.

"Unfortunately, my lovelies, I do have to take this one away. We have much to attend to, but I will be out this evening to make my rounds and work with anyone who'd like to." Micah lightly grasped my elbow and steered me away from the women. I called out my goodbyes over my shoulder and turned to Micah.

"'Now, ladies, what have I told you?'" I teased. A red flush crept up his neck and he shoved me a few feet in front of him.

"Go, you wretched girl, and deal with your mate. He's inside and far too patient, if you ask me," he said, eyeing me.

My smile fell to a scowl, which Micah ignored.

"I'm going to pull the others together in my apartment so we can really start planning," he said. "But, Amelia, he's right. You do need time to determine what you two can do together. The rest of us can feel it. We feel the strength between you, we feel the...uh, *emotion*, between you, and you need to understand what all that means. Go apologize for being your defensive, intolerable self and let the man keep a shred of his dignity. He keeps putting you first and that would wear on anyone."

"I am not intolerable," I muttered as he walked away. I heard his snort of disagreement and shot a small blast of power at his heels. Micah waved a hand and it disintegrated before it even hit. Sometimes, I hated how much better he was with magic than me.

It felt like eons since I'd walked through Uncle Derreck's door for the first time, yet, coming in now, his living room looked exactly the same. Except there was a six-foot-tall, smoky-eyed boy stretched out on the couch with his hands laced behind his head and tattoos visible as his sleeves bunched around flexed biceps.

I felt Aidan's frustration, but also his resolve. He knew I was there and waited for me to make the first move. It was a miracle we were the only two people in the room, but most people were eating, so the main living space was ours. Instead of curling into his lap and whispering my apology in his ear, which was what I wanted to do, I decided to do something I knew he'd appreciate more. And, I had to prove to myself our connection was more than toe-curling kisses and roaming hands. I knew we were drawn to each other, but there was more. I knew there was.

I closed my eyes and relaxed, allowing my power to build. My mind saw the living room in a new way, an elemental way. I saw traces of power here and there, the remnants from others who had recently been in the room, but I was drawn to the clouds of blue and orange electricity congregating in front of me. Aidan's body had been replaced by the life source that made him an Immortal. I was surprised at how much his power was laced with orange Hunter magic, but it only made him more intriguing.

I sent my violet smoke toward him, a wisp that grew into a thread and built into a rope. The closer my power got to Aidan, the more his responded, reaching for me. Unlike with Micah, there was no feeling out process. Our souls recognized each other and the power was our visual confirmation of that.

Tears pricked at my eyes as my heart rate increased and his breaths became shallow. He felt it. He felt the overwhelming need to be close, to be joined together. What had been a slow creep toward each other ended as the two stopped, just centimeters apart. In one sudden motion, our powers swirled around each other, the cords spinning so quickly, I couldn't separate violet from blue from orange. As they merged, the cord snapped into one solid gateway between our minds. Aidan, along with all of his over-protective alpha tendencies, was in my head, and it felt right.

Hello, there, I said the words softly, putting my pitiful game to the test.

Well, hello yourself, doll. What exactly was that we were just doing? He didn't get up, or even pull his hands from behind his head, which only made our exchange more fun.

We've been circling this for a while, but I decided it was time for us to finally seal the deal. Now, you're stuck with me.

While I was joking on one level, on another I wasn't. I wanted the security of having access to Aidan and I wanted him to have the same with me. To test our new connection, I sent him the emotions skimming through me. The ones that wanted to hop over that chair, wrap around him, and kiss him breathless.

I expected to hear him in my head, so his voice surprised me, especially since he was now standing directly in front of me.

"You can't do that," he murmured as he dipped his head to kiss me. His stubble was rough on my chin and I didn't want to like it as much as I did.

"Do what?" I asked between kisses.

"Make me forget why I was mad in the first place by using your wily charms," he responded.

I reached up and pulled him down to me. "Oh, but I can, and I did. And now, we have to go downstairs to plot our rebellion, so I can't even make good on my charming ways."

He sighed, but then grabbed me by the waist and hoisted me up. I wrapped my legs around his waist and giggled while he nipped at my neck, and said, "Fine. We'll go, because I know I don't actually have a choice in the matter."

"At least you're learning," I said, grinning wickedly and feeling quite smug.

"Oh, you should have quit while you were ahead, doll," he said, his tone immediately concerning. I felt his intention a second before I found myself slung over Aidan's shoulder, my ass in the air—again—for the world to see as he strode out the front door and around the cabin.

I gave up pummeling his back when the catcalls started. The hooting and hollering from the AniMage crowd made me want to disappear, and all I felt was Aidan's cocky swagger. Damn it all if I didn't like him more for it.

It took a few minutes for the flames in my face to die down, especially once Aidan set me on the floor and I turned to find Rynna and Uncle Derreck staring back at me. Rynna was trying to stifle a smile and my uncle looked anywhere but at me. A smile froze on my face, then I almost tripped over Charlie as I rushed to find a seat on the other side of the small living room.

I hate you, I hissed at Aidan.

You do not, he goaded. *You think I'm goooorgeous. You want to kiiiiss me. You want to huuuug me.*

Oh, SHUT UP. And, by the way, I'm totally judging you right now.

His smug laugh was interrupted by Micah.

"If you two are done, we can get started. This is actually quite serious." He stood in the kitchen, leaning back against the counters, and I immediately felt guilty. Aidan and I were just making out and acting like idiots, and Micah was right. This was not the time.

"They cannot help themselves, Prince Mikail. Their passion and focus on each other is the true sign of mates, much to the dismay of the rest of us." Baleon was standing in the corner near the front door and he shocked me with a quick wink.

"Fine, fine, but let's get on with it," Micah grumbled as he waved a hand in the air. "As you all know, the connection I have with my mother is such that I know her health, and I know she is conscious, which means she has the ability to send the Hunters after us. Now is the time to make choices quickly and to act."

I looked across the room at Derreck and Rynna, feeling a small measure of happiness as he slid his arm around her.

"My mother's journal directed us to the castle," I started. "But only Aidan and I are going." I hadn't made my plans known to anyone else before that point and no one was pleased. Cole shouted, Derreck lectured, and Micah paced and muttered, likely cursing my name.

It was actually Charlie who put them all to shame. He let out a deep, deafening howl and the room quieted. He looked across the room at Onyx, who sat by Cole, and Onyx trotted to stand just in front of Aidan. Charlie stood in front of me, staring and whimpering.

"What, boy?" I asked as I leaned down. I reached out to scratch his head when he dropped his giant paw in my palm.

You must take us. You cannot go alone. You need us.

His voice rang clear in my head. I could only stare into his depthless black eyes.

This is our purpose. You must take us. We must go home.

My head shot up and I stared over Charlie at my uncle. Charlie's tail started to thump a rhythm on the hardwood, as if he saw the dots connecting in my mind.

"Tell me again where Charlie was born," I demanded of my uncle.

"Amelia, we need to focus—" My hand shot up, a violet flame dancing in my palm, and Micah shut up.

Derreck shrugged. "I've always felt a little guilty about it, even though I don't see why it matters now, but I stole Charlie and Onyx from the castle when I left. So many people were already gone. The Elders had been forced to leave the castle to find their mates and families. While I liberated the castle of a few items I knew would make me some money, I found these two huddled together on the floor."

"Wait…Sentinels…what are Sentinels? Why can't I remember where I've heard this?" Aidan cut into the conversation abruptly, his frustration clear. All heads turned to him with looks of confusion, except Bale, who looked impressed.

"What do you know, Baleon?" I asked. I looked between him and Micah, and the confusion on Micah's face confirmed it wasn't something he was hiding.

Baleon stayed silent for a long stretch and finally, Micah walked over to him. "Bale," he said, "you will dishonor no one by helping us to use the tools we've been given. What is a Sentinel?"

Baleon grimaced, but then nodded. "The Sentinels were the guards of council chamber and only the royal guard knew of their existence. They guarded the innermost secrets of Elders, and of our people. No one knew what race they truly were. When the Elders disappeared, so did the Sentinels. We assumed they were dead."

Charlie and Onyx sat right next to each other, tails thumping, tongues hanging out of their open mouths as they breathed quickly, the excitement bouncing between them palpable. I was excited to understand them, but I was also hesitant. It was another unknown—another unexpected piece in the puzzle.

"But Rhi knew," Aidan said. "He called Charlie a Sentinel when they took Cole. Wouldn't he want Charlie if he was so important?" Aidan questioned Bale as he put his arm around me and pulled me closer to him. Instantly, the fear subsided.

Baleon shrugged. "Why would he want a dog that used to be a guard of a place that no longer mattered, at least in his mind? Leaving Charlie may be his most generous act to date. Typically, Rhi would have killed anyone who didn't matter, and clearly, Charlie and Onyx matter."

His declaration was met with a chorus of booming woofs from the dogs. Onyx ran circles around the couch we sat on. It took a sharp whistle from Bethany to stop him from trying to lick Aidan's face and shut them both up.

"So, you're just going to leave, then? What about the rest of us?" she demanded. I was surprised by the accusation in her tone. Bethany sat next to Cole, who wore a similar look. It was hard to remember that they now had the common denominator of being powerless. That their bond likely led to a fear not all of us shared.

"I do need to go, but we aren't going to leave you defenseless," I responded. "That's why we're all in this room. Micah, Derreck, let's talk about the power and the shields. Aidan, what do we do with the AniMages? Rynna, how many women still need to have babies? When can we start to spread people out and get them to safer places?"

I peppered them all with questions, but if I were honest with myself, I had no idea what I was talking about. I didn't know how to organize armies, or make sure people stayed alive, or do any of this. I didn't know what most of it meant. All that mattered to me right now was getting to that castle and finding out where this was all going to end. I was worried. I cared about all the people in this room and on this property, but this was not my area of expertise.

"Whoa, Ame. Why don't we back up and take this one step at a time?" Aidan asked as he squeezed my shoulder and took control of the conversation.

I heard the discussion continue, but my mind was elsewhere. I needed to read the journal again. I needed to see if I had missed something that would make this trip quick and focused. I got lost in my own thoughts and then felt a wet nose in my palm. I looked down to find Charlie's massive head dropped onto my lap.

I leaned over him, scratching both ears the way he loved, and whispered, "We're going home, buddy. Don't you worry."

Except, I did worry. And so did everyone else in the room. The more they all spoke, the harder it was to breathe in the space. The combination of the Keeper being bound, my familiarization with my own power, and my growing connection to Aidan, meant I felt the emotions of others more strongly than before. They were louder and harder to block out.

Finally, I moved Charlie out of my lap and stood. "I need some air, I'll be back," I said to no one in particular. As I made my way to the door, an arm looped through mine.

"And I'm coming with you," Bethany said as she fell in step with me. In that moment, with the drama and the boys behind us, and the reality of what could come in front of us, it felt right to be walking beside my best friend.

I turned to Bethany, and was concerned by how exhausted she looked. "We need some girl talk, don't we?" I asked.

"Oh, honey, you have no idea," she replied with a sigh.

Chapter 23
Amelia

We stepped out into the night together. I shivered a little and sent heat from my core into my limbs. I continued the push and through our looped arms, sent the same warmth to Bethany.

She jolted a little and then relaxed again. "Hmm, fun trick. Maybe ask next time, though? Being around all of you is strange enough without it creeping into me."

Her reaction surprised me. "I didn't realize we bothered you," I said as I started to pull away.

Her hand clamped down on my arm. "Now, be fair, Ame," Bethany said sternly. "The last month has been a little over the top, even by Grimm's standards. I'm all for saving the Immortal race, but right now, I'm feeling a little cabin fever."

She sighed and we walked in silence toward a small bench-swing hanging from a tree limb. "What I'd really like is Starbucks. Or Orange Leaf. Or sushi," she said wistfully.

I grinned, and added, "Or McDonald's fries. Or a bookstore."

"Shampoo that doesn't smell unisex."

"A reason to wear makeup."

"Clothes I haven't already worn once this week."

"Quiet," we both said simultaneously.

"Jinx." Bethany got it out right before I did. We laughed together as we sat down on the swing.

My shoes sunk into the soil at first, but I moved us backward, feeling that familiar swirl in my stomach as I let go and we started to float forward, and then back again.

"It's all a little much right now, yeah?" I asked.

She snorted. "Ya think?"

"It's pretty hard to wrap my head around it all, but I'm being drawn to the castle. And now, with Charlie and Onyx being Sentinels…we have to go. I wish I could explain it better." I looked up at the constellations lining the sky and tried to breathe through the mix of anticipation and fear.

"I don't really get it, but I don't need to," Bethany said as she looked up as well. "You do. And it's clear you and Aidan are the real deal. He was hell bent to get to you, and whatever you have is only getting stronger. We can all see it. Heck, even I can feel it. That's…great for you." Bethany's attempt at enthusiasm fell short.

I put my hand over hers, and said, "Hey, B, truth…right?"

She looked at me without turning toward me. "Right," she whispered, her anxiety rolling off her.

"It's okay to miss him, and to maybe still want him. It's okay to admit it if it's what you want." I let the words sit between us.

I heard her heart beating. I felt it pick up as she took a deep breath. "But what am I?" she asked. "I'm not one of you. And even if that were okay for the average magic wielding putz, he's a Prince. *A Prince.*" Bethany fell back against the bench and let her head drop, closing her eyes.

"I wish I knew what to say, B," I said. "I wish I knew how it all worked before, or how it will work when this all ends, but I don't know. What I do know is he still wants you, and your lack of power doesn't seem to concern him in any way. And if it doesn't matter to him, why should it matter to you?" I felt good about my advice. It seemed like advice she would give me.

Bethany actually laughed—a short cackle that erupted from nowhere and was gone as quickly as it came. She shook her head, her long, blonde hair catching the moonlight.

"So, let's say we get past that part, Ame," she said, her disbelief obvious in her tone. "Everybody is hunky dory with a human and a magical Prince hooking up. Great. But there are still those pesky Hunters. And his whack-a-doo mother. And who do you think will be the one they come for? Who will get used, just like with Melinda?" She swallowed, and I felt her sadness, and the fact that she thought she was betraying our friendship, but I also felt her fear.

Bethany's next words were hoarse, forced past the emotion she tried so hard to contain. "I've stood next to you through all of this, even when you weren't here, but I don't know if this is the place for me anymore."

I couldn't argue with her. I couldn't tell her she was wrong when she was right. But we could protect her here.

"Where will you go?" I finally forced the question out as I squeezed Bethany's hand in mine.

She looked at me, tears welling in her eyes. "Maybe back home. Or just anywhere for a while until this is over. I don't want them to hurt my parents. Maybe Mexico? I could make a killing bartending down there," she joked. She always tried to lighten the mood in moments like this.

We swung back and forth slowly, holding onto each other, our hands clasped so tightly, I lost feeling in my fingers, but I didn't care.

"You're my best friend, B. My only best friend. Ever. And I'm sorry you ended up a part of this. I really am. It's my fault." My voice was thick, the lump in my throat growing as tears started to slowly fall.

"Don't be. I'm not. Amelia, look at me." Bethany's tone was sharp, and I turned to her, surprised.

"You listen to me, Amelia Bradbury," she said, her own cheeks wet. "You are doing what's right. You're doing what's right for all of these people, even the unsavory sort who treat humans like second class citizens.

"You're part of something, something big and important. And they were right, I am a liability. You can't do what you need to if you're worried about me. So, I'm going to go. And, so are you. You're going to go to that castle, and you're going to find the answers, and you're going to solve your mother's riddles. You're going to knock that Queen on her ass and stomp those damn Hunters a new one. And when you're done, we can go to the spa, like proper ladies."

I could only smile and shake my head. I hadn't known how much her being here had grounded me until the idea that she'd be gone wiped away my foundation. I knew I still had Aidan, but there was something to be said for having your best friend around. It was just different.

Bethany shrugged. "The spa was all I could come up with. I don't give a damn what we do, but we will need serious alone time when this is over."

I stood and as Bethany did the same, I pulled her in for a hard hug, wrapping my arms around her. The thought of her leaving, and being hurt, sent stabbing pain into my gut. She had to be protected. No one could find her. Holding her tightly, I willed the universe to watch over her and hide her from the other Immortals. I only let go when Bethany cried out.

Stepping back, I looked around. "What? What happened?" I was instantly half-crouched, my hands out and ready to fight.

The door to Micah's apartment burst open and the whole brigade came running.

She stared at me, open-mouthed. "You. It was you. You did something to me. You...zapped me..." she trailed off as the surprised looks on our friends' faces stared back at her.

"Oh," Micah said as he stopped next to me.

Aidan came up on my opposite side, his mouth open, eyes wide.

"What are you looking at? Why are y'all staring at me?" Bethany was starting to panic. I couldn't exactly explain the violet haze she couldn't see surrounding her, but it had clearly come from me.

"What happened? What did I do?" I asked, not taking my eyes from her.

"You have cloaked her, Amelia," Baleon spoke from behind us. "In the next few minutes, your trace will fade and she will only be visible to Immortals she chooses to show herself to. Rowena was the last Elder I knew with that ability. She tried to save her mate's life with it, but he chose to reveal himself, thinking those who took her would stay true to their word and allow her to live if he gave himself up."

As soon as the words left Baleon's mouth, Micah was in front of Bethany. His hands were on her cheeks and his speech was a hurried slur. "Please don't hide from me, love. Please don't disappear from me. I will be here for you, just as I said I would. You don't have to leave. I know that's what you want, but it does not have to be that way. We will fix this. I will take care of you."

Bethany shook her head sadly. She put her hands over his and pulled them away from her face. "For now, I have to. I have to go, and I have to do what I need to do for me. Maybe another day, Prince Mikail."

Bethany leaned in and softly kissed Micah, lingering a moment as a tear slipped from her closed eyes. When she pulled away, I knew I was the only one who could see her.

As I scanned the others, everyone looked in every direction. There was only one who looked directly at the spot where Bethany stood—Cole.

Micah saw him, too, and faster than I'd seen any Immortal move, he was in front of Cole.

"You must help her. You must protect her. It doesn't matter if anyone can see her, she is vulnerable. She is human. She should never have been a part of this, and that's my fault, but you have to do this. If you care about her—"

Micah's tirade ended when Cole punched him. One good right cross to the jaw and Micah was on his butt in the dirt with Cole leaning over him.

"You will not tell me what to do. You are not my Prince anymore." Cole's voice was deep, his anger raging as he pointed his finger down at Micah. "And I don't need to be told that Bethany needs anything. She's quite capable of handling herself, human or not. But, of course I'm not going to let her leave here alone with everything that's happening, you ignorant, self-absorbed ass. She's my friend, and I'll take care of her because that's what I do. I don't lie. I don't cut and run. I take care of the people I care about."

Cole didn't spare Micah another glance as he walked over to Bethany. Micah stood, fuming, but silent.

"Do you want my help?" Cole asked her.

Bethany looked shell-shocked. "I…I do," she stuttered. "I don't know what just happened, it sounds like a good thing, but I…I just want to leave. I can't do this anymore."

Cole didn't acknowledge anyone else, just held out his hand and waited for Bethany to take it. "Then, we'll leave," he said.

Chapter 24
Micah

My jaw throbbed, but my soul screamed as I watched Cole's outstretched hand hovering in the air between them. Though I couldn't see her, it was clear he held her hand as they walked away. He was leaving with her. Rationally, I knew there was no other choice, but I hated him in that moment.

"Mikail…" Aunt Ryannon's voice seemed far away, but I felt her hand on my arm.

I jerked away, then immediately started to apologize. It was ingrained in me to do as was proper, but this time, I didn't care. I stopped just a few words in and clamped my mouth shut. Aunt Ryannon stood next to Amelia's uncle, her lips pursed with a look of worry she couldn't hide. Amelia and Aidan were holding hands, ever the mated pair. And Bale looked at me with quiet concern.

"I'm fine," I declared to all of them. "I'm fine. This was for the best. Now we can get on with things. Let's go back inside." I turned on my heel and tried not to stomp my anger through the soles of my feet as I made my way into the small apartment.

At first, the dogs were the only ones to follow me, but eventually, the others trickled in. As soon as they were seated, I launched into the plan. I needed to control something. She was gone and I had to do *something.*

"Amelia, you and Aidan are right, you need to go," I said. "And if you're going all the way to the castle, then you need transportation. We have a private hanger near Brighton. The jet isn't huge, but it will make the trip. And I know we have an AniMage out there who is a pilot. They call him Hawk, for obvious reasons. The three of you should leave immediately."

I didn't give them time to argue, or even process the information I'd thrown at them before I continued.

"I believe Derreck and Rynna should be left in charge here. They can protect the women, children, and families who have been reunited. With fewer of us here, there is less likelihood the power will draw the Hunters this way."

Finally, I looked at Bale.

"Baleon, our duty is to find help. There are more Immortals than not who would like to see my mother dethroned. Who better to convince them than her son?" Bale nodded, but he would have come with me wherever I went.

I stood. "Okay, then? Let's go." I took one step before they all spoke at once.

I clenched my jaw and fought back the urge to use my power to silence them. I had done it to my mother once, and then spent three days locked in a small room for it. Baleon sat outside the door, his fingers wedged underneath so I could hold on to him, and made sure I was fed, but no one was allowed to speak to me. She said if I wanted silence, then I would understand what silence meant. I was seven. I hadn't used that particular skill since.

I held up both hands. Eventually, they quieted. Aidan was the first to speak again.

"You can't make that decision for all of us, Micah," he said. I felt Aidan's control slipping, but appreciated that he held back the wolf wanting to put me in my place. Right now, I did not need an excuse to let my power run freely either.

"Your offer of the jet is great," he continued, "but I lead the majority of those people out there. I need to speak to them. I need to give them a plan and someone to follow. And, I'm sorry, but Derreck isn't exactly on my list of trusted advisors, and Rynna is a caretaker. My people need a leader. Elias will have to take my place."

Derreck reclined on the sofa and looked at him with bordering indifference. "I'm not offended, Aidan, don't worry," he said. Then he turned to me. "And, you and I are not friends, Mikail, but you've proven your place. You've proven me wrong. I believe your aunt when she says you will fight for us. But if you think you are the right person to convince *our people* to fight, you are wrong." His tone grated on me and my tenuous grip on my emotions started to slip as he continued.

"You have convinced the people here to trust you, but out there, they are not your people. They are not your mother's people. They will see you as a spy and they will turn you in for treason so they don't suffer your mother's wrath themselves. You are the last person who should be out spreading the word. It should be Rynna and me, and possibly a few others."

My aunt sat, her hands in her lap, waiting her turn, always the patient one. "Mikail, Derreck is right. No matter how pure your intentions, Immortals who have not met you will not trust you. It would be dangerous, especially if you take Baleon with you."

I opened my mouth to argue. "I'm not finished," she scolded before I got a word in.

"Aidan," she said, looking across the room, "you cannot leave Elias in charge. He is distracted, rightfully so, and he has led for too long. He deserves this time with his family and doesn't need to be asked to sacrifice yet again. You should put Mikail in charge. The women love him, the AniMage men have come to respect him, and there is much Baleon can teach all of them about fighting the Hunters." Aidan was nodding thoughtfully, clearly open to the idea.

She turned to me again, this time her eyes burned red when she spoke. "Mikail, if you do this, if you choose to fully take this path, you will be dead to your mother. She will never forgive you. You will be disgraced, just as I was when she banished me. You will have made a choice you cannot come back from. Be certain, nephew. It can be a lonely path to lose your family, no matter who they are." Her unchecked sadness was stronger than I'd expected.

My eyes scanned the room as I let her words and emotions sink in. They landed on Amelia, and I realized she had yet to speak. "You have to have thoughts on this, you have thoughts on everything." I tried to banter, but it fell flat.

She just stared at me for the longest time.

"My best friend is gone. My brother is gone," she said, matter of fact. "In all likelihood, it's better that I don't know where. My father is dead. My mother is dead. I'm about to get on a jet, fly halfway across the world, and search the ruins of a castle that looks like who-knows-what so I can figure out what this prophecy really means, and what I'm supposed to do to end your mother's reign." She used air quotes around that last part, her irritation with the prophecy clear. "There's a solid chance the Hunters could find the people I care about while I'm gone. At this point, Micah, you're either in or you're out. I never had a choice about being in, not really, so be sure. I won't choose for you. I won't tell you what you should or shouldn't do."

I swallowed the dry lump that formed in my throat. I'd known this choice would come, and it always seemed so easy when it was merely hypothetical. Now, even after everything I knew about my mother, and everything she'd done to me and everyone else, I hesitated for a brief second. Then, her voice rang clearly in my mind.

It is quite disappointing to think you were one of the last children born, Mikail. I do hope the history books realize our world wasn't filled with failures like you, but great men like your father. They will see. They will see that only the strong survive and the rest serve, or disappear completely.

"There is no question. I'm in," I said. I stepped toward Aidan and held out my hand. He looked puzzled. "If you'll have me, I would be honored to fill in for you. I will train them. Bale and I will teach them, and we will build our army from the inside out."

Aidan smiled and grasped my hand, shaking it slowly. "We'll tell them together. Then, Amelia, the dogs, and I will head out with Hawk."

Relief bloomed in my chest and spread quickly through me. I would stand on my own. I would lead. I would help save my people.

Chapter 25
Aidan

Surprisingly, the AniMages and Mage women took to our plan rather quickly. They were anxious for movement and action. The realization that Julia was awake, and we were no longer safe, made them ask the right questions.

The women who could fight wanted to know how to prepare. The AniMages focused on what could be done to actually damage the Hunters and stop what felt like unstoppable power. Those with families, or still pregnant, wanted to know where they could go to stay safe. The group rallied around Micah and Baleon.

I struggled through the conversation with my pack. I wanted them to trust Micah and Baleon, and was proud they embraced our plan without complaint, but a small part of me wanted them to rebel in some way. I wanted them to need me, to demand that I stayed.

I had been their King for less than a month. Only this small group even knew the AniMages had a King again. It was a ridiculous notion and I would leave with

Amelia anyway, but the pull of my own duty created conflict I hadn't expected. So much of this journey had been about getting to Amelia, and then getting her back. But, during it all, I had grown attached to the AniMages. They were my family—my real family—and I hated leaving them vulnerable.

They had an odd mixture of fear and hope when we told them Amelia and I were going back to the castle. AniMages came forward to impart whatever knowledge they could about the area and what they remembered from their time at the castle before Julia drove them from their homes.

More of them than I'd expected were around when Julia took the throne and the Immortal world crumbled. It was heartbreaking to hear their stories, but Amelia and I gave each one the opportunity to speak their piece. We heard about how the Hunters ransacked the villages, how they burned homes to the ground and forced the AniMages to scatter. Some now questioned whether their wives had died or simply became a part of Julia's experiments. Either way, they'd lost their families and they lived on the run, always waiting for the Hunters to finish the job. Their stories helped me gain perspective. If the answer was really in that castle, we would find it.

Before we could leave, we needed to also send Rynna and Derreck on their way. They had friends all over North America, and Rynna knew of a few places they might find Tragar—the man who saved Amelia's mother's journal. The four of us stood awkwardly in Derreck's driveway. I held Amelia's hand, a current of anxiety running back and forth between us.

Rynna was the first to step forward, holding her arms out to Amelia. I missed our connection as soon as she stepped away, but the relief I saw in Rynna's eyes as she pulled Amelia in helped put me at ease.

"You're off on another adventure, aren't you, dear?" Rynna asked as she cupped the back of Amelia's head in one hand and wrapped her arm around her. Amelia chuckled. "Just promise me you'll be careful," Rynna said soberly. "Promise me you'll make the decisions in your heart. You will know what to do when the time comes, I am sure of it.

"Remember there was a time when the castle was filled with life and laughter," Rynna continued. "There was a time when Immortals didn't want to leave the surrounding lands and they rejoiced in the lives they led. Things fell apart very quickly and there are no clear explanations for how it began or what could have been done to stop it. My sister sits at the center now, but I have always believed there is more to our story. Be wary. Be vigilant. Be careful." Rynna squeezed Amelia's hands and let her go.

Amelia stepped back, nodding. When the time came, I wondered whether she would be careful or go running head first into danger, like usual.

Derreck took his turn, awkwardly holding out a hand. Amelia shook her head and wrapped him in a hug. "You're my uncle, we can hug. And I know. I have to think of our people, not myself, and I need to make the decision best for the whole because it is my duty."

Derreck hiccupped a laugh as he stepped back, holding her by the shoulders. "If I'd thought you were actually going to listen to me, I would have said a lot more, you know." Amelia laughed quietly as he pressed a kiss to her forehead. "You are just like your mother in so many ways, Amelia. You make me miss her even more, but you honor her memory. She knew this day would come and you are as prepared as you can be for it. Trust your instincts and trust each other. It is what brought you this far."

Amelia stepped back to my side. Her energy was calm as her palm slid into mine. It had been long enough since Cole's power merged with hers, I no longer felt the difference between the two. Our fingers intertwined as Rynna and Derreck mimicked the motion. I looked down at her and knew the determination in her eyes matched my own.

"We're doing the right thing by leaving them, aren't we?" I asked quietly.

Her eyes moved across the crowd of Immortals who stood, waiting for us to leave. "Too much has happened for this all to be coincidence," she said. "We met and my power went through the roof. That power started to break your binds. Uncle Derreck stole the Sentinels from the castle.

"I allowed myself to be taken to Cresthaven," she continued. "If I hadn't, these women would be dead, and we would have never understood the full extent of Julia's insanity. We have a Hunter and the Prince of Immortals on our side. We have a journal telling us where to go and, hopefully, what to do when we get there. Fate brought us this far. Now, Aidan, it is up to us. If not us, then who?"

Chapter 26
Amelia

We walked through the Syrian forest in silence. It wasn't strained or awkward in any way. It was actually rejuvenating. The quiet was welcome after days and days of conversation, decisions, arguments, and emotions.

I needed space to clear my mind and wrap my head around where we were and what we were doing. I was still reconciling the fact that I fell asleep over the Atlantic Ocean and woke up in Syria, a hotbed of civil unrest. It was beyond comprehension. But, we hadn't seen a single soul and the closer we got to the castle, the more I felt the pull of it. I didn't need Charlie and Onyx to lead us. I could have found my way there with no guide in pitch black from the way it drew me in.

I had expected that, though. When we first boarded the plane, I pulled out the pages of my mother's journal and organized them chronologically again. I read every word. Bethany had been right. Reading about her relationship with my father had been pretty wonderful. It reminded me of how I felt about Aidan. She talked about how she was drawn to him. How he calmed her, yet sent her heart racing.

She detailed her visions, and so many of them had already come true: Julia getting pregnant, Cane dying, the villages burning, the Hunters killing so many. She had seen so much and it brought tears to my eyes to know she carried that burden alone.

She talked more about her quest to find the chamber, but the journal ended before she could tell me where to find it. The only thing I knew was, much like I felt now, she was pulled toward it. It was one of her last entries and she described the feeling perfectly.

I know the time is coming. The dominoes are poised to fall and each event will trigger the next. They still plan to marry me off, but they don't know what I do. Lavignia won't listen. She won't listen, so neither will I.

Nathaniel stopped me on my way to the castle today. He scared me, pulling me off the path into the bushes. He looked at me with such concern and tenderness, I struggled to keep the tears at bay. Then he told me he would leave the castle forever to allow me to do my duty, or we could run together. That I could choose love and let the rest of the Elders handle what was to come.

He doesn't know what I do, but I will leave with him. There will be nothing but death here soon, and I am one of the few who can still bear life inside me.

I walked the halls earlier today, willing the visions to show me how to stop this when I felt it. A light tugging, right over my heart, as if someone tied a string to my breastbone and gently pulled me toward them.

One step at a time, I was pulled forward. With each step, my heart pounded and my pulse beat in my ears. I cannot say for sure, but I believe something, or someone, has sought me out. I would have found them, too, if it weren't for Julia. I heard the click of her heels against the stone and knew she was following me again. Even while the pain of separation stole my breath, I had to turn away from the one pulling at me to stop her from finding what only I was meant to find.

I felt that same tug, that same pull. Something, or someone, was drawing me in.

You're quiet over there. Everything okay? Aidan's voice interrupted my thoughts and I smiled, loving the fact that we could talk like this.

I stepped over a log and held a small tree branch back so we could both pass by. *I can't believe how much my mother took on. The visions, the searching, sneaking back here, absorbing the power of the Elders...I don't know how she knew to do all of that. But I reread her journal and now, I feel just like she did toward the end. Something is drawing me there. We're close.*

Since landing, our connection had strengthened and our power intensified. When Aidan's anxiety spiked, I felt his wolf stretching through him. It was a strange, yet comforting feeling. There was Aidan the man, who wanted to protect me. Then, there was Aidan the wolf, the AniMage King, who would take down an army for me.

When the wolf came to the forefront, everything was instantly heightened for me as well. The power transfer between us meant I felt my own senses sharpen. The frozen soil hiding beneath the fresh snow, the wet fur on the Danes, even my own shampoo…it was all so heavy in my nose. I could see deeper into the forest and the ache in my legs eased as new energy filtered in.

It doesn't feel threatening, I assured him. *With everything I can feel from you, I'm surprised you can't feel it, too.*

I watched Aidan's eyes squint as he concentrated. Finally, he shook his head and said out loud, "I don't feel drawn anywhere. It's the first time your emotions haven't also transferred to me, and I don't like it. Stay with me, Amelia. Stay with me and don't take off. Promise me."

I walked ahead of him, and threw, "Of course I will," over my shoulder. He grabbed my arm and pulled me to a stop. I turned, irritated. I already knew where the conversation was going and neither of us was going to like it.

"I just told you I can feel your emotions, Amelia, and you aren't telling me the truth," Aidan said, glaring at me. "I've tried to block you out and give you privacy, but ever since we landed, I can't keep my walls up and that means right now, when I told you to stay with me, I felt your hesitation. I felt your indifference. Why?"

I didn't know what to say. I hadn't directly thought I would go where I had to whether he liked it or not, but it was the truth. I pulled my arm out of his grasp, frustrated, finally admitting to myself what I had to tell him.

"I have to do what I have to do, Aidan," I said. "You can't solve this. I'm the Elder. I'm the one who can get in that chamber. We don't know what's in there, but it's me they want. If they wanted you, you would feel them, too. I won't apologize for doing what I have to do."

I didn't miss the hurt in his eyes as his arm dropped and he looked at me like I'd hit him. Guilt crept in, but I couldn't take it back now, so I turned back to the path.

"We have to keep going," I said as I started to walk again.

"Bullshit," he said loudly. I turned.

"Excuse me?"

He leaned in a little, over enunciating this time. "Bull. Shit. That's what I said. This is what you do, it's what you've done since the beginning. You don't know the answers, no one does, but you find something out and make decisions that impact everyone.

"You become the martyr, decide which risks to take and then you are the first person to put yourself in danger." Aidan crossed the short distance between us. He stood a foot in front of me and rocked back on his heels, his arms crossed over his chest. "So, I'm calling bullshit. This prophecy is about both of us. It takes both of us to stop this. You aren't that special. *We're special.* We're a team. Without *us*, none of this happens. I left my pack to fend for themselves because I believe in what we're doing *together.* So, you're either going to let me do my job and protect you, even if it is just from yourself, or I'm taking you back to the plane."

I was in a boiling rage before he even finished his little rant. "You're going to *take me back to the plane?*" I screeched out. Even the integration of Cole's power couldn't tamp down whatever was pushing our power and emotions to new heights. I didn't want to fight with him, but I couldn't stop myself.

Both of our eyes lit at the same moment and the power spike from Aidan matched my own. Our power swirled in the air around us. It poked and prodded, whipping back and forth. He and I were squared off and neither of us was giving an inch.

My knees buckled as something slammed into me from behind. As I tumbled to the ground, I found myself next to Aidan, our heads inches from each other, but our bodies pointed in opposite directions. Before we could move, paws planted on either side of our faces and wet noses pressed against our cold ones.

I looked up into Charlie's coal-black eyes and felt his warm snorts of breath huffing down at me, clearly annoyed. A low growl came from Onyx as I stared up at Charlie, his words clear in my head.

Enough. Stop this now. We are finally home. You are home. And he is right. This cannot be done by you alone. I know the power of her call, but you must stay focused.

Aidan must have gotten a similar speech because as we stood, he looked over at me sheepishly.

"I'm sorry, Aidan. I don't understand what's getting me so riled up, but you're right. Neither of us can do this alone. More than that, I want it to be you beside me," I apologized, holding out my hand. He took it and brought it to his lips, then we fell in line behind the Danes.

As we came over the hill, the first homes appeared. Or, more accurately, the burnt and broken shells of what used to be homes. Aidan took my hand as my eyes filled with tears. We followed Charlie and Onyx through the wreckage, stepping over the remains of lives forever changed by Julia and her Hunters. Not only was seeing the homes around me jarring, it was like falling back in time. While Julia's wrath had begun only thirty years ago, the Immortals had lived separately from humans and hadn't been so quick to adopt our modern architecture.

The homes had been made of some type of clay mixture with stone foundations. Thick chunks of wall remained on some and the wood frames of doors and windows still stood on others. Thirty years of weather had degraded the homes even further — each one a handful of broken bones no longer making the full skeleton of a village.

Charlie and Onyx picked their way through the piles of wood and decrepit belongings, turning back every so often to make sure Aidan and I continued to follow. After Charlie's scolding, I kept my distance. Each time he looked at me, I felt like I had let him down. When Charlie and Onyx moved off of us, Aidan and I hadn't argued anymore. Instead, we helped each other up and agreed to focus on what was in front of us, together.

Unease lumped in my stomach, a ball growing with each step we took. I felt nauseous and weak. Aidan reached for me and as soon as he wrapped my hand in his, I felt the influx of power push me closer to normal.

I gave him a grateful smile and we continued. It was roughly a mile through the village. The homes had been on the outskirts in a lower, flatter area. As we climbed uphill, we found more defined streets, what had been shops and clearly the city center. We hiked up the side of the mountain, curving around and between the buildings until finally coming to a massive gate. The stone wall around it reached into the sky, seemingly ending amidst the clouds.

The dogs stood on either side of the wooden gate and stared at us. Aidan looked at me, and asked, "Do they think we know how to get in there?"

"Apparently," I said, cocking my head and moving closer. The wood was old and splintered, beaten by weather and wind. The large metal rings toward the center were as big as beach balls and appeared to weigh hundreds of pounds.

I turned to the dogs. "Shouldn't this open automatically? You don't expect us to open it ourselves, do you?"

Charlie ambled toward me, closing the short distance and sitting down. I squatted and looked into his eyes once again.

I felt him there, lingering in my mind, and wondered if we had always been able to do this.

Your abilities are amplified here. This is our home. We also have access to parts of our magic that had been unreachable until now. You do not even have to look at me to hear me. Though, I still find the ear scratches quite wonderful. So, if you would oblige, we will explain.

I laughed out loud. Charlie's combination of formal speech and puppy ways was more than a little amusing. As his tongue lolled and he leaned into my hand, his tail thumped a rhythm onto the ground. I looked over to find Aidan doing the same for Onyx and both dogs appeared to be in heaven.

Are you both listening? he asked.

I hadn't realized Aidan had heard him the whole time as well, but we answered yes simultaneously. While the guy drove me crazy, I couldn't deny that he had fit himself snugly into my heart. My practical mind tried to keep him at arm's length, but my body and power had other ideas. I wished I'd had a few more minutes to savor the beginnings of what we were becoming back in the bedroom at Uncle Derreck's cabin, but having him here with me was more than I could have hoped for. Prophecy or not, I wasn't alone, and I didn't want anyone else beside me.

This time, it was Onyx who spoke. *You must work together and move the gate yourselves. Between you, you have the power. Use your gifts and prove you are who we believe you to be. Prove you belong together and are meant to be here.*

The two dogs trotted off behind us and sat down. Apparently, that was all the direction we were going to get. There were times I missed what the Keeper had been capable of. Now was most definitely one of them.

I turned to Aidan. "Any thoughts?"

He scratched the back of his head while looking at the gate and further up the massive wall it was attached to. "It looks like we're opening the door to the mountain itself. Where's the rest of the castle?"

"Well, behind the gate, I'd imagine." I couldn't help it. I started to laugh as he scowled initially and then joined me with a chuckle of his own.

"Touché, doll," he responded drily.

"Maybe we should try the little trick from the other night…out in the clearing?" It had only been the most intense few minutes of my life. Every one of my senses had been heightened and I felt Aidan in every cell. He had consumed me in those few minutes, just as I had completely consumed him. The power that built between us had been the stuff of legends—or, at least, it felt like it.

It was that good, was it?

I bit my lip, trying to hold back a smile. *Damn it, Montgomery, you aren't supposed to just listen in whenever you want.*

Can't help it, like Charlie said, the power is amplified here. Anything else you'd like to compliment while we're here?

He stepped toward me, the bright blue bursting from his pupils to cover his smoky iris in a giant sunburst. Those eyes pinned me in place, and I felt heat radiate through me. I swallowed, my throat dry. I licked my lips and Aidan cocked his head, his hooded eyes narrowing. I felt my own power build to match the pitch of his. It was a buzz in the air, crackling between us.

My violet smoke thickened as the intensity grew and my need to be close to him, to touch him, overwhelmed me. Aidan was still steps away and he stood still, watching me. I wanted the distance between us gone.

Blue fire circled his hands and reached out to surround him. It swirled around his wrists and up his arms until the two segments connected, each cut with orange bursts to remind me exactly what made Aidan special.

Each of us encased in our respective magic, we took a step toward each other and held one hand up. The action was innate, my hand rising of its own accord to the same height as Aidan's. We took another step forward, our hands inches apart.

Power ricocheted back and forth, the current flowing between us. Violet, blue, and orange bounced between our palms. Between the wolf howling in our shared mind and the Hunter strength emanating from Aidan, I couldn't focus. I wanted to be in his arms. I wanted to feel his lips.

As we closed the final distance, Aidan lowered his head, his lips hovering just above mine. I felt his breath and needed to move only the tiniest bit to meet him. Before I could move, he whispered, "Focus, doll. Let's open that gate."

I didn't take my eyes off him, but focused on the gate and the need for it to be gone. Through our shared connection, I felt Aidan mimic my efforts, and we both directed our power to our palms.

I saw the quirk of his lips as he whispered, *Now*, in my mind. We turned our palms out at the same moment and lightning shot toward the gate. It was a concentrated energy that swirled and mixed as it raced toward the wooden door. I was too busy closing the distance between us to see the two collide.

With my free hand, I gripped the back of his neck and felt his smiling lips as they crushed against mine. We had broken open the damn of power and now, as his tongue swept into my mouth and his hand came to my waist, I felt more from him than I ever had.

Aidan's emotions were stronger than I'd expected. With the door between us blown wide open, I caught glimpses of his memories, his thoughts about me, and his true feelings.

Our kisses slowed and his hand moved to grasp mine as he pulled away.

"When did you know you loved me?" I asked, still lost in the intimate thoughts I'd seen. Embarrassment burned my cheeks and I looked down at my feet.

Aidan pulled me into his chest and wrapped his arms around me. "There was no one moment that I knew. It was every moment combined. From the first time you spoke to me out on that beach, to the day you absolutely failed at convincing me you were training MMA with Micah, to the nights we stayed up until sunrise asking each other a hundred questions.

"Every day you said something else that surprised me. You wanted so much from the world, but you wanted to give it so much as well. You didn't want to be held back by your family, but you wanted to be close to them. You were fiercely protective of Bethany and equally hesitant to let me in. You were a riddle I knew I would never solve, but I wanted to spend the rest of my life trying."

I opened my mouth to respond when Aidan exclaimed, "Holy shit!"

I whipped around to find that we hadn't just opened the door, we had destroyed the door. It was toothpicks. Slivers of wood shattered and tossed in every direction. Charlie and Onyx had already crossed into the castle and stood waiting for us, clearly impatient.

"Ohmygod, can you believe this? Look what we did!" I took a few steps toward the open door, hardly containing my shock.

"Were you going to say something before?" Aidan asked, a sly smile telling me he knew I was.

"Oh," I stuttered. "I…um…I'm really glad you didn't let me go. I'm really glad you came for me and you're here now." I stumbled through the words I hadn't actually intended to say. *Coward*, I berated myself.

Aidan looked at me, his hopeful expression slowly fading.

"Shall we?" he asked, gesturing forward.

I exhaled and mentally thanked him for not pressing the issue. I knew what I wanted to say and what he wanted to hear. After all this, he deserved to hear it. I only hoped he would stay patient as I unraveled the mystery of my own heart.

Chapter 27
Aidan

I nudged Amelia along as I tried to keep pace with the Danes. Her eyes were wide and her movements slow, just as they had been since we'd entered the castle. We were both astounded that so much remained.

I tried not to dwell on what happened outside. I had allowed her to see me, unfiltered and emotionally vulnerable, and yet again, she found a way around her feelings. I had stopped second-guessing my feelings for her a long time ago. I accepted whatever part of them was tied to being her mate and realized beyond the obvious physical attraction we had for each other, the way I felt couldn't be manufactured. She was clearly still hesitant, and I wasn't sure how many more times I could put myself out there for her to reject. Whether she knew that's what she'd done or not, that was how it felt.

Charlie and Onyx led us past rooms filled with furniture and hallways lined with paintings and photos. No one had closed up shop, so to speak, and many of the rooms had clearly been raided. Drawers hung open, furniture shoved askew, and unidentifiable broken items littered the floor. The castle itself was cold. The chilly air from the mountain whipped through the empty hallways, making us both glad to have winter jackets.

The dogs yipped and barked at us if we took too long, and eventually, Onyx came to take up the rear so he could physically push us forward. I considered shifting to show him who was really in charge, but that would have been poor judgment on my part since the dogs clearly knew where they were going and we had no idea.

Amelia stopped in front of yet another frame. "Doll, we have to keep going. Onyx is going to take a chunk of me before long," I said as I tried to pull her along. Amelia yanked her arm from my light grip and stepped even closer to the photograph.

"It's my mom. With Rynna and Julia," she said quietly.

I looked at the portrait again, this time really focusing. Rynna was the only one of the three I'd actually met, so it was easy to pick her out. She stood between the other two in a long dress with her hair in a long braid, as it typically was today. Of the other two, I knew which was Amelia's mother based on the fact that Amelia was a carbon copy and the other woman was bright blonde. Rynna and Liana looked maybe fifteen in the picture and stood in front of a water fountain. All three were laughing, their arms around each other's waists.

"They were all friends?" I asked.

Amelia nodded. "I think so. I wonder what happened," she mused.

I pulled at her arm again. "We can ask Rynna when we get home." Reluctantly, she came with me, but her eyes darted back to the photograph as we walked away.

We continued up staircase after staircase. As we made our way higher into the castle, the walls weren't just made of stone, they were stone. I looked closely as we climbed and was certain the castle was built directly into the side of the mountain.

Charlie finally diverted from the stairs and made a beeline down a hallway. It didn't look different from any other hallway we had passed, but as we approached the last door on the right, Charlie sat down and a warning bell went off inside me. It was the first time I'd felt anything out of the ordinary since we'd landed, and that meant something.

I pulled Amelia back to the top of the stairs in a second. She swayed on her feet as I called out, "What's going on, Charlie? Something's off here. I can feel it."

We must go this way. You have to trust me. I am leading you home.

"You keep saying that. You keep talking about home, but aren't we already home? We're in the castle," I said. "You need to give us more information."

Amelia stepped from my side and turned her back to the dogs. "Come on, Aidan. We have to go. We have to trust them. Why come here and follow them this whole way if we aren't going to finish this? Whatever it is."

This could be a trap, I growled in her mind.

If it were a trap, we wouldn't need to walk up eight flights of stairs. And Charlie's protected me since I've known him. He wouldn't let me get hurt now.

I crossed my arms and surveyed the situation again. Charlie came back down the hall halfway, but Onyx stood next to the door, sniffing with his tail quickly swishing back and forth. Amelia was in front of me, and looked mildly impatient herself.

"What?" I asked. I knew there was something she wasn't saying.

"I can feel it again," she said, her gaze darting between me and the door. "It's pulling me. It's pulling me that way. I want to go in that door, Aidan. I need to." She was trying to remain still, but kept shifting her weight from her right foot to her left, her fingers twisting in front of her.

I still couldn't feel the pull she was talking about. I searched myself and the connection between us, hoping for a better understanding of what everyone was so anxious for, but I got nothing. I didn't like nothing.

"If we're going, I'm going in first. You stay behind me, got it?" I was trying to be stern, but she nodded with such excitement, I couldn't keep the face going. I sighed and held out my hand. "Okay, let's go then." She took it and dragged me toward the door. I really didn't like the idea that something was influencing her, but she was right, there was no turning back now.

Onyx moved to the side and Charlie stood right in front of the door. I felt the same excitement coming from him and struggled again with my inability to know what was coming. I reached out slowly with my free hand, grasped the door handle lightly, and twisted it.

I'd expected it to be locked, but the door opened with a quiet *snick*. I shoved it in, slamming it against the wall while keeping Amelia safely outside. Immediately, we were bathed in a bright glow.

We stepped in slowly, both of us staring at the river of rainbow-colored light that ran ceiling to floor. It moved, a continuous current of energy that was both beautiful and terrifying. It reminded me of a combination of both our powers—the electric look of my energy, snapping and popping as it streamed along, and the wispy threads of Amelia's, flowing and shifting. Colors streaked down the wall—orange, green, red, violet, and blue. They flowed together, drawing both of us forward. As we got closer yet, I saw bright white interspersed among the colored river.

Both dogs paced in front of the door. They strode opposite directions, their paws hitting the floor at exactly the same moments, turning in stride and crossing past each other again. They didn't look around, they didn't speak to us at all.

Charlie's mammoth white body, which was covered in small black patches, moved with a precision I'd never seen the lumbering giant have. Onyx disappeared into the shadows as he walked his route. His nails clicked on the floor and his black body shined in the firelight. The cavernous room was most definitely built into the mountainside. The rock walls were jagged and the room appeared chiseled out.

I made Amelia stay a step behind me, but we inched forward. The unease I felt in the hallway only grew, and the reaction from the dogs only worried me further. "Hey, guys, what are we doing here?" I asked, but neither animal responded. They didn't acknowledge my presence at all, just kept pacing.

"Does this concern you in the least?" I asked her, gesturing to the Danes. Amelia shook her head.

"We're supposed to be here," she said, breathless and unfocused. "I can feel it, Aidan. This is exactly where we're supposed to be. Can we get closer?" she asked as she stepped forward. I jumped in front of her.

"Can you please let me go first?" I asked, ready to toss her over my shoulder if she didn't stop running headfirst into the unknown. "I know you're completely capable, but let me be the guy right now, okay?" I thought she'd appreciate the compliment, but Amelia only nodded absently as she stared over my shoulder.

"Holy shit," she whispered. I whirled around, power flooding my system. Instead of something terrible, I saw symbols floating down the wall. Somehow, we had gotten close enough to trigger this. We watched bright, silver glowing emblems flow from top to bottom. They disappeared at the floor and reappeared at the ceiling, slowly drifting down again.

Amelia pulled the small backpack from her shoulders and dropped it to the ground. "She talked about this," she said excitedly as she pulled the journal pages out. "My mother talked about this. We are in the right place, Aidan!" Amelia looked up at me, beaming.

I couldn't help but smile down at her, even though I knew in my gut this wouldn't be as easy as she thought.

Amelia flipped the pages until she found the one she wanted and stood so we could both read it together.

Lavignia sees all. I know she does. It was no coincidence during my trek to the chamber today that she removed the blind before they finished unlocking the door.

It was unlike anything I'd ever seen. A wall of power—a rainbow of color and continuous stream of symbols. The ancient markings Tragar and I only found in books were lit up—silver and effervescent against the swirling colors of the door.

I watched as Lavignia and Vivian stood side by side, their arms moving in a slow pattern as they snatched certain symbols from the cascade of power running from floor to ceiling. I couldn't move. I didn't know if Vivian understood the gift Lavignia was giving me, so I was only able to see a portion of the symbols.

As Lavignia snatched the last symbol from the wall, it burned brightly in her glowing, violet palm. Vivian placed her hand over Lavignia's and the door disappeared. Then, I was blind again. I've walked through this interior room every time on our way to the chamber and I always feel the pull strongest in this place. I only wish I understood where it was coming from.

Together, we stared at the wall standing between us and answers. Just as her mother described, the flow of power was continuous and every race was represented.

"These symbols, I've seen them before," Amelia said. "They are the same ones on my cuff. Micah started to explain them to me, but he didn't finish. I wonder why they are this color, this silverish white. The only white power I've ever seen was a piece of the Keeper. This is all so strange," she mused.

Amelia took a step forward and leaned in to look closer, interrupting Charlie's path. His growl was deep, intense, and I snatched her by the waist, pulling her behind my outstretched arm. As soon as she moved, Charlie resumed his measured steps, disregarding us completely.

"What's wrong with him?" Amelia asked.

I gritted my teeth against the overwhelming howls of my wolf. I had controlled him thus far, but with Amelia in actual danger, I couldn't anymore. He wanted us out of here, back on that plane, and halfway across the world on the way home. But, we had to do this. She had to do this. There was no going back now.

"They act like they've turned back into guards," I said to her as I watched the dogs continue their patrol. "Baleon said they guarded the chamber, and that's what they're doing. But it's strange that they are so focused." My mind whipped through the possibilities of what all of this could mean.

I worried that behind this door was going to be something bigger and scarier than Amelia imagined. She had this misguided notion that because she was sent on this path, everything would be sunshine and rainbows. That wasn't what we'd experienced up to this point, and I didn't see it changing.

"We need to know what those symbols mean," I muttered.

"Micah!" Amelia exclaimed. "Micah knows, and I can get to Micah."

Amelia walked backward, further from the door and Danes. I followed. She reached out and I took her hands, grateful for the contact. My wolf calmed when I touched her. As our powers swirled together and our connection solidified, I felt like I could take a full breath again.

"Do you think he's been bitten yet?" I joked.

Amelia rolled her eyes, and said, "I wouldn't doubt Melinda tried. I hope he let Baleon pin her to a wall and the Mages use her for target practice."

Her retort dripped of sarcasm and her eyes narrowed when she said Melinda's name. I couldn't stop from laughing out loud. Amelia shook our joined hands. "Focus, Montgomery. I need your help to find Micah."

"Right. Yes. Let's do this," I said, still chuckling. I closed my eyes and focused myself in her mind. I lingered on the edges and allowed her to give me whatever access she wanted. I found myself matching the rhythm of her breathing and as we both took a slow inhale, I felt an openness, like someone had been in a heated room and suddenly opened a window. The air was sucked out and a chill sent shivers up my spine.

I've never tried this over a long distance. Give me a second.

I didn't reply, but I did pull at my power and send it to her. What would have normally been blue smoke was a swirling tangle of orange and blue. Since touching down, the Hunter side of me that had never really felt integrated was everywhere. My senses were further developed, my fear was less, and my intuition more.

I watched my power filter into her space, mixing with hers. As they threaded together, a multi-colored braid, she spoke again.

Micah? Can you hear me? We need your help.

I saw the thin, red glowing thread that was her connection to Micah. As she reached out, it pulsed brighter and became thicker. I continued to feed my power into her until finally, we heard him.

This is not a fabulous time, Amelia. What can I do for you? Micah's irritation was blatant. I was about to interject when Amelia spoke.

We found the chamber, but there are symbols on the wall and I don't know what they mean. We have to know which symbols to use to get through it.

It was silent. Micah said nothing and I was about to pull the plug on the whole thing when he spoke again.

Quickly, can you show me?

What's happening, what aren't you saying? I interrupted, knowing something was wrong.

Not now. If you need my help, you have about one minute to get it. Micah's fear invaded my mind, forming an ugly ball in the pit of my stomach. He was supposed to be protecting my people.

Amelia started rattling off descriptions of the symbols, and Micah named the ones he could, but I barely heard their voices. I could only think about Cora and Dillon. Elias, Nell, and their children. Willow. Sully. My wolf tore my insides apart trying to get out, trying to force me to move. I was letting my people down, out on a wild goose chase for something that could be nothing.

Tell me. I swear to God, Micah. Tell me what's happening, I interrupted again.

Damn it, man, I don't have time for this. They are coming for me and if I'm to stop them from killing each other, I can't be doing this right now. You take care of your business and I'll take care of mine.

And then, he was gone.

Chapter 28
Micah

This is what I get for taking charge. For signing up to be the one who taught them how to use their power and allowing Bale to show them how to truly fight. I ducked as a bright blue fireball erupted above my head and the top half of the door exploded. I crouched, still inside the stall in the barn where I'd taken refuge to try to help Amelia and Aidan.

"We know you're in there, Prince. Just come out. We don't want to hurt you…much." I heard a high-pitched laugh and knew it was Melinda. "No one can defeat the Hunters. We finally get that. So, we're taking you back. We'll give the Queen her baby boy and she'll spare us."

I slammed my fist into the dirt floor. Melinda had started all of this. I had made such progress since we'd been here, but she'd slowly poisoned enough of the AniMages to cause problems.

"Don't make us come in there for you, *Prince Mikail.* Your Hunter doesn't understand we won't actually harm the women and children, so he continues to fight a worthless fight. Elias is exactly the traitor we always knew he was, ready to abandon us when it became convenient. Let's take care of this quickly and it can end." I didn't recognize the male voice, but it didn't matter.

"You don't understand what you're doing," I yelled. "You think my mother will want me back? She won't. You think she'll reward you somehow? She won't. She hates you. She will welcome you into Cresthaven and the Hunters will never allow you to leave again. This is madness. We are here to fight for each other, all of us, not against each other." I tried to talk some sense into them while I reached out to Bale. They tipped their hand by confirming what we assumed when this all started.

You need to put a stop to this, Baleon. They won't hurt the women, they are simply keeping you busy. I know this is child's play for you.

He grunted inside my head. *They are ill-equipped to fight even the youngest Hunter. But if I do what needs done, the protective shields will be broken and we will no longer be safe here.*

I sighed. I knew it would come to this. Between what happened with Bethany and the attempted mutiny the AniMages had tried with Aidan, it was clear these people had been without a leader for too long. Many relished what they saw as freedom.

Bale showed me the view from his eyes. He and Elias created a half shield in front of my apartment where they and the AniMages still on our side had corralled all the women. Those who weren't pregnant held a second line and helped as they could. I saw AniMages blown backwards, tree branches flying and an array of colorful fireballs being thrown back and forth. The rogue AniMages weren't aiming their shots and they weren't smart enough to know we were on to them. I guessed there were ten total between those in the barn and the ones attacking Baleon.

Do it. We will move. We will adjust.

As the threats began again from the AniMages on the other side of the stall door, Baleon allowed me open access to his mind. It was a bond we'd forged many years ago when he stood in my bedroom and knelt before me.

I was six years old and my mother had a particularly bad day. She barreled down the hall and stood outside the library door, screaming my name. I looked up to see her open palm close before I was thrown across the room. Landing in a heap at her feet, I was quickly at eye level, an invisible claw digging through the back of my shirt and into my skin.

"I told you I wanted you training," she shrieked. "I told you that you needed to be with Rhi, learning how to take your father's place." It was always uncomfortable looking into her eyes. They glittered with spite and rage, and I loathed that mine were the same color.

"I am not good at fighting. They are mean to me. They hit me and they laugh. They tell me I will never be strong and I don't belong there." I tried not to mumble. She detested mumbling, but I detested Rhi more.

"You will do as you're told, Mikail," she said, her voice echoing off the walls. "You'll let them hit you and you'll learn to hit back. You cannot lead our people unless you eliminate fear from your soul. Let them break you. We will build you into the man you were meant to be and you will stand beside me as your father should have. We will lead these people into the future. We will reign. Do you understand me?" she hissed and leaned in, her face pinched into a scowl.

"I will never be him! I don't want to be him! I HATE HIM!" The words erupted from my heart before I had the good sense to stop them from coming out and she flung me across the room. I smacked into a wall of books and landed awkwardly, breaking my arm. I couldn't stop the pained scream and began crying. I begged my mother to help me, to have the Hunters heal me.

She said, "Learn to live with pain, Mikail. We all do." Then, she walked away.

Baleon gently picked me up and laid his hand over my arm. Before I was in my room, the bones were already knitting back together. We healed quickly, but he sped the process and dulled the pain. As tears streaked down my face, he stood me up and knelt.

He spoke quietly, but firmly, his head bowed. "Prince Mikail, from this day forward, I pledge myself to you. I will protect you. I will place your wellbeing above my own. I will guard your life with mine. I make this choice of my own accord, under no duress, and I swear on the Mother who bore us, the Earth that provides for us, the Water that replenishes us, the Fire that sustains us, and the Air that gives us life, I will fulfill this oath until my soul goes back to whence it came. You will see as I see and hear what I hear. I am yours to command."

When he lifted his head, Baleon's eyes swirled a mix of orange and yellow that frightened me. But when he held out his hand, I took it. As his large hand engulfed my small one, I felt a rush of energy that made me wince. "Do not fear, Prince Mikail. That was only my mark. It allows you and me to connect, to communicate. I will always be able to find you and you will always be able to call for me. I will never leave you alone again." And he hadn't. Even in Brighton, my Hunter had never been far.

As Baleon stood in the yard, allowing his power to build, he motioned for everyone else behind him to stay back as he stepped forward.

He brought both hands up and orbs of orange light crackled, cut with white lightning. A wicked grin twisted his features before he started to speak. "This was unnecessary, you understand," he said to the AniMages, who were slowly backing away. "We came to help you. I meant to share my secrets with you, to betray my brothers and sisters so I might save them. But now, you have made your choice, and for that, you must pay the consequences."

Through his eyes, I watched the light from Baleon's palms grow, the orbs the size of basketballs, then beach balls, then encompassing his massive frame. Bale crossed his arms in front of him and when he whipped them back wide, every AniMage who stood against us howled in agony. The iridescent blue faded from their eyes and those who were shifted instantly reverted to their human form. In seconds, every AniMage who fought against us was frozen in place.

I slid open the remnants of the stall door to find Melinda and three other AniMages frozen, their hands at their ears, their faces twisted in pain. What they didn't know was when the freeze thawed and they could move again, they would have no access to their power or the ability to harm anyone.

Baleon had bound their power and given us the time we needed to escape. The Hunters would surely feel the energy Bale had expended, and they would come. We could not be here when they arrived.

Chapter 29
Amelia

Aidan and I timed our return to the wall so we could pass between Charlie and Onyx, who had yet to stray from their perfect line, marching back and forth in front of it. As we approached, I felt the pull again. It made me want to dive head first into the iridescent waves of color. My chest ached as I forced myself to stand still.

I turned to Aidan, who was clenching his jaw, staring straight ahead, but clearly not at the wall. I moved in front of him and put both hands on his cheeks, drawing his gaze down. His blue eyes were glowing brightly as he continued the strained silence he'd maintained since Micah disappeared.

"Talk to me," I requested. "You've done everything you can to help me get here and get through this. Let me help you."

His eyes were pained. Aidan looked down at me and I felt the inferno of emotions tearing him apart. I funneled the calming energy toward him, hoping to help reduce the intensity of what he was going through.

"No," he said as he pulled away and shoved my hands down, shaking his head. "Don't do that. I need to feel this. I am finally part of something, Amelia. They are my family and it's my job to take care of them."

The anguish in his heart and eyes killed me. I reached back up toward him and laid my hand on his cheek, holding my power back.

"I'm sorry, Aidan. I was so focused on the end, on what I was supposed to do, I didn't think about what this might do to you." I was ashamed, and I didn't hide it. He deserved the truth.

Aidan reached out and wrapped his hand around the back of my neck, lightly pulling me toward him. He touched his forehead to mine and his words were choked.

"How am I supposed to make the right choice? What even is the right choice?" he asked, his voice thick with conflicted emotion. "I can't walk away from you, Amelia. I couldn't leave you if I wanted to, but I left them. I left the people I was supposed to protect. My people, my father's people. People who trusted me and made me their leader. I left them because I will always choose you, but how do I know I made the right choice? Since we came into the castle, I haven't been able to hear them. We don't know what's happening over there and I left them to handle it alone. If anything happens…" he trailed off, and I was left with the weight of his guilt and the soul-crushing shame he felt at failing his duties as AniMage King.

My heart ached for him. Aidan was so patient. He fought for me, for this cause he barely understood, with everything he had. We were always so busy making the next choice, I hadn't stopped to think about what it cost him.

I reached up and threaded my fingers through the hair on the back of his head, pulling back to look into his eyes. "Aidan, we won't ever know if the choices we make are the right ones. We have to trust our instincts, trust our hearts, and trust each other. I know you can't feel it like I do, but we are in the right place. We are on the verge of solving this puzzle. When we do, we will get back to the States as fast as we can. We'll find the AniMages, we'll find our friends, and we'll end this. Together, we will end this. There is no other option. We have needed each other every step since we got off that plane. I can't do this without you, Aidan."

He swallowed and closed his eyes, nodding. When he opened them, a forced calm layered over his frustration. I felt his power stretch and unfold through him. "I'm with you, doll. Just tell me what we need to do."

I balanced on my tiptoes and softly kissed him, both a thank you and a promise.

I turned to stand next to him and we stared at the wall of light. "We need to identify the symbols and decide what order to pull them down in," I said.

"These are clearly the sun and moon," he said. "This one looks like the Elder symbol you drew me, and these are fire, earth, air, and water."

"I know you weren't listening while Micah explained these. Impressive, Montgomery." I smirked and gave him a playful shove. "These four are the symbols for our people." I waited and watched, finally pointing as they drifted down toward us.

"You were right," I confirmed. "The four intersecting circles surrounded by a circle is the symbol for the Elders. The shield with two arrows intersecting is for the Hunters. The circle with the small offshoots that look like claws represent the AniMages, and the one that is a diamond with two of the edges extended into what looks like tails, that is for the Mages. Micah also explained the two moon-looking slivers on each side of the circle is the symbol for mother. I have no idea what to do with that one."

We stood and watched the symbols repeat, floating from top to bottom. It looked like a flashlight was behind each one, setting it off from the sheen of light making up the wall.

"Elements, the sun and moon, the races, and a mother," I mused, running the options in my mind. "We know the races are having issues getting pregnant, so what if this is tied to that? The mother is first, followed by the races, who use the elements, which are influenced by the sun and moon?"

Aidan didn't look away as he replied, "Makes sense to me. What's the worst that could happen?"

I shrugged, having no real idea. "Think we should ask Charlie and Onyx?"

Aidan took a step into Onyx's path and he immediately started to growl. It came from deep within Onyx's chest and with each step, we saw more of his teeth. I grabbed Aidan and pulled him back to my side.

"I'm going to venture a guess that we're on our own here," I said sarcastically. "But they would have warned us, don't you think? I mean, really, why would they bring us all the way here and then give us nothing to work with?" I asked. My rationalizations didn't sit well in my gut and I felt Aidan's wariness, but neither of us voiced our fear, so we stepped closer.

I reached toward the full moon offset by the two slivers, the symbol for mother, when the nagging in the pit of my stomach stopped me and I turned to Aidan. I looked up at him, and he watched me, questioning. I reached out and grasped his hand in mine.

"We're going to do this, and we have no idea what it means or what will happen, but I wanted to tell you…" The words stuck in my throat as his eyes widened. "I…um…thank you," I croaked, and his face fell, but he quickly hid it.

I rushed to salvage the moment. "Thank you for not giving up on us—on me—and thank you for coming for me. For embracing Bethany, taking care of Charlie, and being more than I ever expected." It was all true, but once again, I had chickened out.

Aidan squeezed my hand, his expression morphing into amusement. He cupped his free hand under my chin and tilted my head up, leaning down to brush my lips with his. "You're welcome, Ame. And, I appreciate that. But, let's get on with it."

I smiled against his second kiss and resumed my position. I reached up and as soon as my fingers grazed the river of magic, I felt a tingle all the way to my toes. It was euphoria, but also distracting. I wanted to curl up inside the feeling and lose myself there.

With a quick shake of my head, I stood on my tiptoes and reached for the mother symbol. With my other hand, I grabbed the Mage symbol. As I pulled the shiny symbols from the stream of magic, the glowing silver faded to a dull metal. Each one became a small weight in my hand, the size of a golf ball, while retaining its original shape.

"Now, you, Aidan. Get the AniMage and Hunter. Charlie said we have to do this together." I felt the weight of the two symbols in my palm and watched as Aidan turned. Without hesitation, he grabbed the two symbols as they reached him.

As the magic stream closed in on the space where the Hunter symbol had been, I heard a *crack*. We turned, looking into every corner of the room. Seconds later, both dogs stilled and Aidan shoved me behind him as the ceiling above the first door we'd come through crashed down around us.

Chapter 30
Micah

A caravan of vehicles headed south on Route One. We didn't know where we were headed exactly, but we knew we had to outrun the Hunters who would be at Derreck's property soon. There were too many women still pregnant and unable to shift, so we traveled the old fashioned way. And I hated it.

I sat in the passenger seat, Baleon behind the wheel, both of us silent. In order to pack all our supplies, we had to bring multiple vehicles. The pregnant women were spread across them, just in case we were ambushed. Lilith took up the back of Elias's Suburban, the massive Tigress ready to give birth to her kittens at any moment. Willow brought up the rear. The healer who helped remove my mother's spell was now a leader among the women.

Our SUV held the most occupants, but the majority were unbound and not pregnant, which meant they shifted into smaller animals to stay more comfortable. Most took the form of small cats, curled up together and sleeping through the journey. The rest watched out the windows, likely holding conversations telepathically.

My thoughts drifted back to the AniMages attempted coup. They believed I was leverage. They believed that even now, my mother would allow me back. That she would want me to take my place as the Prince of Immortals.

And she would.

I sat straighter, looking at everything and nothing at once as my mind churned with possibilities. She would take me back. She would trust me if I told her I was coming back, because she couldn't prove otherwise. It had irritated her to no end that she could never read my mind, but she had at least acknowledged that it gave me some right to my position. I was more than "just a Mage."

"Prince Mikail?" Bale questioned softly, giving me a sideways look. "I do not like the look on your face."

I smirked, and responded, "No, Bale, I don't suppose you do. You won't like this at all."

He sighed. His eyes closed briefly as he shook his head. Bale was used to following me into situations he disliked. The fact that I was able to keep him out of sight in Brighton was a feat of wills, especially the day Bethany and Amelia showed up at Esmerelda's. Bale had been around a corner with a message from Tragar when they arrived to ambush Aidan and me.

Bethany. That memory took me in directions I did not want to go. I hated not knowing where she was or how she was. I hoped Cole was taking care of her like he'd promised. If he didn't keep her safe, there was a good chance I'd kill him myself. And it wouldn't be hard now that he had no power and Amelia wasn't around to protect him.

I sighed. Bethany deserved more than me, though. She deserved someone who could truly protect her, and love her, and age with her. Her frustration with Immortals was apparent when she left. She didn't need me, even if I needed her.

I had to focus. Realizing what I had to say next couldn't be overheard, I switched to telepathy.

We're going back to Cresthaven.

We will not, he responded. His knuckles were white as he gripped the steering wheel, his eyes flaring orange. I dug into the glovebox and handed him a pair of dark sunglasses.

We will. We must. She will never expect it. I settled back in my seat, looking out at the road ahead. We were on the Pacific Coast Highway and the winding road gave me the opportunity to stare out at the ocean.

I heard Bale grind his teeth together. *What is it she will not be expecting, Prince Mikail?*

Me, to come home, and kill her, I responded without looking away from the crashing waves.

The car jerked as Bale swiveled in his seat, his mouth open. He quickly righted himself, and the car.

Of all the statements for you to make, that was the one I had hoped you wouldn't. He sighed. *You do not understand the weight of a life, Mikail. It will take a part of your soul. And your own mother? That is not what you want. Why now? What has changed?*

I held out my hand and a thin piece of leather appeared. I yanked my hair back and quickly secured it before rolling the window down halfway. The salty sea air rushed in, taking his words away and giving me renewed strength.

In a low whisper, I said, "We searched for her hidden chamber for years, Bale. We knew she was taking women, but we didn't know why and were never able to find them. My mother was kidnapping our people, essentially raping them, and then forcing them to have children she either killed or took. She would have made Amelia do the same, or likely worse. She is mad, and this cannot continue. I am the Prince of the Immortals. If she is gone, I can rule. Amelia and Aidan may or may not find anything of value in Syria, but in the meantime, I can put us on the path to the right future. And she will never suspect a thing."

It seemed like the only logical solution, yet Baleon looked at me like I had lost my mind. He flipped on his signal and pulled to the side of the road. When the SUV was in park, he ordered everyone to stay inside, got out, and came to my side. As he opened my door, he waved at Elias and Willow to stay in their vehicles. I slowly got out, wondering where this was going. Bale looked down at me, his eyes suddenly sad. Then, he knelt in front of me, and I immediately understood.

He tried to speak, and I yelled for him to get up. I pulled at his jacket and eventually launched at his shoulders, trying to knock him over, to stop him in some way. Left with no other choice, I finally yelled, "I command you to get up and be quiet!"

Baleon's mouth snapped shut and he stood, but his eyes burned orange and he glared, furious. He couldn't refuse my command, it was part of his original oath to me.

"I will not allow you to make that oath, Bale. You have already made one to me and I will not put that on you. This is my choice. My mother damaged our people, our future, my friends, and…me," I finished quietly, my eyes dropping as my anger deflated to resolve. "This is my choice, Bale. I appreciate what you tried to do, but the best you can do for me now is help me. We both know the world will be better for it. Now, speak your turn."

His glare faded. "It has been many years since you exercised that ability," he said with a smirk. We both remembered the night I decided I would run away. I commanded Baleon to help me. He packed my bag and ushered me through the halls toward the grounds of Cresthaven. We were almost at the main gate when he started to ask me questions. "Where will we go, how will we eat, what will we do for money in the human world…?" Questions I had no idea how to answer at eleven years old. Eventually, I was more scared of the outside than the inside.

"I will not dissuade you now as I did then," he said. "You are a man, Prince Mikail, a fine man. And you know your own soul and what it can withstand. If this is the will of the Gods, then so be it. I will protect you as I always have." Baleon pulled his fist to his heart and gave me a small bow.

Once back on the road, the cell phone we'd picked up from a gas station along the highway started ringing. Elias explained since we were already heading toward Brighton, we should just take everyone back to the caves the AniMages had previously used. There were supplies, it was well hidden, and magic barriers helped reinforce the cloaking. I couldn't disagree with his logic, and was glad to know we had a destination. Now, I also knew how quickly Baleon and I could get back on the road.

To Cresthaven. To kill my mother.

I said those words in my mind, over and over, waiting for them to make me feel guilty. The guilt had yet to show. The only reaction was a need for action. My foot tapped a quick rhythm on the floorboard and I jumped as a hand reached out and grasped my shoulder.

"It's only me, Micah, don't be alarmed." Cora's soft voice floated up from behind me. She crouched just behind my seat. I turned to her and brought a forced smile to my face.

"We should be to our destination in a few hours," I said. She nodded, sliding her hand from my shoulder to my elbow.

"I know. Dillon is quite anxious to show me where he's been living while I was…away." Cora looked back over her shoulder to Dillon's sleeping form. Her eyes were filled with such love and I hated the twinge of jealousy that rose inside me.

"But that's not why I'm here," she continued. "Micah, you should wait for Amelia and Aidan to return. I know you're planning something, but they will bring back knowledge you need. Do not act hastily. What has happened to our people occurred over decades, it cannot be undone in a day."

I sat straighter. Indignant, I leaned in, my words just above a whisper. "I would kindly ask you to stay out of this, Cora."

Her hopeful expression faded as she nodded. "I see. I will do that then. Good luck, Prince Mikail."

I turned to face forward and caught a knowing look from Baleon that I chose to ignore.

I hadn't actually been to Elias's caves, though I'd made the trek there from the confines of Amelia's mind when she went to rescue Bethany. The steps were foreign, though the landscape was familiar. I picked my way through the trees, distracted by my own thoughts. I was ready to go. I was ready to be alone in the car with Bale so we could make our plans and get on with it.

Once on the larger path, Willow stepped up beside me. "It's strange not being able to read you like we can normally read each other. Your emotions are a blank space, but your body is not. I see the weight you carry. Would you like to talk about it? I've been told I'm a good listener."

Her voice pulled at me and I briefly considered asking her opinion, but I shook my head quickly and dismissed the notion. "No," I barked out, before backtracking. I swallowed my defensive tone and tried again. "I mean, thank you, Willow, but no, I do not need to talk."

Willow looked up at me, her green eyes the same color as the magic flowing through her. Green grass on a summer day after a good rain, that's what her eyes made me think of. She continued to stare at me, both of us stopped in the middle of the trail. The moment I decided to look away, she brought her hand to my chest and placed it over my heart.

"Your pain is buried, but it won't stay that way. Be careful what reason you give it to come forward. You can either rid yourself of it, or it will consume you," she said, eyes filled with compassion and worry. Then she turned away and continued up the path, leaving me standing there, missing the warmth of her hand and wondering how she knew.

At that same moment, Dillon streaked past me, a jackrabbit in human form. I caught a high-pitched "'scuse me" as he rushed past. I shook my head and followed him. Baleon was a few steps behind me and I motioned him forward. As we walked in stride, he spoke.

"Do you feel right leaving them so soon, Prince Mikail? We cannot guarantee their safety here, and we need them for the same reasons your mother did. They can carry life. We have no future to protect without offspring." Bale's words were true, and I'd thought over this issue myself many times.

"Elias says they will be safe. And we won't be gone long. We have to do this, Bale. There is no other way into Cresthaven. You know Rhi will have taken charge of the Hunters. My mother will want vengeance." I squeezed my fists, the muscles in my body coiled tight. I had never fought my mother overtly. I made choices she didn't know of and I helped those opposed to her, but I never stood against her like I did the day we rescued Amelia.

It felt good.

It felt good to fight for the right side of this war, to fight for my people. I was their Prince and we had lived like this for too long. Tragar couldn't remember a time before my grandfather's rule. He couldn't remember a time when people hadn't whispered about the Elders and wondered why there wasn't more information about where we came from and what we were here for.

We weren't human and we didn't fit in with humans. Before my mother lost her mind, we were cloistered in one area, required to stay there. It was ridiculous. All of it.

I wanted my people back together, by their choice. I wanted to sit on my family throne and make decisions that would help us grow, help us come together as one Immortal people, no matter our individual races. My mother wouldn't be the only issue, Rhi was sure to be a challenge of his own, but it was a beginning. If I could take the throne, at least I could start to bring people together. I could show them the Clair blood was not tainted through and through.

We finally emerged into the clearing leading to the caves. Bale and I were the last to arrive and it was already a busy scene. People went this way and that way as they aired out blankets, unpacked supplies, and rested after the hike.

I hadn't taken two steps forward when I heard, "Thank you, sweet baby Jesus." I knew that voice. My head shot up and swiveled back and forth. I had to be hearing things. I was scanning the campsite when she spoke again. "Micah, I'm here. Goddamn all this magic shit, I'm right here!"

Her voice came from directly in front of me, but there was nothing there. "Bethany?" I questioned. I waved a hand in the empty space in front of me and felt something I instantly knew I shouldn't have. I had felt that particular part of her just once, and had to get permission first. I started to apologize when Bethany's still invisible palms connected with my chest, shoving me back a step.

I grunted, always impressed with the force such a small girl could put out. "You have to show yourself. Bloody hell, woman, I can't see you!"

"I don't know how! Amelia did this to me and then we just left. I don't know how to show myself!" Bethany shrieked, her panic unnerving. Bethany didn't panic.

I held my hands out, trying to calm her down. I wasn't even sure I was looking in the right place. "Concentrate on me. You have to focus on the fact that you know me and want me to see you."

Baleon interjected at that point, but stayed back away from us. "You can also decide to show yourself to everyone here, but if you do that, you cannot be cloaked again. The spell will be undone."

"Undone? Like completely undone? I don't know. No, I do. I can do that." She still sounded panicked. I was starting to worry. It wasn't like Bethany to lose control like this.

The air in front of me started to shimmer. It was what I would guess heat visions to be like, where everything behind that space was wavering and broken. Slowly, Bethany appeared, her eyes closed and nose wrinkled in a way I shouldn't have found as adorable as I did. But, I had long accepted that she undid me by simply breathing.

"I can see you now," I said, unable to hold back my smile of relief or the hand that reached forward and tucked a stray hair fallen from her ponytail behind her ear.

Bethany shook off my hand and I let it drop. She surprised me when she took a small step toward me, looking like she might actually reach for me.

"Thank God you came. I don't know how you knew to come, but I swear to everything good and holy, I'll do everything right from here on out because I prayed you would find me." Tears started to fill her eyes and Bethany's hands shook.

"What happened?" I asked, stepping forward. She stepped back, looking over my shoulder. "Bethany, this is not the time! What happened?"

"Not you," she said, her head shaking back and forth. "I wasn't backing away from you. Him. I was backing away from him." She pointed her trembling finger toward Baleon.

"How can you trust him? He is one of them and they found us. They took Cole. They took him even though they said they could tell he didn't have any magic. And they hurt him! They hurt him because he wouldn't tell them where the women were or where Amelia was. And he didn't tell them about me. I had to hide and watch while they hurt him and then took him!" Bethany was breaking down, tears streaming down her cheeks and hiccuping sobs interrupting her words.

"What? They took Cole? Who? Where?" I pelted her with questions as AniMages surrounded us. They knew who Bethany and Cole were to Amelia and me. They knew what this meant.

Bethany opened her mouth, but the sobs took over as she collapsed against me. I slowly lowered us both to the ground and held her to me as I looked over at Baleon. He nodded, his mouth a tight line. There was no question now. We were going to Cresthaven.

Chapter 31
Aidan

A pile of jagged rocks and crumbled pieces of the mountain wall covered our exit. I strained my hearing, making sure no other rocks would fall. The jolt of energy and amped up power ran through me, my wolf on high alert, ready to go. I was close to shifting, but wasn't sure whether I'd be more of a help or hindrance for Amelia in that form. She crouched behind me as we both silently scanned the room, still positioned just in front of the wall of magic.

"Have you seen either dog move?" I asked, staring at the two Danes who now stood sentry on each side of the room. They were close to the edges, their backs almost against the side walls.

I didn't wait for her to answer. "I don't like this, Amelia. I don't like—"

Hearing another faint *click*, I didn't finish my warning. She couldn't hear it, but my wolf howled inside my head, yelping for me to look up. With one hand, I shoved Amelia down as I leapt over her so my body shielded hers. A quiet *whoosh* told me something was falling at the same moment both Danes started howling.

Sounds assaulted my ears. The dogs baying, Amelia's screams, a roaring wind I heard but couldn't feel, and finally, my own wordless shouts. I threw both hands in the air as light glinted off dark metal bars and registered the spiked grate plummeting toward us. It moved too fast for me to get us both to safety, and the wall blocked our path in the other direction. I had seconds to make a decision.

Crouching over Amelia, I flung everything I had at the grate. I didn't know how to stop it, but my AniMage instincts took over and I had no control over them. I pulled at the power and then forced it back out, focused only on protecting Amelia. It was blue fire and orange lightning, a concentrated stream of continuous energy that shot from my palms and hit the grate dead center, slowing it down but not changing the trajectory.

I redirected the stream of crackling power to the right half of the grate and pulled at the deepest parts of me. I screamed, the power scorching my hands and shredding my insides as it yanked energy from every cell. I directed the blasts at the right edge of the grate and it started to lift up and away from us.

As I forced more power out of my body to move the grate, I struggled to breathe, my body scrambling to heal the burns and replenish itself since I refused to stop. The last burst of power propelled out of me, a basketball-sized orb of swirling light hitting exactly where I'd intended, sending the grate toppling to the left, landing with a deafening clang on its top in the center of the room.

I exhaled in relief, but my body quickly responded to what I'd put it through. Exhaustion overtook me and I couldn't stop from laying out on the cold stones. They were cool against my hot skin. My body was limp and my insides raw.

Amelia hovered over me, her voice far away, though her face was inches from mine. Her words stopped and a soothing energy slid through me, relieving the aches and pains, and acting as a salve on my internal blisters. I didn't want her to stop when she did.

"Thank you," I mumbled as I sat up. "I don't know why I couldn't take care of that myself."

She steadied me. "You feel really depleted. I should probably give you more, then you can tell me what the hell just happened." She sent a wary look over my shoulder, and I turned to see the spiked grate halfway across the room, upside down and partially melted.

"You did a number on that thing," she said wryly. "I could have helped you, you know. You didn't have to take that on alone."

The room wouldn't stay put. I swayed with the movement in my head. Amelia took both of my hands in hers and I felt her filter in again. The Elder power combined with what she gained from Cole felt like a nap in the sunshine. Nothing hurt and I could feel my energy being renewed. I wanted to lay back and let the euphoria take me away, but we needed answers and there was only one way to get them.

I released her hands, pulled away, and pressed them against the stones, slowly making my way to standing. Amelia rose at the same speed, her hands out like she expected me to topple. Once at full height, I took a deep breath and reassessed. Nothing wobbled, spun, or ached…much.

"Come on, we need to try again," I said.

"Are you sure, Aidan? What if we're wrong again?" Amelia stared at the wall of power, gnawing at her lower lip.

"We've come this far. We can do this. We have to," I said, holding out my hand. She took it and we stood together in silence, watching the symbols float slowly toward the floor before disappearing and then reappearing at the top of the wall.

I focused all of my attention on the wall, seeing nothing but the flowing colors and symbols. Up and down. Up and down. Then, it started—faint strains of a melody I'd fought to remember as a child and wished I could forget as I grew up. A melody that had sent me over the edge when Amelia hummed it in the courtyard of our college.

My head whipped back and forth as my eyes scanned the room. "Do you hear that?" I asked. "Where is it coming from?"

"Aidan, I don't hear anything. What are—"

"Shhhh," I said, putting one hand up. "There. It's there again." I closed my eyes and the notes grew louder.

"Aidan, I don't hear anything," she argued.

The song overtook my mind, blocking out anything else Amelia might have said. It triggered a memory. One that hadn't arisen when my binds were broken and my wolf was freed. I didn't trust this room or what had happened here, but as soon as the scene began and I saw my parents, I knew I had to see the rest.

I heard them say my name, but knew they weren't speaking *to me*. Their Aidan was in my mother's arms, wrapped in a blanket. She swayed back and forth as they spoke in hushed tones.

"This was the right choice, wasn't it, Zen?" my mother asked. My father came up behind her and wrapped his arms around both her and me, his chin resting on the top of her head. He swayed back and forth, the three of us forming a family unit I'd never seen until now.

"Kayla, you know we had to do this. I didn't want to abandon my duties and leave the pack any more than you did. But, Lavignia came to us and told us to leave. She said our son would help save our people. She said he would help stop Julia's madness and lead the AniMages. He will be King and our people will be whole again," my father said quietly, and tears fell from my mother's cheeks.

"How have our people strayed so far from their purpose, Zen? When did Immortals become so selfish, so conceited to believe that they were the only ones who mattered? How did this happen?" she asked quietly.

"Your heart has always been so big, Kayla. Since we were children and I learned quickly capturing toads would only earn me your ire and not your favor, you've always seen the world as so black and white. Nothing was ever insignificant to you. Every life held value." My father smiled as he kissed my mother's temple. "Unfortunately, it is not so simple and clear to everyone."

"Shouldn't it be so simple though, Zendrick? We know the truth. Lavignia told us everything. We understand who we were meant to be and our purpose in this world. How could she tell us and no one else? Why would she impart such knowledge and then send us away?"

She didn't wait for him to answer. Instead, she pulled me closer and continued.

"Will any of us remember what truly happened? How can we blindly believe someone who has lied to us for years? The world Julia has built…I don't want that for our son. He shouldn't have to run from his home and be afraid. I don't want this life for him, Zen." She stopped speaking and another tear fell.

My father only pulled her more tightly to him, saying, "I know, doll, I know. Lavignia came to us and offered us the truth. But she said it came with consequences, and it has."

Neither of my parents spoke as they swayed back and forth. Soon, my father started to hum and my mother's voice filled the air.

She plucked the sun from the sky,
She borrowed the moon for one night,
She looked down at this place,
And knew the timing was right.

She poured drops from the ocean,
Breathed fire from the core,
She exhaled her breath,
Dug her hands into the soil.

She gave of herself,
It flowed freely within,
But without her love and light,
Our souls will grow dim.

The keepers of men,
Caretakers of fur and fin,
Sworn protectors,
Guardians of all of them.

Her light shines bright,
We are never alone,
We need only look in,
To finally be home.

"Be with us now, Mother. We need you," my mother whispered.

My eyes snapped open, connecting with the symbols on the wall. I watched them float as the song repeated in my head. The sequence of symbols changed and I continued to stare. By the third time, they were organized perfectly, and I finally understood the memory.

"That's it," I said, the words riding my exhale.

"What's it, Aidan? What just happened? You zoned out on me for a second." Amelia stepped in front of me, her eyes narrowing as she searched my face.

I filled her in on the memory and tried not to allow the emotion of feeling so close to my parents choke me up. Her eyes were bright, ripples of violet light behind glass as they filled. As I got to the end of the story, I found the melody of the song my mother sang and sang it myself.

Amelia watched and listened, her eyes never straying from mine. I could feel her ache to hold me, to touch me. The need for our connection was in me as well. I reached out and pulled her to me. With my arms wrapped around her the same way my father had held my mother, I finished the song and dropped a kiss to the top of her head.

"That was beautiful, Aidan," she said, her voice wavering. "I've never been able to forget that melody."

"I wish you could have heard my mother sing it. That was something truly beautiful," I responded. We were quiet as we both stared at the wall. The memory of Amelia humming my mother's song and the afternoon we ditched so I could take her up to my favorite cliffs was one of my favorites. It was the first time we truly opened up to each other. It was hard to believe how far we'd come.

The symbols started their fall again and this time, I knew exactly what to do. I sang the song again and as I got to each symbol, I reached out and pulled it from the stream of light. Each time my fingers dipped into the power stream, I felt the electric shock vibrate to my core. But with each one I pulled correctly, the shock lessened.

Amelia stood next to me. As she watched, a smile developed. Each symbol I plucked, I dropped into her outstretched hands. I expected them to dull, to lose the silver sheen they held as they had before, but they didn't. They glowed brighter. Her palms filled with their own light source.

I pulled the last symbol down, the one for mother. It was the only one that made sense to end the song and the only symbol still floating. I dropped it into Amelia's hands and the light grew even brighter.

Neither of us could take our eyes from Amelia's palms and the glowing symbols. The room was silent, our quick breaths the only sound. I was drawn to the light, to Amelia, and turned to face her completely.

A need I couldn't stop or explain engulfed me. I reached out and covered Amelia's hand with my own. When the outer edges of my hands met the skin of hers, the cascade of power from the door dropped, a thunderous *whoosh* echoing across the room. At the same time, the light between our hands flared and we were both thrown backwards.

We landed in a heap, limbs tangled. My head smacked on the cold stone and I fought dizziness as I tried to get to my feet. I had no idea what would come through that space and I needed to protect us. Thankfully, Amelia's healing had done the trick. My power was no longer depleted and the dizziness cleared quickly. I helped Amelia to her feet when the light in the room strobed.

Our heads whipped around and we both shielded our eyes against the brightness streaming in from the doorway we'd opened. It was blinding at first, permeating the cavern with stark white light. It filled every nook and crevice, bringing with it a warmth that wrapped around me like a blanket. I instantly lost the need to fight or protect. I only wanted to be close to whatever was coming.

The vibrancy dimmed slowly and a silhouette appeared. A woman shaped like an hourglass wearing a one-shouldered dress that clung to her figure and fell to the floor. She came across the threshold, and said, "I am Gaea. Mother of all Immortals, Mother of all beings, Mother Earth. And you are the saviors of everything I hold dear."

Chapter 32
Amelia

"Gaea?" I croaked out. My voice echoed the disbelief running through my brain.

The woman continued to take measured steps toward us, her hands clasped loosely in front of her. Had I ever envisioned a run-in with a Greek goddess, I wouldn't have imagined her to be this tall, curvaceous woman with salt and pepper hair flowing down her back and life's wrinkles crisscrossing her face. I spent enough time with my head in mythology books to know who Gaea was, but my mind couldn't reconcile the deity with the woman in front of me.

She gave me a small smile, amusement dancing in her eyes. "Gaea is indeed my name, Amelia. And I have long waited for you to come. For my children to finally save themselves and send me the ones who would bring me home."

I couldn't begin to pick my gaping mouth up off the floor. Maybe I shouldn't have been shocked to have a

Goddess standing in front of me, I was an Immortal after all, but I could only sit there and stare at her.

Both my and Aidan's power had been on full tilt since we'd entered the cavern. Our eyes glowed in the semi-darkness of the room now that the light from the wall was gone.

"Before we begin, allow me to restore you fully," Gaea said as she held out her hands. A swirling white mist rushed from her palms and enveloped us both. I wanted to step away, but as soon as the droplets landed on my skin, as soon as I breathed the fine vapor in, I felt the change. My body felt less battered and my mind felt clear. I stood taller. I felt Aidan's change as well. I brought him back from the edge, but through Gaea's power, his strength returned fully and the internal wounds from his episode completely healed.

Aidan tightened his grip on my hand and I returned the gesture, grateful he was beside me.

"You said we were saviors. Of what exactly? What is a Goddess doing trapped in a mountain? And why do you need us both?" As I peppered her with questions, her smile only grew.

I wanted to feel uneasy as she moved closer, but I was drawn to her. That same pull in my chest made me want to walk into her arms and allow her to hold me. To fill me with everything inside her, all the love from a mother I'd never known. Aidan must have felt my warring emotions. He let go of my hand and locked me to his side.

"We're in this together, doll. You stay with me," he whispered in my ear and I nodded, though I wasn't sure I entirely agreed.

"Don't be scared," she said softly. "I will tell you my story, but first, you must know I have been waiting. So long, I've waited. Yet, you are still a surprise, Amelia. Your mother went to great lengths to protect you and our people. Her only downfall was she didn't know everything she needed to. I called to her, just like I called to you, and just before you opened the door, to Aidan. In the same way I unlocked his memory, I tried to draw her to me, to show her the truth before she made her choices. I feel the darkness she put in you. I can make it go away, but we will get to that."

Gaea stopped, waved a hand, and the ground started to crack. Stones in front of her ruptured as saplings emerged. They began to weave themselves together, a quick dance of bark twirling around bark, interlacing and creating a beautiful chair.

"The earth is only one element you can manipulate, Amelia," she said as she laid a hand on the bark. Leaves burst from the intricately woven tree limbs, creating a plush cushion for her to sit on. She repeated the movements and Aidan and I both jumped as stones behind us cracked apart and a small couch for us to sit on knitted itself together.

Gaea snapped her fingers and the room lit up. Fire danced above us, creating a glow that touched all corners of the room. Finally, I watched her eyes land on Charlie and Onyx. Her smile widened, and she whispered, "My loves, my sons, come to me as you were."

The Great Danes I loved morphed before my eyes into men. With a snap of her fingers, they were both dressed. They stood tall, as tall as any Hunter, and with the same light brown skin and white hair. They both walked quickly to Gaea and fell to one knee.

"Mother," Charlie said, his head bowed and white hair gleaming as it fell around his shoulders, "we have missed you, but we have done our duty in your absence."

She reached down, cradling both of their cheeks in her hands. "I rejoice knowing you are still here with me. Stand so you can properly introduce yourselves."

The men stood and turned to us as Gaea sat down. Aidan pulled me tighter to him, but I refused to be held. My curiosity was too much. I stepped forward and he was quickly beside me, muttering his displeasure.

"Charlie? Onyx?" I stared at them, my eyes shifting from Onyx's dark features to Charlie's broad stature. Onyx had yet to speak, but his almost-black eyes danced with amusement.

"The Hunter was right, we are Sentinels," Onyx said with a wry smile. "We are the guardians of the Great Mother and her children. When we could no longer get to her, we took a shifted form to protect ourselves and hide from the Queen. It was serendipity that your uncle found us and led us to you and your brother. We knew we had to bring the chosen ones back here if we were ever going to free Gaea. As your power has grown, so has ours. We had been apart from our mother for too long and became more animal than man. As her power manifested in you, it provided us the connection we needed to find ourselves once more."

Charlie interjected. "To answer your first question, we are most closely tied to Hunters and AniMages. Close to Gaea, we can do things others can't, and we have the ability to share our gifts." Charlie's eyes shifted to Aidan and his gaze settled there, clearly waiting for something.

I heard Aidan's quick intake of breath and felt his heartbeat racing. "You? It was you?" He breathed out the words. I looked from him to Charlie, confused.

Charlie nodded and explained. "We took the form of puppies knowing they are more desirable and people would protect us. In the beginning, we were able to shift back and forth and continue our duties. Your uncle's home allowed us the freedom to roam, and he didn't worry when we were gone for long stretches. We tracked the Hunters who searched for Zendrick and Kayla, and masked ourselves to join them the night they attacked. I found Aidan and did what I could to hide his presence and ensure his survival, including imparting some of my gifts upon him."

I looked past Charlie and saw Gaea's eyes shine with unshed tears of pride. Aidan still hadn't spoken, but I felt the conflict brewing inside him.

Charlie continued, saying, "I also told Cole to give everything he had to Amelia. I knew the power he held wasn't his to keep, and that Amelia wouldn't survive the Keeper without it."

My dog gave Aidan additional Hunter power and told my brother to give up his power to save me. *My dog.*

"While I do love all creatures, Charlie and Onyx are much more than dogs, Amelia," Gaea said. "They were the first Immortals I created on Earth. I made them to protect me, but to also help me carry out my mission. While I was unable to come back to Earth fully, they continued to make a difference."

"What we didn't understand was that they needed me," she said sadly. "Everything we do has a price, never forget that, and while I was able to give them so much, they needed me to thrive. Charlie infusing Hunter power into Aidan was one of the last times he was able to use his full power. Too far from me, he was incapable of gathering what he needed to replenish, and hasn't been able to leave his shifted form until now. As Onyx said, they regressed into being more animal than man."

Gaea held out her hands and each Sentinel took one. She looked up at them, her affection obvious, squeezed theirs hands, and let go.

"So, it's true? What Julia has said all along, that AniMages were more animal than man?" I asked the question as my mind rebelled against the potential answer.

Gaea shook her head, a sad scowl deepening the lines in her face. "Charlie and Onyx were something special, something different. They were the first and therefore, the test. Please sit, and I will tell you my story. It needs to be short as you have choices to make and places to be, but there are truths you must know to survive."

I turned to Aidan, and his shocked expression matched my own.

Are you ready for this? he asked.

No. But that doesn't matter. Everything I've done has led me here. She is the first person who can truly give me answers. I can't run from this.

He reached out and I took his hand, mine shaking slightly.

Neither can I. We are both tied to this in ways I had never imagined. I'm here with you, doll. Every step.

I nodded and we sat on the couch to face Mother Earth and hear the tale of how we came to exist.

Chapter 33
Aidan

Amelia sat next to me on the lush pile of leaves that made our seat, her knee bouncing up and down as she tapped one finger on her leg. Her mind raced, the anxiety a ball of nausea that started to get to me as well. I grasped the rough bark of the tree supporting us and allowed it to dig into my skin, forcing me to focus.

I looked up to find Gaea staring quietly at me. It was unnerving. I couldn't tell whether she was judging me, expecting me to do something, or waiting for me to freak out. Any combination of those was a real possibility. I'd never sat in front of a Goddess.

Jesus. This is actually happening.

Gaea chuckled, a high ting of laughter that immediately drew my brows together as I scowled in her direction.

"Let me guess, you do the mind invasion thing, too?" I asked. Her quiet calm was really getting to me. It was easier for me to handle people who couldn't handle themselves.

"Yes, Aidan. That is one of my many talents," she said. I hated the fact that I was drawn to the way she said my name and that her approval was suddenly something I craved. I clenched my fist and willed myself to focus. We needed information.

"There are things happening out there we have to deal with. We can't sit here forever." It came out gruffer than I'd intended, and Amelia gave me a dirty look.

"I'm sorry, Gaea, he doesn't mean that," she hurriedly apologized. "I mean, um, we do have a situation out there, but we want to hear what you have to say," Amelia stuttered, and preened as Gaea smiled at her. Gaea's approval was something we both wanted, like it or not—and I did not.

With Onyx standing over one shoulder and Charlie over the other, Gaea finally began her tale.

"I won't be so self-absorbed as to think you know my history since children don't cling to the stories of the Gods the way they once did," she said. She waved a hand in the air and a light breeze floated through the room.

"I am called many things," she continued, "but the one most known is Mother Earth. The universe, the stars, this planet, the Gods and Goddesses of Homer's stories…they all came from me in one fashion or another. I've created many things in my time, but this planet has always been one of my favorites. I always watched over and loved the humans. But, as the years have passed, I realized they are a self-destructive species, not just destroying themselves, but the planet I adore. I decided they needed help. I went against the wishes of many, as I am prone to do, and created the Immortals."

Gaea paused, her lips twisting into a thoughtful smirk. "To be fair, I was acting impetuously, as is also typical of me, and created this new race without fully thinking it through. I thought as long as I left someone in charge, my children would do as I asked and play the roles I gave them. It did not work that way. Few things ever work out as you intend." She stopped, staring off into space.

It gave me the opportunity to watch her, to study Gaea, Mother Earth. The breeze she'd conjured still floated through the room, rippling the long dress she wore and catching in her long hair. She put her chin in her hand, her expression relaxed and her mind clearly wandering. Her eyes glowed white when she actively used her power, but settled to the color of mist. If it weren't for the strangeness of her eyes, I pictured this woman in a kitchen, her hands buried in dough and flour on her face. She was the grandmother everyone wished they had.

Caught in my own thoughts, I was surprised when Gaea sat straight in her chair and addressed Amelia.

"Amelia, you have something in you that was never meant to be," she said, her tone tender. "Your mother didn't understand what being an Elder meant. She didn't get close enough to me to see the truth of what was happening around her.

"And now, though the darkness is tethered, your safety is not going to last. The power inside you, as you've learned, is instinctual and primal. In its current form, it cannot be contained. The choice is yours to make—the first choice that's truly ever been yours." Gaea smiled. I didn't like it. I didn't like the way she was playing to Amelia, or the way Amelia was leaning in, eating up her words.

I reached for Amelia's wrist and pulled her to my side. She scooted toward me, but glowered at the interruption.

Gaea looked at me, her curiosity obvious as she leaned in and tilted her head to the side. "You don't trust me, do you, Aidan? Though, I suppose after all you've been through, you have no reason to trust me. To really trust anyone," she mused quietly, and I wondered if she meant to say it out loud.

"There are people—your people—who need us, who rely on us. Can you please tell us what we're here to know? What I think right now doesn't matter," I said. All I wanted was to get what we needed and get back to the AniMages. To protect those I could from whatever was coming.

"Ah," she said as she sat back in her chair with a small smile. "Your protective instincts are just as I'd hoped. Let us move forward. We will come back to Amelia's choices once I've explained.

"This began close to a hundred years ago. After Charlie and Onyx, I created Mages, AniMages, and Hunters," she said. "Mages to protect the humans from themselves, AniMages to protect the animals and nature from the humans, and Hunters to protect the Immortals from the rest of the world. The Hunters were fashioned after Charlie and Onyx, given instincts allowing them to foresee enemies and the fortitude to do what had to be done to protect those whom I created.

"I only wanted my children to help maintain order on this planet, and I took much grief from Olympus for it. Not that I hadn't been enough of a pain throughout the years, but to create races specifically to protect those lesser beings who were mortal…" she trailed off and clutched her chest, rolling her eyes. Images of Zeus holding a lightning bolt and threatening to kill us all had me stifling a chuckle. Amelia giggled a little and Gaea laughed. "While I created them all, I have been a thorn in their sides for as long as they can remember. I like it that way.

"The Clairs were meant to rule," she said. "They were Mage and the only family to have direct access to me. They were the only ones who understood who I truly was. As it tends to be, after a few decades, I paid less and less attention to my creations and they did as children are wont to do—exactly what they are not supposed to.

"Instead of keeping the Immortals in the shadows, silently correcting the humans and their balance with nature, the first King decided, because he was Mage, the Mages should be considered the most important Immortal. He abandoned his duties and put my children against each other. He said it was in my honor, as if I would ever condone such a thing," Gaea sneered, her face twisting into a grimace for the first time since we'd met.

"What he didn't anticipate was civil war erupting," she said with a sad sigh. "It didn't take long for him to come crawling to my altar, begging for my help. By the time he showed me the truth, it was too late."

Amelia and I exchanged shocked looks as Gaea paused, tears dripping from her eyes. Charlie knelt next to the arm of her chair and she grabbed his shoulder, slowly breathing in and out. The leaves she sat on shriveled, transitioning from bright green to brittle brown, crumbling beneath her until only bare trees remained, a twisted throne.

"You cannot understand the loss of children," she said, her voice thick with emotion. "I have lost so many in my time, and so often for such senseless reasons, but this was something I never expected. Of course, I told him I would do anything it took. Much to my surprise, anything ended up being everything.

"There were so few of them left, and the hatred he had bred was so prevalent, so violent, the only thing that could turn them back into my loving children was a total change." Gaea paused again, her pain obvious in the way she gripped Charlie's shoulder.

"So," she continued quietly, "I did what no Goddess had done before. I sacrificed myself to give my children a chance. To give this planet and the human race a chance. Love drives us to do the most illogical things, but I thought my love was the only thing that would save them."

Chapter 34
Amelia

I couldn't look away from her. I gripped my hand firmly around Aidan's, ensuring I didn't lose myself to the pull of Gaea's power. I could feel it tugging at me and I refused to lose myself to anything again. Aidan's hand was an anchor, his wariness and distrust of the situation a reminder.

Gaea sniffled, allowing a few more tears to drip down before she spoke again. "The next part I must show you, because words will not do it justice. I had no idea my children were capable of such savagery against themselves." She waved a hand and a white orb appeared between our couch and her chair.

"It was you!" I said. I pulled myself away from Aidan and shot across the small space between us. I stood in front of the elusive white orb that had haunted my every interaction with the separated Keeper power.

"It was you inside me," I said again. "You were there, with the Keeper. But you wouldn't come to me. You wouldn't help me. Why wouldn't you help me?" I stared into the bright light and lifted a hand to reach into it, the one thing I'd never been able to do, when Aidan grabbed me around the waist and yanked me backwards.

You can't trust her or any of this yet, Amelia. If she's a Goddess, who knows what touching that will do.

I turned to him, his face stricken, panic etched in his set jaw and rigid posture. He was right. I knew he was right. Gaea's allure was stronger than I wanted to admit. I nodded and we sat back down. It was harder to stay still than I'd anticipated.

Gaea watched us with clear curiosity, but continued once we were seated again. "I could not help you because you were not meant to have the power inside you. Had I allowed you to access everything in your soul, it would have devoured you. I learned many things from your mother's choices, but chief among them was the need for balance.

"The power she placed in you was nature-based," Gaea explained. "It was core to each of the races, but had no counter. I realized what she had done to make the cuff once you put it on—the love she embedded, the tears she cried, and the blood she shed. You were able to access the other power through a mix of her magic, her love, and your will. I understood then what the Immortals were missing was balance. I had concentrated too much on what they were and what I wanted them to be, I did not provide the love and guidance they needed. I did not temper instinct with affection." Her words were so simple, so matter of fact.

"Your mother was determined to save you, and her people," she continued. "Truly, her devotion was admirable, if only she knew the truth. If only I had trusted the Elders, but I did not. It is the curse of power. You believe the burden is yours alone to bear." Gaea went quiet as she leaned back in her chair. She suddenly looked like a grandmother who had seen too much. Not a Goddess who created and destroyed so many throughout her lifetime.

"I made a choice that day to wall myself off from Earth," she finally said. She gestured behind us. "Beyond that door is a portal to other worlds. They are worlds I created and worlds only I can travel between, but in those worlds, I do not need a corporeal form. It is only here on Earth that my body is needed.

"I decided the Clairs would not continue to lead alone. They clearly could not be trusted with the task. I created the Elders, men and women with combined power stronger than that of the average Immortal. The Council Elders, specifically, were a special group of women who would be required to marry into the other races so both the races and their magic would evolve, as everything should. They also had to visit this room and pay their homage to me.

"Unbeknownst to them, each time they interacted with the elements of my altar, power was exchanged between us. What they gave allowed my spirit to exist across many worlds at once. What they unknowingly took was a part of me. I was forever etched into their souls so I could watch and know what was happening with my people. I believed if anything were to go wrong again, they would come to me to pray, and through them, I could return." Gaea's lips turned down, flattening into a thin line.

She sighed, and then continued. "And then came your mother. She was intended to be a Council Elder. She was days from understanding her path and the connection we would have. But, she left. Her gift of sight did what all gifts tend to do and only showed part of what should be known.

"She left with your father and when she returned, with you growing in her womb, she convinced the other Council Elders her vision was the truth. They saw what Julia was trying to do and they were afraid. They didn't come to me as they should have, so I could return and stop the madness before it began. Instead, they gave Liana what they could. She saw you, and she saw the end. She never saw the middle and what her choices would mean, but they never do."

"Don't," I warned. "Don't talk about my mother like that. Don't talk about her like she didn't do what she thought she had to. I'm here because of the choices she made. Her choices were clearly better than yours." I bit my tongue as words that shouldn't have left my mind slid out of my mouth with a warning I couldn't take back embedded in them.

Charlie and Onyx both took a step forward. A growl came from beside me as Aidan scooted to the edge of the seat. He was propped on the balls of his feet with one arm across the front of me, his eyes burning bright blue.

"Now, now," Gaea scolded, "that is just unnecessary. Everyone relax." Her tone was soft, but there was a demand no one could refuse. "You are right, Amelia, your mother did what she thought was best. The fault was more mine than hers. Had I been there, none of this would have happened." My muscles relaxed of their own accord and I slumped against the leafy seat. Charlie and Onyx floated back to their original position and Aidan was silent beside me.

Are you okay? I asked.

I feel like I could pass out and sleep for days. That's more impressive than the alpha power I have over the pack. Also, slightly terrifying. Tread lightly, Amelia. We still don't know exactly what we're dealing with here.

He was right. The deeper into this we got, the more nervous I became. And yet, there was at least one more lingering question in my mind. Something I had to know.

She had already acknowledged this wasn't my mother's fault, so I moved on to another awkward topic. "You, um, mentioned marrying, but you didn't elaborate on the mates. Why were they so important?"

I didn't look at Aidan when I asked. We both knew about my trust issues, but I wanted them gone. I wanted her to tell me my emotions were mine and what we had was real.

I hated the knowing smile that appeared on Gaea's face. The tiny quirk of her lips and crinkle of her eyes that said she saw right through my question.

"We must back up one step, Amelia, because it is a crucial one," Gaea responded. "I tied the fertility of the Immortals to the Elders and myself. I believed someone could again threaten what I created, so I did two things. First, I mandated that each Elder must marry someone with a magic mixture different from their own, so lines could not be so easily drawn between the races. Many of those fighting in this so-called war have mixed blood and do not even realize it.

"Then, I cast a spell ensuring the Council Elders replenish their power by visiting me regularly, or fertility would slowly disappear for all Immortals. If the Elders were killed, all of my children would eventually die, because that meant they had become something abominable. Your being alive is the only reason any children have been born since Julia took the throne."

Gaea abruptly stood and smacked her hands together. "Come," she commanded. She strode toward the door without looking back and Onyx fell in right behind her. Charlie raised an eyebrow at us, silently gesturing for us to follow. I missed the goofy dog; I didn't entirely appreciate the impatient Immortal.

I don't know that we should follow her in there, Aidan warned.

I don't think we have much of a choice, I responded.

Aidan caught my hand in his and laced our fingers together. *Then we go together and stay together.*

I couldn't agree more. It looks like it might be you and me against the world, Montgomery.

He smirked. *Always has been, doll, you just didn't know it.*

What he didn't understand was I was actually starting to believe that myself.

Chapter 35
Aidan

Alarm bells I didn't know I had went off in every corner of my mind. My wolf howled and what I surmised as the Hunter part of me sent power flooding through my system, heightening my senses to a new level.

Amelia admitted to more than just being happy I was breathing and I couldn't even enjoy it. Gaea was a dozen paces ahead of us in the portal room while Amelia and I still stood in the main cavern. I tightened my grip on her hand and sought out our connection. Power flowed back and forth between us in a continuous loop. Her energy calmed the anger and helped me think clearly. Mine made her more alert.

I peered through the doorway and made out five small, stone statues. They looked like birdbaths, but with a vertical piece of rock attached to the back, creating a small wall. Each wall was engraved with a different symbol, but it was hard to make them out. The room was dimly lit and

Gaea stood still, her back to us, clearly waiting for our entrance.

We collectively took a deep breath and Amelia squeezed my hand just as we crossed over. Immediately, pain ripped through me. It tore down my chest like I was being slit from throat to navel and I couldn't stop the scream that followed. As quickly as it began, it ended. I was sprawled on the cold floor, struggling to pull in a full breath. I forced myself to my feet, prepared to unleash hell in whatever way I could when I saw Amelia.

Sweat collected on her forehead and at her temples. She bit her lip and her hands shook like she held an invisible jackhammer. I felt the truth of what had just taken place as Gaea started to speak.

"This room is where my power is the strongest," she said, her arms spread wide. "It is the place where it finally has the ability to come home. You are not a Goddess, sweet Amelia, and your mother did not understand the power she took from the Elders. What is inside you—what did you call it, the Keeper power? It is more of me than any being anywhere can sustain. I'm honestly surprised you have lasted this long."

That curious look was back again. Gaea leaned in, inspecting Amelia, clearly looking for something. Amelia's strength was waning. I felt the spread of darkness as the Keeper unfurled in her system. Her breaths were quick and shallow, her legs now shaking. I tried to move, but my own legs were like lead. They refused to budge, and I knew it was Gaea.

I wanted to connect to Amelia, but the last time I had, the Keeper almost sucked me dry. In Cresthaven, she drained most of my power in seconds. But then, Amelia cried out and fell to her knees. Her eyes rolled back in her head and the reverberations of the Keeper's torturous ministrations echoed through me. I knew it didn't matter anymore. I would die to save her.

I latched onto our connection with everything I had and blasted power into Amelia's system. My hope was to beat back the Keeper long enough to find where Amelia hid herself this time and get her to fight with me. I pulled at the power buried deep in my physical body and allowed my soul to seek out hers.

The darkness of the Keeper was like oil, moving slowly, but coating every inch of Amelia internally and creeping through her mind. I felt her intention, a disgusting mix of anticipated pain and high expectations for what was to come. If she was able to bring Amelia back and control her, I might lose her forever.

Fear and determination drove me forward. I used the light inside me to fend off the darkness. I blasted through her inky barriers and decimated thick, syrupy blockages in Amelia's body and mind. But, as soon as I cleared one area, it was swallowed again. With each space I made it through, the Keeper siphoned more of my own power.

Finally, I saw her—a faint pulse of violet light in the back corner of her own mind. Hidden behind stacks of dreams and files of memories, Amelia laid there, curled in a tight ball. I flew to her side, wrapping my body around hers. I struggled to stay present, so much of my own energy gone. I watched the black pool spread toward us. It inched forward and Amelia whimpered. I lashed out, sending a flare of blue and orange light into the center, dissolving it from the inside out, but it immediately closed in on itself like I had never been there.

"You won't go alone, Amelia," I whispered. "She'll have to come through me to get to you. You and me against the world, doll." I closed my eyes, pulled her tighter to me, and prepared for the pain.

"Enough. That is enough." I heard Gaea's voice and a thunderous crack that sounded like lightning striking inches from me. When I opened my eyes, Amelia was still wrapped in my arms, but we were in the portal room once again. Gaea had one hand on Amelia's head and one outstretched. A rainbow of light erupted from her palm and blasted the stone below, eroding it to dust.

I had no idea what she was doing and I struggled to wake my sleeping limbs. They were dead weight as I tried to smack at Gaea's hand.

"Hush now," she scolded. "I am removing power she should have never had. You showed me what I needed to see, Aidan. You did what a mate would do. Sleep now." Gaea gave the command and I had no choice but to close my eyes and follow it.

I awoke and bolted upright. The memories were hazy. For a minute, I didn't know if I was still dreaming. Amelia was sprawled out beside me and Gaea was perched on a chair, this one made of stone wrapped in vines. I drew short breaths as no part of me moved but my eyes.

We were still in the portal room, but now each of the birdbath-looking sculptures was filled. A small waterfall dripped down the side of the stone, backing to fill the bowl with water. One with fire; a single flame in the center of the bowl, hovering above the basin. The third held a mound of dirt, rich and dark, with a lone daisy reaching up from the soil. I swallowed down the irritation that came with knowing Gaea somehow saw Amelia's reaction to my first gift. The last sculpture I knew signified air, and the small spinning cyclone swirled in the basin.

Amelia's eyes fluttered open. They connected with mine and her relief was visible as she slowly closed them and her body relaxed back onto the ground. She gradually sat up, and I did the same. We helped each other stand, our hands lingering as we silently verified the other was indeed okay.

"The power is gone from you, child," Gaea said, her soft voice cutting through the silence of the room. "It has come back to its rightful home and you will no longer need to fear it."

Gaea stood from her chair and slowly walked forward. The dress she wore was deep green, fitting for Mother Earth, and it skimmed the floor so perfectly, she looked like she floated across the space between us. Amelia gripped my hand and I pulled her close to me. I no longer trusted this woman.

Gaea stopped, and asked, "Why so defensive, Aidan? I have removed the dark power from your mate. I have done what no one else could, and she's safe from it now."

"She isn't safe until this is over," I said, wrapping my arm protectively around Amelia.

Gaea laughed—a laugh that came from her belly and bounced off the walls. "Oh, child, she is not safe from the world, only from the power that was inside her. You will leave here soon enough and she will be less safe outside these walls than in them. Neither of you will ever be completely safe again, unless you make the choice."

"What choice?" Amelia asked, her voice breaking. She stepped away from me and repeated herself, this time stronger. "What choice? I've never had a choice."

"But you do now, Amelia," Gaea said as a smile formed and her eyes shined with knowledge she had yet to share. "I want to offer you something no one else has. Your mother thought what she was doing was right, and as I waited for you and Aidan to recuperate, I realized I wasn't being entirely fair. There are many things I'd like for you to do, but so far, you have been through so much and overcome more than most would even attempt. For that, I believe you have earned the right to choose your fate."

Amelia and I exchanged skeptical looks.

Be careful. It was all I could say. There were more words, but I'd said them all before.

She squeezed my hand. *You and me, Montgomery, against the world.*

It had become our mantra to each other. Our reassurance.

"What exactly are you offering?" Amelia asked.

Gaea paused and her smile slowly faded. She didn't look sad, more conflicted. A tiny shake of her head and the smile was back. "Amelia, you are who I've waited for, but as I said, too much of this was done to you without your consent. So, I am going to offer you a choice. You have the option to go back to being just a Mage, and if you choose this, Aidan also has the opportunity to revert to an AniMage. I will strip the Elder from you, Amelia, and I will remove Charlie's Sentinel power from Aidan. I will erase the memories of those who believe Aidan is their King and those who believe you are their savior. You will be able to leave this place and have whatever life you choose, with or without each other."

This time, as we looked at each other, Amelia and I were stunned. A hundred possibilities flew past in an instant. We could leave and all of this would go away. We could run off to some corner of the world and be happy. We could be normal. It was what she always wanted.

I saw the same possibilities flit across Amelia's features. She brightened, her eyes going wide and the corners of her lips turning up. But just as quickly, they fell. Her eyes filled and her brow furrowed. I knew what this was, too. Guilt. How could we leave our people to handle all of this alone?

Gaea continued. "The other choice is to embrace what you are, Amelia. You will no longer be tied to a prophecy, you will make an active choice to take on this responsibility. You will allow me to provide you with the amount of my power you can sustain. Power you can wield with a thought. It will allow you to call on the elements," she said as her hand lifted. One by one, each element independently boiled, brightened, bloomed, and blew. "There will be no question in your mind how to use what I give you. I will always be accessible. I will not come every time you call, but if I feel the need is there, I will respond."

Amelia stepped forward, her excitement palpable in the air as she opened her mouth to speak. I knew she was going to say, or maybe yell, "Yes!", but Gaea raised a hand and cocked a brow. "I am not finished." Amelia's mouth snapped shut.

"If you choose this path, you are also choosing Aidan. You cannot sustain me alone. A mate is necessary for this process to work. If you choose him, you are choosing to share yourself fully with him. You have felt the beginnings of mating. The passion, the connection, and the intensity will all be there. Stronger now than before.

"You will never be able to hide your true emotions from him, nor him from you. If you feel pain, so will he. If your heart breaks, his will sit in shards next to yours. You are forever tied to each other. But, the joys in your life will be doubled as you feel them from him as well. You will feed each other's souls and replenish each other's power. His duty will be to help carry the power I provide you and ensure you can handle using it. He will share the strength of his wolf and the knowledge of the Sentinel, which is even greater than that of Hunters. If you make this choice, your heart is no longer yours to guard. It will be his forever."

Amelia was quiet, and I refused to speak. I refused to believe the girl I nursed back from the other side, who I'd carried out of a deranged Queen's laboratory and told all my secrets to, would walk away. There was too much between us. But this had to be her choice. Gaea was right about that. I would be the choice she made, or I would let her walk away.

"Before he knew I was an Elder, or part of this Immortal world at all, Aidan fought to be with me," Amelia said, turning to me. She looked at me with such curiosity, as if she were surprised I would fight for her, or love her at all. She wasn't talking to Gaea anymore.

"And then, even when you knew, you still came for me," she continued, shaking her head. "You embraced your own wild and magical truths and came to Cresthaven for me. You fought for me to come back to you. You found me in places neither of us knew existed, and you never gave up on me. You told me you loved me over and over, and I've never said it back even though I should have. You fight for me, and with me.

"You always fight with me," she laughed, a soft melody that barely echoed through the room, but sent reverberations through my body and soul.

I will always fight for you, and with you, I thought to myself.

"You came here and you've stayed, even while you know your people are in trouble. Right now, I can feel you, so patient, letting me have this moment to sort through my fear and my hope to find the truth. You are the only person who has never asked me to be anything but myself, in whatever form that took. You accept me, Aidan, and that's why I choose you. I love you, Aidan, and I choose you."

Chapter 36
Amelia

He didn't speak. I told Aidan I loved him for the first time and he was silent. I watched his pupils dilate, a black dot growing against the vibrant blue of his irises. His head tilted to the side and brought his hand to my cheek.

"Say it again," he said softly.

"I love you, Aidan. I do," I said, assuring him. "You've shown me in every way you could, and I was afraid to believe it. Afraid if I did, you'd leave me, too. But before you say anything else, before Gaea does anything, I need to know you choose me, as well. I don't want to make choices for both of us. This is a lot. This is insane. So, I have to know you're in before we move forward."

My heart rattled in my chest. It beat so quickly, I was sure my ribs would rupture and it would skip across the stone floor.

I studied Aidan's face. Watched the corners of his eyes wrinkle and his lips spread into a wide grin. His adorable dimple appeared and I wanted to push up to my toes and kiss it. That dimple was his tell. Only when he was truly happy did he smile big enough to bring it out. I couldn't help but smile back at him, even though he hadn't said anything.

"After everything we've gone through in the past few months, doll, you really think there's any other option for me?" Aidan's voice was low, a husky whisper meant just for me. "You've wound your way around every defense I've ever built and taken up every inch of my heart. There is nowhere I wouldn't go, and nothing I wouldn't do to keep you safe and remind you every day I will not leave you. I will love you every day. I will love you when I want to lock you up and throw away the key, which I'm sure will happen often enough. You couldn't get rid of me if you tried, Amelia. You have always been my choice."

Gaea clapped her hands, a girlish squeal surprising both of us and reminding us of her presence. Aidan and I turned just in time to feel a tiny shock work from our feet to our foreheads. Our jeans and jackets disappeared. Aidan wore long dark brown pants, a cream, long-sleeved shirt, and no shoes. The material looked light and comfortable.

I looked down to find a beautiful cream dress. Long-sleeved, a fitted bodice, and a flowing A-line skirt. It was made of the same material as Aidan's clothes. I also wore no shoes, yet the stone didn't feel cold beneath my feet. My hair was down around my shoulders, and Aidan reached up to play with whatever was in my hair. I looked up at him, the question obvious.

"A flower wreath made of daisies," he said with a grin. Of course.

"You are wearing the traditional dress of our mating ritual," Gaea said from behind us. "The clothes were typically blessed by either the oldest living Immortal, or the Elders. This time, they are blessed by me. Your mating will bind you to each other, me, and this earth. Are you ready?"

Gaea positioned herself the same way a priest would in a wedding. She stood in front of us and Aidan and I faced each other, our hands joined between us. We didn't look away from each other when we simultaneously answered, "Yes."

Gaea placed her hands over ours and began to speak. "Two hearts, two minds, two souls, forever linked. Your mate is not merely a companion, they are the fulfillment of your very essence. From this point forward, Amelia Bradbury and Aidan Montgomery, you have chosen each other. Before all others, against all enemies, even between friends and family, you will put the other first. It will not be a choice. It will be vital to your livelihood.

"Together, you will hold power no one has ever seen. You will be charged with changing the future of the Immortal race. Your collective power will bring back the light for those who have lost it. Your power will give and take life from this Earth. You will sustain each other. You will feed and replenish each other's souls.

"Aidan, you will carry the portion of my power Amelia cannot sustain continually. When the time comes, you must give her what she needs, even if she doesn't understand she needs it. Do you understand?" she asked. Aidan nodded, his eyes locked on mine.

"Amelia, you are the light this world has been looking for. You have grown so much during this journey and your heart clearly reaches for your people. Do not be afraid of what I give you. Wield it fairly, graciously, and honestly. Do not fear your emotions, but do not let them rule you. Do you understand?" she asked me. I nodded as well, whispering, "I do."

"Very well," Gaea said. "One heart, one mind, one soul. By the Earth that provides, the Water that replenishes, the Fire that sustains, and the Air that gives us life, I am the Mother of them all, and I join the two of you forever more. As the humans say, you may now kiss to solidify this union." Gaea stepped back.

Aidan didn't hesitate. Stepping forward, he captured my lips in his. Another shock rippled through us as my arms came to his neck and his wrapped around my back. It was a gentle kiss. One steeped in emotion and honesty. When we pulled apart, Aidan recoiled slightly, but quickly rebounded.

"Your eyes," he said, turning to Gaea. "What happened to her eyes?" he asked.

"Don't fear, Aidan. That is my mark. It is the way you will convince others of who Amelia is and who the two of you are now. The change in her eyes is also accompanied by a change in her power. It will no longer be only the violet of Elders. When she calls on our collective power, it will be white, yet another sign. Also, memories that were once blocked by me, in the hopes of allowing the races to start over and begin anew, will return. My children will remember their prayers and my origins. They will see Amelia, hear my name, and know."

I wished I could see them for myself and with that errant thought, a mirror appeared in my hand. While shocked, I couldn't resist looking down. My dark hair was still down and the daisy crown sat upon my head. Violet eyes stared back at me, the same bright glow I'd always known. Now though, white starbursts extended from my pupils outward, the spires varying lengths and cutting into the purple. It was a mixture of who I was, now infused with Gaea's spirit. It was beautiful.

I looked up at Gaea and the mirror disappeared. "Just as quickly as you conjured the mirror, you can rid yourself of it," she explained. "My power is embedded in you, Amelia. You can call on it at will. Do not fear it. Embrace it. Allow it to be as much a part of you as the power you received from your brother. This power was also meant for you. You proved that with your ability to work with the Keeper.

"I must go now, but know I am never far. You also must go. Much has happened while we've been here together, and if you don't hurry, much will go wrong. I am counting on you both to make the right decisions for my children. Do not let me down." Gaea stood, her hands clasped in front of her. She nodded, almost bowing, before she disappeared.

Charlie and Onyx stepped forward. A boyish grin came over Charlie's face as I closed the distance between us.

"Do you have to go?" I asked them. I had grown accustomed to Charlie's presence. He was another grounding influence in my life. Even when he'd been my dog, I felt better with him nearby. Onyx wasn't as familiar to me, but knowing they were brothers, and that he had taken care of Cole while I was away, was enough to make me concerned.

"We must," he responded. The Sentinel Charlie had been so serious, it surprised me to see his expression soften.

"We will meet again, Amelia," he assured me. "I have seen who you are and know who you can become. Your best decisions have come when you trusted yourself and used what the great Mother gave you for the good of the whole. Remember that, and you will see you do not need us." Charlie gave me a quick bow and I stood taller. He had seen everything from the Keeper power initially manifesting in me to us finding Gaea. It meant something to have his words to carry in my heart. I looked over to find similar compassion in Onyx's eyes. Wherever they went, I was certain those two would be watching out for me in some capacity.

I returned to Aidan's side and we faced Charlie and Onyx. They looked at each other and then back at us. Both gave a short wave and then faded as Gaea had done.

"So, it looks like you're stuck with me now, Montgomery," I joked, a sudden shyness taking hold as the reality of the last few hours set in.

He tucked a rogue strand of hair behind my ear and let his fingertips linger on my cheek until I looked up at him. As he spoke, he lowered his face to mine, his lips millimeters from my own. "I do believe you chose me first, Amelia, which means *you* are actually the one stuck with *me*."

"Mmmhmmm," was all I could muster as I waited for the kiss his tone promised. He made me wait, his voice low as he said, "Say it one more time."

I laughed and acquiesced. "I love you, Aidan Montgomery. And if you don't kiss me right now, I'm going to figure out just how mean I can be to you without hurting myself."

"Well, we wouldn't want that," he said, covering the inches between us in an instant and muddling any retorts I had with a mind-blowing kiss. After a few moments, Aidan pulled away and touched his forehead to mine.

"We need to go. Gaea warned us and I think we've learned she isn't to be ignored," he said.

"I know. We can do this, right?" I asked.

Aidan stepped back and held out his hand. "You and me against the world, doll. Forever."

"Forever," I agreed, taking it.

We quickly left the castle, knowing no matter what came next, we would face it together.

Chapter 37
Micah

We reached the small cabin Aidan had used before storming Cresthaven and frustration continued to get the best of me. I brainstormed, trying to come up with a plan, but Baleon rejected idea after idea of how I'd get back into the castle to get to Cole.

Bethany interjected, doing what she always did. She made things simple. "Why don't you just walk in the front door like you live there? You do technically live there, right?" she asked tartly.

I turned to her, prepared to chance her wrath by telling her to find somewhere else to hover, when Baleon said, "She does have a point, Prince Mikail. Why not walk through the front door? It would create less suspicion for you to make your presence known than for you to attempt an entrance and be found out. We have no idea what we're walking into right now. We could find out. And then you could tell Amelia."

Bethany's eyebrow rose. She dared me to speak the words on the tip of my tongue. Her feistiness had slowly returned and it only made it harder to maintain myself in her presence. She kept herself at arm's length, though. Outside of her initial breakdown, she had not cried, nor had she allowed me to come close to touching her. Even after leaving Brighton and spending a day in the car together, she said as few words to me as possible.

The only question she had was when we were getting Cole back. It was only making my edginess worse to hear her concern for him. They had spent days together. We had spent months together. Yet, she seemed to care more for his wellbeing than mine. She didn't flinch at me walking back into the lion's den, but he had to be rescued. Though, he had no magic, so her concerns were likely founded. Damn logic.

So, now I strode up to the front door of Cresthaven as if I hadn't turned against my mother and her Hunters. As if I hadn't allowed her precious baby-making factory and the girl she'd spent my whole life trying to control get away, and then run from her clutches myself.

When I left, I did not believe I would ever return. I did not believe I would ever have to face her again. But, I should have known better. The demons of your past are never far away. You can never outrun them—you can only face them head-on and fight them to the death.

Baleon was only steps behind me and as I'd anticipated, the door opened before I even reached the stairs. I was shocked to see Joran step out. The last time I'd seen him, he was fending off Hunters as Baleon and I escaped. Joran barely acknowledged me, saying, "Please, stay here, Prince Mikail. Rhi will be down shortly," while looking out over our heads.

Baleon stood at my side and we waited. Finally, unable to stand it any longer, I said, "Joran, you don't look well. Is everything okay?"

He was thinner than usual, his movements slower and his eyes dull. He had never been indifferent or mean to me, like most of the Hunters, and I had always appreciated that. "Ye-yes, Prince Mikail. I am fine. Things have been…different since you left." He would not meet my eyes and I saw the slight tremor in his hands as he held them clasped in front of him.

Before I could react, the door opened and Rhi stepped out. A swagger in his step stirred a latent rage inside me, but I swallowed my aggression to play the part. Baleon and I discussed this at length. There was only one way I was getting inside.

Rhi stepped up beside Joran and the Hunter did his best not to flinch. I could not reconcile the intimidating, tattoo-covered behemoth man I knew with the twitchy shell standing in front of me.

"Have you come groveling home, Prince? Tossed out by the little purple-eyed Keeper and her boyfriend? You're not much use to anyone, now are you?" Rhi's grin was wide as he stood with his arms crossed over his chest, his feet planted as he blocked my path.

I didn't rise to his bait. "Tell me, Rhi, what oath did you take?" I asked pleasantly.

"Excuse me?" he replied.

"Your oath," I said slowly. "You took an oath to my grandfather that you renewed to my mother. What were the words of that oath?" I only allowed a slight smile to develop as he finally understood where I was going. His arms dropped to his sides as his eyes hardened.

"I took an oath to protect and serve the Clair line for as long as they would have me, just like every other Hunter." As he spoke, his eyes began to swirl, the orange and black mixture giving away his anger. My smile widened.

"Mmm, I don't believe those were the exact words, now were they, Rhi?" I took the steps two at a time until I stood next to him. I looked up at him until he finally moved two steps down.

"I am sworn to protect *and obey*," he forced out, "the Clair line." I looked down at him, nodding.

"That you are. Which means, as *Prince Mikail Clair*, you will obey me. You will not disrespect me again. You will take me to my mother and you will not speak unless spoken to. Understood?" I stood there, waiting for confirmation. He could not see the sweat running down my back, but he could likely hear my heartbeat race.

"Yes, *Prince Mikail*. I will remind you, though, your mother is the only one who can force my compliance," Rhi's warning did not fall on deaf ears. I knew this charade would only last so long. Hunter honor and pride would keep him in check, but would it be for long enough?

"Very good. Lead the way," I said, standing aside so he could pass. I looked over my shoulder to see Joran's amused expression. His eyes lit up and I watched him stand a bit taller as he finally met mine. His small nod was all I needed to know we had one more on our side.

Of course, I knew how to get to my mother's rooms, but I wanted to observe. As we walked through the house, Rhi leading the way, I watched how the other Hunters reacted to him. Some he nodded to, and they returned his greeting. Some he stared down, and they quickly looked away. There were clearly two camps of Hunters at Cresthaven.

My mother's suite was on the far side of the house, and it gave me time to think. Amelia and Aidan would be back in the States soon, likely already en route to the cabin.

Amelia had reached out to me when they left the castle and I explained Cole being taken to Cresthaven. I told her Bethany had come as well, and Amelia wanted me to wait for them, but I didn't trust my mother or Rhi. If anyone was going in to get Cole out, it had to be me and Baleon, and we had to go alone. It was our safest chance.

I knew Amelia would be angry that we left before they returned, but I couldn't fathom she and Aidan had found anything in Syria that would change our plan of attack. She couldn't walk in here and take on these Hunters. What I was doing was the right choice. It was the safe choice. She could tell me whatever stories she swore I needed to hear in person after we got her human brother away from my mother and Rhi.

Finally, we approached my mother's door. The two Hunters stationed outside stepped apart and allowed us inside after a nod from Rhi.

"You can wait outside," I said to Rhi.

"I will not," he replied, staring down at me. "I serve the Clair line, but your mother is the head of that line. You attacked us. You fought against her. You aided those half-breeds and the Keeper. You cost us years of work and planning. I do not trust you, and I will not leave her alone with you."

"Now, Rhi, at least allow my son to share the story he concocted to reason away his betrayal." Her voice was weak, but it carried from her bedroom.

As it always did, the anxiety that surfaced anytime a direct confrontation with my mother was looming rose sharply, threatening to steal my breath and make me turn on my heel to get as far away as fast as possible. I clenched my jaw and drew in a slow breath as I entered her bedroom door. Before I could cross the doorframe, Rhi stepped in front of me, leaning down so his swirling orange eyes were level with mine.

"Watch yourself in here, Prince. There is nothing I won't do for her," he hissed. He barely got the words out before Bale shoved him backwards. Bale said nothing, and Rhi flashed a smug smirk before leading the way into mother's room.

I crossed the threshold and was shocked to find the drapes drawn. The room was lit by small sconces only. Hunter fire burned in them, casting an orange glow over the room. The four-poster bed was a mountain of pillows and blankets. In the low light, it was hard to find my mother amidst it all. As my eyes adjusted, I saw her in the center. I held back a gasp and worked to keep my face neutral.

"There is no need to hold back, Mikail. I know what I am, and what I am no longer," she said, her hoarse voice barely above a whisper. The woman speaking to me looked nothing like the woman I'd left just a few weeks ago. Her blonde hair was silver, her perfect complexion filled with lines and wrinkles. Her cheekbones stood out and her collarbone was sharp edges threatening to puncture her skin.

"What happened, Mother?" I asked.

Her eyes were sad, the ice blue dulled to a pale shade. "All power comes at a price, Mikail. Sometimes you know what it is up front, and sometimes, the price doesn't matter, until it does."

"It's killing you to control them, yet you still do. You allow it to drain you. Why? How is this worth it?" I cursed the wayward emotion filling my chest. She was my mother and she was dying.

Her eyes flicked up to mine and the stare that had terrified me as a child was back. She could still lock me in place with just a look. "How dare you question me, Mikail? After everything you've done, after all the ways you've betrayed me, your name, and your people? You do not ask questions. You answer them. You tell me, son of mine, why are you here? I thought you made your choice very clear."

She struggled to pull in a breath, the wheezing noise giving away her inability to fully lecture me. She was suddenly more human in my eyes. She was not the woman of my nightmares, and she did not hold the power here. I simply needed to wait this out and do as Bale and I had decided.

"I'm sorry, Mother. You're right. I did not expect this, and I'm acting irrationally, which is not what Clairs do. I am here because I made the wrong choice. I am here to apologize and beg your forgiveness. I was wrong to fight against you. I see it now. I see what you meant. I watched the AniMages and finally understand. They are vile, disgusting creatures. We do not want them in our world. They must be dealt with."

"Is that so? Just like that?" she questioned. "You say you've come around and changed your mind, and I should believe you?" The wheezing was worse, and short coughs accompanied it.

I stepped up to the bed, taking a chance to sit on the edge and reach for my mother's hand. It was a gamble. Her skin felt paper-thin and the bones were too pronounced, so I grasped it lightly.

"You told me to always evaluate all sides of a situation before I made a decision," I said stoically. "My initial evaluation was incorrect, and as soon as I realized that, I came home. They fight for a ridiculous cause. They believe they deserve freedom, but they deserve a quick death." I hated myself for saying the words, but she would accept nothing less.

"My Queen—" Rhi started, but my mother interrupted.

"Silence. My son is speaking." His mouth snapped shut and Rhi took a step back. His animosity for me rolled off him in waves that most certainly wanted to drag me under.

"What did you learn that you can share with us, Mikail?" she asked. I knew she would. I was prepared.

"If your Hunters have not already found the group of AniMages Baleon stripped of their power, then they are likely long gone. But, their power will not return. Baleon bound it and they will live their lives out wishing they had not come at me. They are not dead, but they will wish they were. I made the decision to leave and they didn't want me to tell you the women were birthing and the children were still powerless, but it is the truth. Leaving here did nothing to change what we already knew. Our people are dying, Mother, and we must do what is necessary to save them."

"And the Keeper?" she asked, focusing on me as she struggled to push herself higher on the pillows surrounding her.

"She's gone. She and the AniMage left, alone. They went off chasing stories and rumors. Idiots," I sneered.

"I want to believe you, Mikail, but we both know I have no way to see inside your mind. No way to know if what you say is the truth. You are going to have to prove to me your allegiance is real. Do you understand?" There was a familiar hitch in her tone, and I knew I would not like her next words.

"I understand, Mother. What is it I have to do to prove my allegiance to you?" I asked, keeping my tone deferential, just the way she preferred.

She looked up at Rhi and a wicked smile bloomed across his face. I looked between them as she nodded. He tipped his head in silent acknowledgment, turned, and strode quickly out the door. Baleon and I exchanged quick glances of wary trepidation.

Julia didn't speak to me. She didn't look at me. For a long stretch of minutes, we sat in utter silence, save for my heart beating furiously against my chest. The longer I sat there, the more firm I was in the knowledge of what was about to happen.

There was only one outcome. All I could think was, *Do it now, you have to do it now. Kill her now.* But I couldn't. I was frozen. And when the door finally opened, I was not shocked to see who was shoved through it.

My mother finally turned to face me. The joy in her eyes was the purest form of evil.

"To prove your allegiance to me, to your people, and your crown," she said, "Mikail, you will kill him. You will kill the Keeper's brother and you will do it now. Then, and only then, will I believe the stories you told are the truth."

Chapter 38
Amelia

There was a good chance I'd walked a hole in the carpet of the small cabin. Aidan knew exactly how to get here since it hadn't been long ago he prepared his own attack on Cresthaven from the same place. We arrived earlier today to find Bethany, Rynna, and Uncle Derreck, but not Micah or Baleon.

Morons, I fumed. I told Micah to wait for us. It was *my brother* who hung in the balance. Instead, he'd called in Rynna and my uncle, and took off.

Arguments I wished I could have with Micah and possibilities for the kind of torture they were putting Cole through ran rampant in my mind.

Aidan sat in a recliner, his eyes tracing my movements. Bethany was cooking, even though we all told her we weren't hungry. Uncle Derreck and Rynna were whispering quietly, still trying to reconcile the story of what happened with Gaea.

I stopped, and declared, "We need to go. We need a plan and we need to go."

"You've said that three times now, Amelia," Aidan responded. "Do you have a plan?"

"No," I snarled toward him, frustration and fear for Cole fraying the calm demeanor I'd been working hard to maintain. His eyebrow arched and I took a deep breath. "I'm sorry," I apologized. "No, I don't. But why do we need one? Gaea told me to call on what she gave me and use it however I need to. Let's walk through the front door and do what needs to be done."

"After we left the others in Brighton, that's what I told Micah to do," Bethany said from the kitchen area. The guilt in her tone said everything. She looked up from a mixing bowl and it was like I saw her for the first time that day. Her hair was piled on top of her head in a messy knot, easily day-three hair. She didn't do day-three hair. She was wearing clothes that clearly weren't hers, and her face was clean of makeup; the dark circles were too prominent under her eyes.

"Let's stop a minute and think through this," Uncle Derreck interjected. "Gaea told you your job is to take care of her children. The Hunters are her children, too. You can't walk in there and wipe them out just because Julia has control over them. They didn't all choose that life."

He was right, and I knew it.

"Okay," I agreed, trying to slow my racing thoughts. "Can we use the maze to get in and surprise them? Can we get to Julia and take her out, then reason with the Hunters? We can split up and half of us go each way. A group to find Cole and a group to go after Julia. What do you think?"

Aidan was on his feet instantly. "No way. There's no splitting up. Where you go, I go, doll. End of story."

I knew Aidan was still frustrated after hearing about what happened at Derreck's, and I was pushing his patience. While there was no love lost between him and Melinda, it hurt him to know he hadn't been there for his people when they needed him. I think he also had a few choice words for Micah the next time he saw him.

"If y'all are gonna start arguing, you may as well add me coming into the mix. You aren't leaving me here again. Cloak me, turn me into an animal—I don't give a damn what you do, but I am coming with you." Bethany's voice cut across the room and I saw my friend's tired eyes, but determined expression. She stood in the kitchen, her arms crossed over her chest, shoulders back, lips a tight line.

Aidan, Rynna, and Derreck's voices were one unintelligible sound in the background as Bethany and I held each other's stare, an entire conversation playing out in the silence between us.

"Okay," I said, loud enough to quiet the room. "You deserve this. You've been through just as much as any of us, B. If you want to come, I'll cloak you and you'll stay with us. We won't leave you again."

"You swear you won't stick me in some room or pawn me off on someone to watch? I don't want to get stuck with that weird librarian you told me about," she said as she twisted her lips into a mock pout.

"Don't talk about Tragar like that!" I chided. "He's sweet. And he's likely our lifeline. Don't you think, Ryn?"

Rynna nodded slowly. "But, Amelia, are you sure you're comfortable with this? Are you sure you can do what you think you can?"

I couldn't blame Rynna for her question. I would have asked the same had I been told our outrageous story.

You should show them. Aidan's voice was welcome. In the time it took us to get back home, we explored our new connection. I'd also come to depend on the nearness of him. Mentally and physically, I didn't want to be far from Aidan.

"Come outside," I said, gesturing for everyone to follow me.

We filed out and I had them stay near the cabin while I walked further into a clearing surrounded on two sides by trees.

Gaea was right. It took only a thought for things to happen, so I imagined my desired outcomes carefully. I was learning how to build the barrier between my thoughts and intentions, but it wasn't entirely solidified yet.

This new power was so similar, yet entirely different from the Keeper. I could do the same things, but now, I was in total control. There was no fear tied to this magic. This power was tied to everything around me—the elements, the people, every living thing.

"Earth," I called out, my right hand outstretched and palm pointed down. A sapling shot from the soil. It grew taller and taller, until it reached my hand, then leaves sprouted.

"Fire," I called next, reaching my left hand above my head and tipping it back. White smoke gathered around my palm and a flame flickered. It grew until a ball of heat crackled in the air above me. I drew my hands in and stepped forward. Both the tree and the fire stayed where they were.

"Water," I called next. This time, I didn't move. I didn't need to with the first two, but it helped them to understand I was indeed the one in control. Dark clouds gathered over us and rain poured down. With a flick of my wrist, all of us were sheltered by invisible barriers. The rain came in torrents, but the five of us stayed dry.

"Air," I called. The wind picked up and the trees around us curved under the force. It didn't flutter a single piece of clothing on anyone.

"Enough," I said, and it all stopped. The fire dissipated, but the sapling remained, my gift to the land for sustaining my demonstration.

"And those are only the parlor tricks," I explained. "Don't worry about me, Rynna. I can take care of us. Aidan can also take care of us. As my mate, he has more power than he started with as well. This is our time."

Uncle Derreck peppered Aidan with questions and he was doing his best to answer when I felt a familiar niggle at the back of my mind. I had to search it out, the tickle faint enough for me to question whether it were really there at all. I scanned my mind and finally saw the dim pulse of red light. I grasped onto it, knowing exactly who it had to be.

"Amelia, what's wrong? What's happening?" Aidan spoke out loud, likely for the benefit of the others.

"Quiet," I ordered. "I need you guys to be quiet. It's Micah, but I can hardly hear him. Something's wrong. Really wrong."

Chapter 39
Micah

I had a solid three minutes before Rhi came back with his enchanted cuffs. Killing Cole hadn't been an option, so Bale had leapt for Rhi while I shoved Cole out of the way.

We were still in my mother's bedroom, so there wasn't much room for an actual fight. Bale tried to restrain Rhi, to tether his power and ability to do any real damage. I put Cole's arm around my shoulders and tried to get him to the door. If I could get to the sitting room, we had a chance. A hidden passageway would take me from there to the library. Fifteen paces was all I needed.

Unfortunately, Rhi got loose and took one shot. His aim was perfect and Cole crumpled beside me, screaming as pain ripped through him. His eyes rolled into the back of his head and he lost consciousness. I tried to pick him up when a blast hit me as well. My limbs locked and my power felt like a scrambled mess.

Now, my hands were held behind my back by Joran, who leaned down and whispered, "I'm sorry, Prince Mikail, but I must follow orders. I cannot defy him again."

I barely moved my lips as I whispered, "Tragar will find you. Listen carefully before you decide."

Then I sought out my connection to Amelia. With my power on the fritz, I didn't have a lot to put into it, but I found the thread that kept us connected and reached out. Amelia answered immediately, but I struggled to keep our connection solid.

Micah, what's happening? Where are you? Why did you leave?

I don't have time for all that. Listen carefully. In two minutes, you won't be able to find me. I'll be with Cole, held in a prison cell beneath Cresthaven. Only Hunters can get through the doors. Use the maze, find Tragar, and tell him to find Joran. Joran will help you.

He hates Rhi, but he fears Rhi. I don't know what was done to him after we left with you, but he fought for us and Rhi wouldn't let that go unpunished. If you tell him why you're here, that you want to kill my mother and free him, I believe he will do it. I will protect Cole and myself as best as I can, but Bale was also taken, so I can make no guarantees. Time is short. You must hurry, Amelia.

Is Cole okay? she asked.

For now. My mother anticipated the need for him as a bargaining chip. I think she was surprised I was the one she was bargaining with, though.

Tell him we're coming. Micah, we'll find you both. We'll get you out. Things are different now. I—

She was gone. Rhi was taking extreme amounts of pleasure in yanking my shoulders nearly out of their sockets to put my wrists behind me as he affixed the enchanted handcuffs, and the pain caused my concentration to break. "I've been waiting for this, *Prince.* You were never worthy of being my brother's son. I look forward to the time when no one can stop me from showing you how worthless you truly are."

Rhi's voice was low, since my mother wouldn't have approved of his little speech. I gritted my teeth against all the things I could have said, and replied, "Yet, I am still alive and he isn't. Interesting, isn't it?"

That earned me a shock up both my arms. What felt like boiling water scorched the insides of my veins, but I refused to give him the satisfaction of crying out. My head fell backward as my body stiffened, tears springing to my eyes.

"Rhi," my mother said sharply as I tried to control my body once again. He stepped away from me, sending one more jolt into my hands before doing so. I breathed deeply through my nose, still afraid of the sounds that would come from my mouth if I unlocked my jaw.

Cole was still unconscious next to me. I envied his position.

"Mikail, come here," she ordered, her voice barely carrying across the room. I wondered if she might die before Amelia actually got here. Would that be better or worse for me?

I stepped to the end of the bed and waited silently. Was any part of her bothered by what was happening? Did any part of her hold remorse for the things she'd done and the choices she'd made? It didn't seem worth asking anymore.

"Mikail, I had such high hopes for you," she said, not bothering to hide her scorn. "I wanted to believe you truly learned from your mistakes, but you never do. You never have. Now, I must teach you the lesson I have been trying to teach you your whole life. Power is held by those who take it. It is kept by those who wield it unflinchingly. It is earned by those who are willing to compromise anything to achieve their purpose."

"No, Mother," I interjected, "that is where *you* are the one who has it wrong. Power is earned by those who *refuse* to compromise their ideals and beliefs. It is kept by those who put the greater good *before* themselves. It is held by those who are supported and believed in. Power is merely having the resources to accomplish your objectives, and it is fleeting to those who throw people away like garbage when they don't conform.

"Power is celebrated and revered by those who benefit from it," I continued. "You have maintained your power through coercion and fear, and *that* is why you are dying. You couldn't sustain your power because it was never meant for this purpose. You are dying because your life is not worth the air you need to breathe. You are dying because you are evil and the world needs rid of you."

I spat the words, and the relief I felt surprised me. In that moment, I let go years of pain and anger as she stared at me, her gaunt face flushed, eyes wide and nostrils flaring.

"I am capable of more than you think, Mother," I finished with a satisfied smirk. "I just wasn't willing to do it for you."

Chapter 40
Amelia

After Micah disappeared and I relayed the information to the group, it was no longer a discussion of whether we'd go to Cresthaven, it was when. And when was as soon as humanly possible. Bethany forced us to eat, citing an inability to fight without sustenance. I scarfed down the homemade biscuits and gravy, barely taking time to swallow.

Images of Cole in the same room as Rhi fueled a deep panic inside me. I took his power—okay, he gave it to me—and now, he was defenseless, which was my fault. There had to have been a way for me to take what my mother meant for me while leaving him with something. I hadn't even tried to give him his power back, and I couldn't believe I left him with nothing. I should have tried.

Amelia, you have to calm down.

Aidan's voice ruptured my internal tirade.

I can hear your heartbeat racing and feel your guilt. Cole wouldn't want this. He wouldn't want you to feel like this. He made a choice, the same as you. Focus forward. We're going to get him out of there.

I knew Aidan was right. His concern also hovered on the edges of my mind. If I focused on him and not on myself, it was easier. I let his love wash over me, stopping my erratic thoughts. I had to focus. I had to be ready.

I looked around and noticed everyone, having finished eating, was staring at me. I stood from the table. "Let's go," I said calmly.

Getting to Cresthaven and navigating the maze had been a cinch. With each potentially life-threatening situation I helped us make it through, my confidence grew. I had cloaked the group—me, Aidan, Bethany, Rynna, and Derreck—so we could approach the outer gates unnoticed. The door to the maze popped open as soon as I stood in front of it.

Rynna and I agreed we wanted to be farther into the maze before we attempted a door. As we ran down leafy corridors, surrounded by the eight-foot-tall hedges, I'd realized I could no longer separate Gaea's power from my own. She was a part of me and I prayed I could control what she gave me to save my brother and friends. And that we could fulfill her wishes to help all of our people.

Sensing my anxiety, Aidan provided a wave of reassurance. Feeling him there, always in the back of my mind, was a relief. To some, perhaps it would have been an intrusion, but fundamentally, I had changed so much since he and I met. My power growing, the Keeper taking hold, my experience at Cresthaven, and then with Gaea…my power had been held hostage, amped up, combined with Cole's, stripped of the Keeper, and merged with a Goddess. Aidan was my anchor. He reminded me of everything I was beneath the magic and prophecy. Amid a host of impulsive, half-baked decisions, his presence confirmed there was something I had done right. I had chosen him.

I love you.

He grinned over at me. *I know. But you can keep telling me.*

Shaking my head, I laughed. I slowed our jog to a walk and then stopped. "Here goes nothing," I muttered as I plunged my hand into the hedge like Micah had. The leaves brushed my fingers before I felt the cool metal of the handle. I lightly traced the circular knob before grasping it and focusing on the door leading us to the library. I heard the *snick* of the latch and the hedge popped inward, revealing giant shelves and stacks of books.

I kept our cloak in place as we filed in. I led the way and was pleased to find Tragar in the center of the room, his back to us. "I knew I would see you again, little one," he said. I lifted the cloak as he turned around. It was hard to know whether his immediate joy was seeing me, or Rynna and Derreck. They ran to him first and I heard Aidan and Bethany laughing quietly behind me.

I used another one of our newest tricks and lurked in Aidan's mind, listening to their conversation.

"It just so happens that your friend here is only *mostly dead*," Aidan said, his voice high, attempting to match Billy Crystal's.

Bethany giggled. "Humperdinck! Humperdinck! Humperdinck!" She perfectly mimicked Miracle Max's wife from Princess Bride and I found myself laughing along with them. They both looked at me and we erupted as a trio.

"Will you two stop!" I attempted to scold them through my laughter. "Tragar is sweet, even if he does look like Miracle Max." I hadn't ever made that connection myself, but the longer I looked at Tragar in his billowing robes with his crazy white hair and big nose, it was all too clear.

Rynna, Derreck, and Tragar all looked at us curiously. "Nothing, it's nothing," I assured them as I gestured Aidan and Bethany forward.

"Tragar, this is my best friend, Bethany, and my mate, Aidan." They each stepped forward and shook Tragar's hand.

"Her mate, you say?" Tragar questioned as he held onto Aidan's hand a bit longer. Aidan nodded. "Yes, sir, made official by Gaea herself." As Aidan held Tragar's hand, I transferred a little of myself into him, directing my power to extend through Aidan's palm into Tragar's.

Tragar's eyes went wide and I swore I could see doors unlocking in his mind. He dropped Aidan's hand and stared at nothing, his eyes unfocused. A few seconds later, he was speaking rapid fire.

"I'll be damned! It's there. It's all there. This whole time, I've searched every book and I've had it all locked away. Gaea. Our Mother. Oh, dear. We've failed. We've failed at everything she created us to be." Tragar looked around wildly, until his eyes landed on me. "Amelia, you must fix this. You must stop this. I can't believe we've allowed it to happen. You have to save us."

I stepped forward and grasped his shaking hands. "Don't worry, Tragar. That's why we're here. Aidan and I are going to fix this. I need you to help me, though. Micah told me to send you to find Joran and bring him here. We need Joran to find Cole and Micah and get them away from Rhi. Can you help us?"

Tragar nodded slowly, his pupils returning to normal as he calmed. Then, he grunted. "That boy knows I don't like bringing them into my library. Damn demons, anyway. But you need Joran, you say? That poor Hunter has been tortured by Rhi ever since you left. I don't know why you'd want him. Shadow of himself, you see. But, if that's what Mikail told me to do, then that's what old Tragar will do."

Tragar continued to mutter to himself as he walked away. "Will you be okay, Tragar?" I called over to him.

"Yes, yes, don't worry, little one. I'm just sorting through pieces of my life I'd long forgotten. I'll go find Joran. Stay back in the stacks, just in case." He quietly left the library and it was back to the five of us.

We stood in a circle. "Okay, we're here. Joran should be here soon, and he can lead us to Cole and Micah. The question now is what all are we here to do?" I asked the question and let it linger in the air between us.

Uncle Derreck spoke first. "We should stay together, at least until we get to Cole. Then, you should let us get him out of here. If we have any hope of converting some of the Hunters to our side, you're going to have to show them what you can do. You're going to have to take out Rhi."

You're going to have to take out Rhi. His words repeated in my mind. Could I do that? Did I have the power for that?

Of course you do. You have a Goddess inside you and me beside you. You won't do this alone. We'll do it together.

Aidan slid his hand into mine and I slowly exhaled, nodding.

"I am going to take out Rhi," I said. I wasn't sure whether I was trying to convince them or myself.

The door to the library opened. We all dropped to a crouch and hid behind the shelves until we heard Tragar call out to us.

I stood to find Joran only feet from me. I knew it was him because I saw the familiar tattoos that wrapped around his bald head and I recognized his gentle eyes, but the rest of him looked like someone else. His body had to be half the size. His long, leather jacket hung off his frame, making it even more noticeable that he'd lost weight. I couldn't imagine what he'd been put through.

"Thank you, Joran," I said. His brow drew together in confusion.

"Thank you for fighting with us. Thank you for helping to save me. Thank you for coming with Tragar."

His pinched features relaxed. "Prince Mikail told me to listen to Tragar before I made my decision. I assume now the decision is whether I will help you?"

"Yes, it is. We need to know if you will help us," I said, gesturing around me. "Joran, this is my Uncle Derreck and Rynna." His mouth quirked into a ghost of a smile.

"Yes, we all know each other from many years ago," he said.

"And this is my mate, Aidan. And my best friend, Bethany," I said.

"I remember your mate from the laboratory. But why would you bring a human here?" he asked gruffly.

"She didn't 'bring a human here'," Bethany shot at him, with full air quotes. "The *human* told her it wasn't optional that I help stop that crazy bitch and get my friends back." She glared at Joran with daggers I hadn't seen before in her eyes. Bethany's hatred for Hunters ran deep, no matter whose side they were on.

An eyebrow rose on Joran's face. "I see. And does the human understand she is nothing but—"

"Enough," I interrupted. "We're not doing this. We don't have time. Every minute we waste is one Rhi could be torturing Cole or Micah."

Aidan finally spoke. "Joran, we are here to stop all of this. We want to get Cole and Micah, find Baleon, and kill Rhi. We want this night to end with Julia and Rhi no longer a threat to anyone, and we have the power to do it." He looked at me and I closed my eyes. When I reopened them, I knew what Joran was seeing.

I extended my arm and flipped my palm up. "Joran, I have power in me no one on this earth has had before. Our Mother, Gaea, put it inside me herself." White smoke built in my palm and started to swirl into a mini-tornado.

Joran looked interested, but not impressed, so I upped the level. I allowed the smoke to drift apart and focused on him. Without a word or movement from me, he rose into the air. Then, so did a stack of books. The books shot around him, creating a wide berth, but circling him like the rings of Saturn.

I watched him squint, clearly trying to fight back. "I won't hurt you, obviously. This is me just having fun. I can feel your power, but it is a candle flame compared to the forest fire inside me. You know I'm telling the truth, I remember your gift. Am I lying when I tell you I met Gaea, that Aidan and I freed her from her prison? And after that, she mated us and gave me the ability to use her power to end Julia's reign once and for all?"

I let the books drift back to their appropriate stacks as I set Joran back on the floor.

"You do not lie, Amelia," Joran responded. "I see her in your eyes and in your heart. But how is it I see her at all? How can I see these memories I never knew I had?"

"When we freed Gaea and she gave me this power to fight Julia, she also explained that she locked away your memories," I explained. "In order to stop the civil war the last King started, she had to wipe away all knowledge of how the Immortals came to that place. With the mention of her name, and the visible use of her power, everyone will remember."

He nodded along as I spoke, finally saying, "I can see why. I may have preferred those memories stayed buried. Now, what is it you want to ask of me?"

"Joran, we need you to take us to where they are holding Micah and Cole," I said. "We need to get into that chamber and a way to get them out. Will you help us? We know we can't get in without a Hunter unless I make it very obvious we are here. If we do that, we lose the element of surprise, and that's the only way we're going to get to Rhi." I didn't want to beg Joran, even though I would if it came to that. I stood between Aidan and Bethany, and we waited.

After a long minute, Joran said, "If you will give me back what he took, I will do anything to bring Rhi to justice. Anything."

I stepped forward and reached up to Joran's cheek. My warm palm met his clammy skin and in that instant, I knew what he meant. Rhi had stripped him down to almost nothing. The power inside Joran was a fraction of what it should have been. The magic that should have flowed freely in his veins and centered in his soul was fragmented. The chunks were jagged puzzle pieces that couldn't find a way back together.

Tears sprang to my eyes as his internal pain hit me. The fact that Joran wasn't insane, that he hadn't allowed Rhi's torture to break his spirit entirely, was shocking. Of its own accord, my power flowed out of me into Joran. I watched the white smoke glide through him and capture the wayward pieces of power in an invisible net. It worked its way through him, until the net was full, and then sat in his core.

Aidan, I need you.

I was getting tired. I wasn't sure what to do next and the only feeling I had was that I needed more.

I'm here, doll. I heard his voice, then felt the influx of energy. As soon as his power met mine, the smoke swirled around Joran's magic. It churned and twirled until the edges of the pieces wore down. Sharp barbs were replaced by rounded corners. As each worn down piece ran into the next, they merged and the ball continued to grow. Once Joran's power was completely coalesced, I heard him sigh.

I started to withdraw and with each inch my healing smoke pulled back, his power reached out. When I finally removed myself from him and my hand from his cheek, Joran looked down at me with utter relief.

"I can breathe. I can feel. You have given me back what I thought I would never have," he said, then dropped to one knee and bowed his head.

"I make this oath to you, Amelia Bradbury. I will do as you bid, I will protect you, and those you love. I am yours to command from this day until you determine my debt is paid." I looked around nervously.

Tragar finally said, "You must accept his oath, Amelia."

I looked at Aidan. He shrugged. *What can it hurt?* he asked.

"Thank you, Joran. I accept," I said.

He stood and pulled his closed fist to his heart, bowing once more. "And now, I will take you to your brother and the Prince. We must move quickly and quietly. We must be ghosts in these halls."

Chapter 41
Aidan

Apparently, there were hidden passages all over Cresthaven. After Amelia cloaked Bethany again, Joran shocked Tragar by popping open a hidden door behind a set of shelves in the library.

"In order for us to be effective at protecting the Queen, we needed access to every part of the house. Many of these passages are rarely used, like this one," he explained to a stammering Tragar. "We knew we were not welcome here." Joran smirked and Tragar relaxed.

"Let me go first, Amelia," I said to her. To my surprise, Amelia didn't argue at all.

"That's probably best," she agreed. "I want to stay with Bethany. Even cloaked, she needs protection."

While I hadn't said it out loud, I was in Joran's camp when it came to Bethany. She was my friend, too, but I didn't agree with her coming with us for this. It was too dangerous and she was a liability. I worried about Amelia protecting Bethany before she protected herself.

It's fine, Aidan. I can do both at once. That's why I want to be close to her. I can feed you power from a distance.

If I could listen in on her, it was only fair she could do the same to me, but Amelia's voice in my head was still a little off-putting.

I was still lost in my own thoughts when I felt a smack to the back of my head.

"Ow," I said as I whipped around. There was no one there. Then, I felt something lightly brush against my neck, sending shivers down my spine. I spun around, looking in the other direction while everyone else watched me with amused smiles.

"What?" I asked, turning around again.

"Ah ha. Very funny, Blondie," I said, and heard her chuckle to herself.

"I had to, Aidan. I just had to," Bethany said. "I mean, if I've got the Cloak of Invisibility, why not have a little fun with it?"

We all laughed, but it was cut short by Joran.

"We must go," Joran said. His seriousness overrode the humor Bethany had brought and we all fell in line. It looked like there was a gap between Amelia and Rynna, but Bethany was there, and Derreck brought up the rear.

"Be careful, all of you," Tragar said as he closed the door behind us.

Joran raised a hand and orange fire erupted in his palm. "This way," he said, and off we went.

We twisted and turned through the passage, moving more slowly than we might have to keep a pace Bethany could maintain. No one spoke and the only sounds were quiet footsteps and quick breaths.

The passage forked multiple times, but Joran never hesitated. More than once, I shut down thoughts of him betraying us. He had made an oath and while I didn't understand entirely what that meant, he also fought on our side once already. But, we couldn't know how deep Rhi's torture scarred him.

Before I could find the right question to ask, a door appeared at the end of the hall. As we got closer, Joran moved even slower. I used my power to even out my breathing and lighten my steps further. I instructed Amelia to do the same. She whispered back to Rynna and soon, we were silently moving, not a sound coming from anyone.

Joran approached the door cautiously. He put a hand to the wood and closed his eyes. When he turned back to us, he whispered, "Micah and Cole are there and alone. For now."

Joran pulled the door open, but as he did, Amelia said, "Just hold on. We shouldn't all go in. Just in case something goes wrong or this is some kind of trick, we can't go barging in there."

Joran stopped, the door open only a foot or so. "That is intelligent. We don't know when the guards will return, but they will."

"Amelia, why don't you and Rynna stay here and let Derreck, Joran, and me check things out?" I asked.

Of course, she instantly disagreed. So did Rynna. And soon, the five of us were arguing in hushed tones. Then, we heard noise from the other side of the door and Joran quickly shoved it closed. We all fell silent.

Voices carried through the wood. The guards were back.

"Now what do we do?" I breathed out, asking Joran.

He put up a hand, and mouthed, "Wait."

I leaned against the passage wall and felt Amelia grip a few of my fingers with hers.

I'm sorry for arguing with you. I'm just scared.

I know that, Amelia. But you have to trust me. I'm not keeping you from fighting, I'm making sure I have solid backup when shit hits the fan. Because we both know it will.

She laughed a little in my mind. *You sound like— ohmygod, where is Bethany?* Amelia looked around, squinting her eyes as she focused further down the passage. *Aidan, she's gone. Where did she go?*

We both turned to the door at the same time. It had been open while we were arguing.

I squeezed her fingers lightly and then stepped next to Joran. I put my mouth to his ear and explained the situation. He swore and rubbed his brow.

"But they cannot see her?" he asked. I shook my head.

Suddenly, the voices coming from the prison chamber were louder. "How did that door get open? Did you leave that open? You damn fool, he could have gotten out!" the first voice yelled.

"I didn't leave it open! And how's he going anywhere? Just because Rhi doesn't use magic on humans doesn't mean he can't inflict pain. Just shut the door and let's go. I'm hungry." The second voice confirmed our fears. Rhi had spent time with Cole. It was only my quick reflexes that kept Amelia from barreling out that door.

I assumed the next sound would be the door to Cole's cell being shut, but it was clanging, a loud *thud*, and more yelling.

"What the hell was that? Did you hit me? You threw that at me, didn't you?" the second voice accused.

"I did no such—ow! I saw that. You used that chain to smack me!" The two were fighting again and I finally put what was happening together.

"It's Bethany. She's distracting them. We need to go, we need to go now," I said, just loud enough for everyone to hear.

"Just for a minute, please stay?" I asked Amelia. She pursed her lips, but nodded. I pressed a quick kiss to her grimace and took my position.

Joran, Derreck, and I leapt out the door and quickly shut it behind us. It closed faster than we'd expected and the sound drew the eyes of the still-arguing Hunters.

"He knew you would come," the first said, lunging toward us. He took two steps before Bethany shoved a steel cell door open and smacked him in the face. The Hunter stumbled backward, the red mark on his face fading instantly as he scowled and scanned the room.

"Get out of the way," I yelled. I hoped Bethany understood I was talking to her. We still couldn't see her, but I had no clue if the Hunters understood what they should be looking for. I didn't want them to.

"You have invaded the wrong place, AniMage. We aren't going anywhere. And, Joran, didn't you learn your lesson the first time? We'll take you ourselves and prove our allegiance to Rhi!"

Fists pounded on one of the doors and I was certain that's where Micah was. "We need to find Cole," I said loudly.

"Your human won't be going anywhere," the second Hunter said. "He's lucky he's breathing." The Hunter rapped on a door, then opened it and shoved his head in, repeating the phrase. The idiot eliminated our guessing game of which one of ten doors Cole was behind. And he left the door partially open when he resumed his position.

I started to goad the Hunters our way. Derreck and Joran did the same. We needed them to come closer so Bethany could get to Cole. The hallway in the prison chamber was probably fifty feet total, with a large open room at our end. Cole and Micah were on the opposite end from us, their cells facing each other.

With each step they took, the two Hunters' eyes glowed brighter—orange swirled with yellow and red. They were white-haired demons stalking their prey.

I saw Cole's door open a tiny bit more and then slowly close again. Bethany had to be in there.

"Will those doors keep out magic?" I asked Joran in a low tone.

He nodded. "They are designed to keep power in or out, but the door is a barrier either way."

I couldn't stop the smile from spreading across my face.

Amelia, get ready to show these Hunters what Gaea is made of. Bethany is with Cole, and both they and Micah are protected behind their cell doors. I want you to come out here and take these two out.

Happy to. Her smug tone actually increased my confidence in her. It was about time she saw it in herself.

I turned to Joran and Derreck, and said, "On three, we bum rush these assholes and give Amelia space."

Chapter 42
Amelia

I had been waiting for Aidan to give me that exact instruction. I exchanged a few words with Rynna and we agreed she'd follow me out and quickly find cover. I didn't think there would be collateral damage, but this was my first test of Gaea's power.

I stood in front of the door and hovered in Aidan's mind. As soon as he, Joran, and Uncle Derreck collided with the Hunters, I threw the door open and strode into the room.

My power was amped to the max and I knew my eyes looked like violet fireballs. The white added to the already potent impact of the purple that defined the Elders. The guys quickly rolled this way and that, getting themselves to safety.

I watched each one bolt behind a cell door and knew the floor was mine. The Hunters leapt to their feet and I had the satisfaction of watching them both swirl their hands in various motions and then look utterly confused when nothing happened. I felt their power come at me like a mosquito I could swat away, so I did.

Then they resorted to actually taking shots at me, shouting various threats as I batted away bolt after bolt of orange lightning. When the taller of the two reached for a cell door, I finally acted offensively. "You will not hurt them, any of them," I warned.

With a flick of my hand, he was thrown across the room. He landed in a crouch, but at least had the intelligence to look impressed. "You are not the same little girl who came here weeks ago," he said, his long white hair falling in his face.

"I am not the same girl period," I said, stretching my arms out in front of me and closing my fists. Each Hunter looked down to find their jacket bunched in my invisible hands. My arms rose and so did they, floating a foot off the ground.

I walked forward, and asked, "Where is Baleon?"

Neither spoke, their orange eyes flaring in revolt of my manipulation. Hunters were used to having the upper hand, always. Gaea had made them for that express purpose. But, they weren't supposed to use that against the very people they were meant to protect.

I shook my fists and threw them wide. The Hunters jolted in the air and then slammed against the hallway walls. The metal bars on the cell doors *clinged* and *clanged*, metal rattling.

"You don't seem to understand what's happening here, so let me make it clear," I said, tipping my head to the side as I stood a foot in front of them. "I am the end of this. I am the end of Julia's reign and your tyranny. You cannot stop me. Rhi cannot stop me. I can take whatever I want from either of you."

I stopped talking and focused on their power. I no longer saw them as blood, muscle, and bones and instead, saw the orange power glowing at their core. I reached out for the threads of that ball and slowly pulled them toward me. I didn't take their power, I didn't want it, but I wanted them to know I could.

I refocused to find stammering Hunters who reeked of fear.

"You aren't used to being the ones controlled, are you? Julia has you so convinced her thoughts are yours, you forget that you wear her collar and do her bidding. I am building a world where you make your own choices. You live where you want and do what you want. Your first choice is now. Either tell me where to find Baleon and do as I say, or find yourselves on the wrong end of this war. Because make no mistake, this is a war, and I will win."

I hadn't even asked them their names. It didn't matter right now.

I'm coming out. I heard Aidan and seconds later, he opened the cell door and joined me.

"Now is when you choose," I said. The two looked at each other and then back at me.

"Fine, we'll tell you, but it won't help. Rhi has him in his chambers. If Rhi has him, then Baleon is doomed. He is likely already broken and gone." The Hunter spoke as I allowed them to drift to the floor. Aidan and I walked forward as one unit.

Their collars. Break them, I said to him. Aidan smiled, a conspiratorial smirk confirming my idea was the right one.

I like it. If she can't find them, they can't rat us out, he responded.

Aidan approached the two Hunters and I fed him my power. It was the reverse of how things may have been intended, but I didn't care who did what. What mattered was we needed to win over these Hunters eventually, and they needed to have as much respect for Aidan as they did for me.

He reached out and grabbed the first Hunter's collar. At the same time, I thought to myself, *snap it in half*, and he did just that. Aidan's hands glowed bright blue and the metal bent and then ruptured under the pressure. The Hunter cried out, meaning more than just the collar had been broken in the process. I wondered how deep Julia's hold really went.

Aidan repeated the movement with the second Hunter, and the result was identical. The cell doors around us started to open and Rynna, Derreck, and Joran emerged. "Into the cell," I demanded, pointing to the room Joran had vacated.

The two Hunters went in without protest and I closed the door behind them, locking it. As soon as the lock clicked into place, I bolted toward Cole's door. I wrenched it open to find Bethany sitting on the floor, tears pouring down her face as my brother's head lay in her lap.

"He's barely breathing," she whispered.

"It's okay, B," I responded, struggling to speak myself. I knelt next to Cole and prayed healing a human was just like healing an Immortal. I felt Aidan's hands on my shoulders and knew we would not let my brother die. Not here. Not after all this.

So, I placed my hands on his chest and sent my magic into his system. I sought out every bruise, broken bone, area of constricted blood flow, and potential injury. Aidan was there with me, on the edges of my mind, reassuring me both verbally and physically as he fed me the excess power I needed to stay focused. When I could watch Cole's lungs fully inflate and his heart no longer struggled to pump, I finally pulled back. He wasn't entirely conscious, but I was afraid to do too much. I swayed on my knees and Aidan wrapped his arms around me from the back, pulling me into him.

Bethany looked at me, awestruck, then she reached down and smoothed Cole's hair out of his face as his eyes started to flutter open.

"You have to get him out of here, Bethany," I said. My voice shook as I watched Cole struggle back to full consciousness. "I need you to get him as far away from this as you can. Take him to Tragar, get him through the maze, and away from here. I need both of you away from here." I watched the uncertainty cross her features, but she locked it down in a hurry.

"I can. I can do that. I need someone to get me to Tragar, but I won't let anyone else hurt him, Amelia," she said. My strength had returned and I reached out, my pinky extended. She nodded and hooked it with her own. "Pinky swear," we both said together.

"I will take them to Tragar," Joran said from behind us. "I can get them there and meet you in Rhi's chambers. We will get Baleon together."

Micah appeared in the doorway of the cell, rubbing his wrists and stretching his shoulders. "I know where we need to go. Let Joran take them and I will lead us. I owe Rhi a visit after how well he treated us."

Cole still hadn't fully come to, so Joran scooped him up as if he weighed nothing at all. Bethany stood as well and yanked me into a strong hug. "Swear to me you're coming back, Ame. Swear to me I'll see you again. Both of you," she demanded. I felt her fingertips dig into my back muscles as she tucked her chin over my shoulder. I assumed she was looking at Aidan as she held onto me.

"Of course you'll see us again, Blondie," he said.

I squeezed her back and pulled away. "You will, Bethany, I promise. Nobody can touch this," I joked, forcing a smile and giving her a sassy look.

"Give 'em hell, girl. And then give 'em some more from your little human friend," she said with a wink.

The room fell silent as she sidestepped Micah without making eye contact and disappeared down the hall to follow Joran.

"Well, boys, I suppose it's time to slay the dragon, don't you think?" I asked, pulling my hands to my hips and rocking back on my heels.

"His fire is about to be put out," Aidan said with a smirk.

Micah followed with, "And then let's chop off his head so he never returns."

I couldn't have agreed more.

Chapter 43
Micah

Leaving Baleon was out of the question. None of us held back as we raced toward the Hunter quarters. I was afraid of what just a few days had done to the only father I'd ever known.

I hadn't even had time to process what Amelia did; blasting into the room with authority and then completely incapacitating two Hunters. I had watched through the small window in my cell door, the metal bars obstructing parts of my vision and making me question whether what I'd seen was actually real.

She and Aidan were behind me now, and with each step, I felt my power returning. The binds were gone and I would soon be able to fight at full strength. Derreck and Rynna brought up the rear of our pack, checking behind us continually.

So far, the other Hunters hadn't come for us. I didn't know why, but I wasn't asking questions. I wanted to get Bale and get out. I also wanted to understand why a part of me felt tied to Amelia in a way I never had before. I felt a deep need to protect her at all costs.

We came to another intersection of hallways and I peeked around the corner. There were no Hunters anywhere and that fact had me concerned. We continued and soon entered Hunter domain, moving as one silent unit. The last thing I expected was to have a door at the other end of the hallway open and Rhi emerge. He took slow steps, his head cocked to the side. He slowly developed a grin that felt gloating and menacing all at once.

"What do we have here?" he asked, sneering, his arms spread wide. "A ragtag group of Mages and one lowly AniMage polluting the bunch? You really shouldn't have bothered. I won't give him back to you." Rhi paused, his chin high as he leaned back. "I have waited a lifetime to do to him what I please. He is protected by no one now. His life isn't worth the blood splatter, though I will still relish in it."

I didn't hesitate. I threw everything I had at Rhi. I had no idea what I yelled at him, but I promised retribution for any of Baleon's pain. I shot quick blasts, waiting for the perfect time to strike, to use the secret Bale had shared only with me.

"If a Hunter comes at you and you truly fear for your life, Prince Mikail, do not hesitate. Aim for his eyes," he'd told me after he'd caught a group of Hunters toying with me in the halls. "A Hunter who cannot see cannot control the power inside him. Every race has a weakness and ours is the need to see. We must see the Immortal and the power inside them to determine how best to attack. If you destroy the Hunter's sight, you take his power." Baleon had drilled this knowledge into me over the years.

As I pelted Rhi with blast after blast, he laughed, shaking them off as if he were walking through a light rain. I knew I wouldn't actually hurt him, but I needed to distract him. The others had spread out around me, but Amelia stayed behind our half circle.

As Derreck and Rynna sent crackling balls of green and red power at Rhi, the stones around him crumbled. I took that moment to aim and send power I gathered from the deepest parts of my core at him. Unfortunately, at the last second, Rhi saw it and spun away. What was meant for his eyes hit the back of his shoulder. The leather disintegrated and blood poured from the wound. Threads of orange power built a web over the wound and Rhi hissed as it cauterized.

It wasn't until Amelia shoved through our ranks that the tides changed. I expected Aidan to hold her back, but he didn't. When we stopped attacking, he filled the gap in our line as she strode toward Rhi. Unflinching, she stared the Hunter down.

"Something is different about you, Keeper," he mused as he brushed at the burnt hole in his jacket. "Did the darkness finally steal your soul? I felt her there; ready to blot you out like a worthless piece of history. Just like your useless parents and good-for-nothing brother. Did she finally win?" he jeered.

Amelia's response shattered my reality entirely.

Chapter 44
Amelia

In one breath, he insulted the three people he shouldn't have. He took two of them from me and I had barely pulled the third from his clutches.

"Today is not your day, Rhi. Today is not the day you want to say things like that to me," I tried to warn him. All the while, I thought about who Gaea was and what she'd given me.

"No?" he asked, barking out a laugh. "I don't want to tell you how your mother groveled for you? How she begged for me to spare your life?" he taunted as he stepped forward.

Earth. My palms glowed white and with one quick movement, the walls around us shook. I cocked my head at Rhi as he regained his balance.

"She did nothing of the sort," I said, my tone intentionally goading him. "My mother saw you coming. She planned for you. She gave me power you couldn't even fathom. You fool. You let me live."

I took pleasure in his face flushing, in the set of his jaw and the way his shoulders rose as he leaned toward me. "What did you say?" he questioned, his threat obvious.

"You. Are. A. Fool," I enunciated. *Air.* I didn't even move. The air whipped into the room, a swirling mini tornado that whirled toward Rhi, blowing his long white hair in all directions. To his credit, he didn't move an inch. He actually looked amused. A small move of his hand and the air fell to nothing.

Suddenly, I was the one lifting into the air. I'd been here before. In Esmerelda's, I'd felt this same hold. It threatened to steal my breath. Shock hit with the realization it had never been Julia. All this time, it was Rhi doing the dirty work. The power had never been hers, just hers to control.

I never took my eyes off Rhi as his smile widened. I kept a straight face as Rhi flung me from side to side, always stopping before I actually hit the wall. Aidan was screaming in my head, but reacting would only make it worse. I let Rhi have his fun, keeping him just on the other side of actually hurting me. I had to stay focused.

After a few more tosses, I finally said, "Are you done?" Rhi's head jolted back. "I asked if you were done," I repeated. His brow furrowed as his hand moved to the left and I didn't follow. This time, it was my smile that grew as I slowly floated to the floor.

Get them back, Aidan. It was all I took the time to say and I heard them retreat. Not far, but far enough to keep themselves from being targeted by Rhi as he dealt with me.

Fire. It was a Hunter's toy, but today, it was mine to own. My hands moved quickly as I tossed flame after flame at Rhi, watching him dance and attempt a rebuttal. He leapt behind furniture and shot orange bursts at me. I slowly strode forward, ignoring the complaints and frustration from those behind me.

Put out his fire, Amelia. Let's end this. We've got your back.

Aidan's words were a light bulb in my mind. He'd said the same thing in the prison chamber. I needed to put Rhi's fire out. Of course.

Rhi started to lower his body into a crouch and I knew I had to stop him before he leapt at me. As quickly as the thought was there, he froze in place. I walked up to Rhi, slowly circling the Hunter who had been the source of so many of my nightmares.

"You know, you aren't invincible," I said nonchalantly. I paused and took a moment to enjoy my position. White smoke gathered around me and I was facing my archenemy, but my heart beat a steady pace.

"You think you are," I continued as I stood in front of him, eye level as he remained crouched. "You've done so much to so many. You've taken so much, and we have all lost more than we should have to you...but not anymore." I leaned in and looked him directly in the eyes. I let him take in the shining violet and the white star that burst from my pupils.

"I found her," I whispered. "Gaea gave me the tools to defeat you. You were never meant to be, and you will never be again."

Rhi's solar storm eyes narrowed, then widened as he took in the full weight of what I'd said. Just like Tragar and Joran, the doors in his mind unlocked and the memories flooded in. I saw it in his eyes, the way they widened and unfocused. In the drop of his jaw and the momentary loss of his precious control.

"No," he whispered, still looking dazed. "We were meant to rule. Lies! You've manipulated me somehow and these are nothing but lies!"

I had a moment's hesitation. I knew what came next. It was so clear in my mind, but I could not undo my next choice once it was made. Rhi continued to rail against me, refusing to acknowledge the truth I'd shown him.

So many times, I'd wished Rhi dead. I daydreamed of killing him in the worst ways possible. But after seeing the devastation of his wrath firsthand, and hearing Gaea's stories, now I just wanted him gone. I would not start the Immortals on a new path that looked just like the old one.

We will never be safe in a world where he lives, Amelia. Let me help you. You won't do this alone.

Aidan was everywhere at once. He physically stood behind me, ready to back my play, no matter what. He was in my mind, constantly reassuring me. His power ran alongside mine, a slow infiltration rippling through me and then merging into my own. We made the choice together to care for the Immortals Gaea put on this Earth. Rhi might be the first to die, but he would not be the last in our quest to right their world.

Be ready to refuel and heal me, Aidan. This will take everything I have.

Water. I grasped Rhi's face in my hands, calling the moisture from my own body and mixing it with the magic running through me. I poured every ounce of water I could into him. I doused his spirit with the cleansing combination and put out every flickering lick of power inside him. Then, I pulled. I looked into his eyes as I extracted every wet, ashen piece of his core out of his body and into mine.

I felt the drain immediately, my organs and tissues shrinking, along with my well of power. But, Aidan was there. He fed my soul and rehydrated my system.

I could taste the burnt, foul remnants of Rhi's magic, and I didn't want it. I didn't want the death and destruction that defined him. I took one hand away from Rhi's face and allowed the residue to flow through and out of me. It was black soot, a dirty rain falling from my palm and collecting on the ground in front of him.

To his credit, Rhi didn't make a sound. As I drained him of every ounce of power he'd ever had, he did nothing but stare into my eyes. When I felt the well run dry, I pulled my hand away, wiping it on my jeans. His eyes no longer burned bright. They were dim, brown, and empty. As his skin wrinkled and his body shrank before my eyes, he said nothing.

It was heady to know I finally stopped him. But it wasn't over yet. I took a deep breath as Aidan stepped to my side. I jolted, shocked, but relieved to see him there. Compassion radiated from him. He took my right hand, interlacing our fingers, then we faced Rhi together.

Air. I called again. This time, though, I called it to me. I reached my left hand toward Rhi and curled my fingers back, as if I were beckoning him to my side. I heard his forced exhale. He began to cough and I called again, this time with urgency. I would not draw this out. I would not do to him as he had done to others. In two heartbeats, Rhi collapsed to his knees and then the ground, his body devoid of oxygen.

Sprawled out, his white hair spread around him and his eyes utterly lifeless, Rhi was no longer a threat. He would not hurt anyone else ever again.

Chapter 45
Aidan

We stood over Rhi's body and it was surreal. We had killed a man. I knew it was a first for both Amelia and me, and that it had taken both of us. As she called the air from his lungs, she drew power from me in a steady stream. Whatever Gaea had done in our mating process provided me with what felt like an unending supply of power to provide to Amelia. Finally, I could protect her.

Micah, Joran, Rynna, and Derreck stepped to our side. Joran had joined them at some point and he looked at Amelia in awe.

"I heard what you said and I believed your words, but to watch this for myself…you are truly the one, Amelia," he said.

Amelia looked at him, the sadness of what we'd just done still lingering in her eyes. "This is only the beginning, Joran. We need to find Baleon, deal with the other Hunters here, and get to Julia. I need to know my brother and Bethany are safe and then…then, we'll figure out what the next step is."

I continued to send waves of reassurance and healing to Amelia. She felt calmer than I'd expected, but I had no idea what the repercussions, if any, would be from what she'd just been through.

"I must find Baleon. I cannot wait any longer. Rynna, Derreck, can you come with me? I don't know how much help he will need, but his wounds will be severe, I have no doubt. Amelia, I know you must continue on. Take Joran, he will help you handle the Hunters." Micah's urgency was felt by all, his concern for Baleon evident in his pained expression and tense posture.

"Go, Micah," I said. "And, please, go with him," I directed Derreck and Rynna, who looked uncertain about leaving us. "Clearly, we can handle ourselves. And, with Joran, we have a buffer. We'll come back as soon as we can to help."

The three took off toward the door Rhi came through, skirting his body without sparing him a glance.

Joran turned on his heel and we followed him back toward the main sections of the house. We moved quickly through the hallways, not caring who knew we were here.

"Where are they, Joran?" I asked, filling the silence as I worried about Amelia. She was lost in her own mind and I was trying to stay out of it.

"They are protecting the Queen. She is weak, but her hold is still there. As soon as she was alerted that you arrived, she gathered every Hunter in Cresthaven to guard her. She knows we are coming," Joran said. His strides were long, his thick boots echoing as they slapped the marble floors.

"Where are the Queen's chambers?" Amelia asked.

I only half-listened to Joran as I stared at Amelia.

What are you going to do? I asked her.

Don't worry, Aidan. I know what to do. I need you to trust me, though.

I was silent. I did trust her, but I didn't like this.

I trust you. Tell me what to do and I'll do it.

We approached the main entrance of the house, the largest gathering space available, and could see the wall of Hunters as we headed straight for them. Men and women, all with matching white hair, black ink, and leather jackets. Their eyes were a blaze of orange against their light brown skin. In contrast to their stark white hair, it looked like we were approaching a group of demons, ready to eat our souls.

"I need you both to stay here," Amelia finally said.

Joran stopped walking, immediately standing alongside the wall.

"What? No! Amelia, what are you doing? At least clue me in on the plan," I demanded.

She looked at me with utter patience. "Aidan, I asked you to trust me. This power…it's a lot. The more I use, the more I understand. I know I should be scared right now. I can see them. But, I'm not. I know what I'm here to do. I know I can keep them from hurting me and each other. I know I will convince them to listen, and that they will let me through. Julia is on the other side of that wall and I will get to her. I won't wait anymore. This has to end."

I looked into her bright eyes and watched the starburst around her pupil dilate and then reduce. The power fluctuations I felt in Amelia were everywhere—in her blood, her eyes, the air around us. Unable to stop myself, I grabbed both of her shoulders and pulled Amelia in for a hard kiss. It was the only place to put my frantic energy. It began with smashed mouths and ended in a needy exchange meant to remind her what she was walking away from.

"I will be fine, Aidan. I promise you. You and me, Montgomery. Always. Trust me to do this, and then follow me once I'm through. They'll let you." She was so sure; there was not a flicker of doubt in her eyes or her mind.

"Okay, doll. I trust you. I'll be here, and never far." I touched a finger to my temple and then kissed her forehead.

I let her walk away from me. I didn't tell her I loved her. She didn't say it either. That was something you said when you thought it was goodbye.

Chapter 46
Amelia

There had to be fifty Hunters staring at me as I walked toward them alone. I should have been scared. I knew that. But, I was focused. There were two things that needed to happen in order for me to get through that wall of Immortal ninjas without any of them, or me, getting hurt, and get to Julia.

I finally exited the hallway completely and the sound of my boots hitting the floor was the only thing I heard. They didn't speak, and neither did I. I walked out into the middle of the room, completely exposed, and lifted my hands as if I surrendered. Aidan didn't speak. I didn't hear him in my mind, or from where he stood, holding his breath while he watched this play out.

As I started to speak, I also focused. I had one true task to accomplish. I let my eyes wander across the swath of Hunters. Their eyes glowed, a swirl of orange, red, and yellow. Most held fireballs in their palms, ready to attack. The smirks and insults had already begun in response to my posture.

"I believe you already know who I am, but in case you don't, I am Amelia Bradbury. I am the daughter of Liana and Nathaniel Bradbury. I was born an Elder and I am the last of my kind," I said calmly. *Focus, Amelia.* I took a breath and slowly exhaled through my nose. The Hunters bordered on restless. There were murmurs between them and more than once, I heard Rhi's name.

"What you don't know is that I didn't ask for any of this. I didn't ask to be part of a prophecy. I didn't ask to have power stowed away in my soul that ultimately just wanted out of me and back to its original owner. I didn't want to be taken by the Queen, to find my fellow Immortal women chained to beds with their power bound and bodies abused. Yet, while I didn't ask for any of this, it still came to me. And with it, came the knowledge that you are among those I am bound to protect. I am no longer bound by this prophecy, I am bound by my own honor. I am bound by the choices I have made."

My hands started to tremble, the white smoke I kept inside too much to contain. My power had built during my speech and this was the moment I waited for.

"I am bound to you," I said, my voice rising as they looked at each other. "Each and every one of you is my cause, my family. I am bound to protect you and I won't have you bound to another," I finished. I clenched my hands into fists and threw them wide. In unison, I heard a chorus of high-pitched *tings* and then a continuous stream of clanging as their collars fell to the floor and bounced off one another.

"I went back to the castle with my mate, Aidan, the AniMage King, and we freed Gaea. Our Mother has returned to Earth. Think about her now and remember who you were. Remember your purpose and step aside. Allow me to end this once and for all." The words hardly sounded like me. I intentionally spoke formally to the Hunters, trying to connect to their sense of honor and respect.

I stood still and watched them. I saw the doors in their minds unlock. I heard their gasps. Those too young to remember Gaea were educated in hushed whispers. It wasn't long before the group split. Hunters stepped to the left and right, creating a path between them to the other side of the house.

I crossed the room and silently walked between them. Some watched with questioning stares. Others shed tears of guilt. I could feel it, and the ache reverberated through me. What shocked me most was the gratitude of the few who stepped forward, brought their fists to their hearts, and bowed their heads to me.

Once I passed through them, my steps quickened. I needed to get to Julia before anyone else got to me, but as I half-ran down the halls, doubt crept in.

Could I do it? I had killed Rhi. Could I kill her, too? I didn't know the answer.

Gaea, you said I could call on you. I don't know what to do. I don't know what's right.

My strides were even. The low glow of the sconces lit the hallway, leading me to the Queen. I would be there soon.

Show her the truth and allow her the choice. We are all accountable to the choices we make. The Fates will have it no other way.

Gaea's voice was soft and comforting in my mind. It enveloped me like a hug while strengthening my resolve.

I closed the last few yards to the Queen's chamber just as Aidan and Joran came around the final turn. Turning to him as I opened the door, I stepped halfway inside and connected my gaze to his.

Forgive me. Trust me.

It was all I allowed between us before I shut the door and used my magic to keep it that way.

I slipped through the suite of rooms, pulled to Queen Julia's bedroom. I knew where to find her. I knew she would be in a regal bed with four posts and a mountain of pillows.

I walked through the doorway. Just as I crossed, I heard a small voice. "I knew it would be you. I thought it might be Mikail, but he was never strong enough. No, I knew it would be you." Julia's voice was faint. If it weren't for my heightened hearing, I would have missed her statement entirely.

I'd guessed right. The four-poster bed was stacked with pillows, but the frail woman situated between them was not the regal Queen I'd remembered. Her blonde hair was silver, leaning toward white. Her icy eyes were dull, like a calm patch of ocean water. Paper-thin skin with crisscrossing light blue veins sagged from her face. She had aged more years than I could comprehend.

I walked to the side of the bed and used my power to bring a chair to me. I sat down at an angle where we could see each other and continued to look around the room. My eyes were drawn to my mother's cuff, which sat on a shelf just five feet from me. My anger boiled and I turned to stare at the Queen.

"I wonder if you knew this day would come?" I asked. "Did you understand what you were doing couldn't last forever? Did you realize you could never fulfill your ridiculous plans?"

"You petulant child. You understand nothing. You have no idea what I gave—" A fit of coughing interrupted her tirade.

Show her the truth. That's what Gaea had said.

I knew what I needed and only Gaea's power could give it to me. As I focused on finding it, I responded to Julia.

"I do. I can see it plainly. You gave up yourself. It was never really you controlling me. We assumed you put the collars on the Hunters to control them, to see through their eyes and force their compliance. How long has it been since you've been able to actually hurt anyone? How long has Rhi done all your dirty work?"

Her smile was almost proud, but then she laughed. A dry, brittle sound came from her stretched smile, making me wonder if the corners of her mouth would crack and crumble. "There is so much about this world you do not understand," she said. Somehow, Julia found condescension even in this state.

"Is there?" I asked. I found what I was looking for. I held up a hand and a white orb appeared. It brightened as I sent the orb through the air between us and it hovered just in front of her. When the orb dimmed, the scenes began. Her smile remained as she saw who they featured.

Cane in the halls of the castle, sneaking kisses from Julia.
Cane with Rhi in the training yard.

Cane with other women in the stables and their beds.

Julia eyes were round, her shock apparent.

Then, the conversation began between Cane and Rhi.

"Do you really think we can do this?" Rhi asked his brother.

"Of course. She's so weak and gullible. She'll do anything I say. We'll marry, I'll be King, and then she'll mysteriously meet her end." The two laughed, maniacal deep roars that ended as Cane said, "I must go entertain the witch. Wish me luck, brother."

The scene faded. "You lie," she whispered. "You lie to taint his memory and I will not have it!" For the first time, I saw red creep across her eyes. Only this time, it stopped midway and then receded. Julia labored to breathe and I had to hold back from helping her. There was one last thing she needed to know.

"I am not lying, Julia. I had no idea what the orb would show you. All I know is Gaea told me to show you the truth, and so I did. Do you remember Mother Earth, the Goddess who created you?" I spoke slowly and clearly to ensure Julia heard every word.

Her eyes smashed closed and then darted around beneath the lids. Her head started to slowly move back and forth, speeding up until she threw it right and then left.

"NOOOOOOOOOOOOOOO!" she howled as she bolted upright in the bed. Her emotion was everywhere at once. I choked on the pain and the hate she let out as she continued to scream in agony, her heart breaking all over again for reasons she never expected. I should not have felt her emotions so clearly, but I couldn't turn it off, or down. I couldn't stop the torrent of suffering she'd never understood until now.

I stood, intending to try to calm her. I reached for Julia and at the same moment, she shot a blast of red fire at me. It barely left her hand before I absorbed it and without thought, latched onto the source. Her power was a single thread inside her and that shot had taken most of what remained.

"This is how it has to be. You have to be stopped completely," I said. Then, I pulled. It was effortless. The thread was tethered to nothing. There was nothing in Julia's core, no true soul to speak of, and the power came easily into me. I turned my opposite palm up and allowed the power to exit, dissolving into a thin mist that dissipated into the air.

She watched it all in silence. With empty eyes, she watched me take what was left, the very essence of what she believed in, and said nothing.

We stared at each other for a few long minutes.

Finally, I said, "There are people outside who want to see you. They want to know this is over."

Before I went for the door, I walked around the bed and snatched the cuff from the shelf. "And this, is mine." I snapped the cuff over my forearm, immediately comforted by my mother's gift. With the Keeper gone, it did nothing, and for that, I was grateful.

I took two steps toward the door, wanting to open it myself and reassure Aidan I was fine in person when she said, "It is indeed over." The resignation in her tone spun me around just in time to see Julia, the covers down, a small dagger in her hand.

"The very same dagger that started this will end it. Fitting, don't you think?" she asked. I stared at her, stupefied and unable to react as she gave me a sad smile and drove the dagger she'd used to kill Lavignia into her stomach.

The sight of blood got my attention and I almost ripped the door from its hinges to get it open. Aidan, Micah, and Rynna were the first in the room. Aidan came to me and pulled me to him, forcing my eyes away from her as I cried.

Micah and Rynna took opposite sides of the bed. Blood poured from Julia's stomach and neither made a move to magically assist her. Instead, each one took one of her hands and they began to sing, the two a perfect harmony.

She plucked the sun from the sky,
She borrowed the moon for one night,
She looked down at this place,
And knew the timing was right.

She poured drops from the ocean,
Breathed fire from the core,
She exhaled her breath,
Dug her hands into the soil.

She gave of herself,
It flowed freely within,
But without her love and light,
Our souls will grow dim.

The keepers of men,
Caretakers of fur and fin,
Sworn protectors,
Guardians of all of them.

Her light shines bright,
We are never alone,
We need only look in,
To finally be home.

Before they could finish the last stanza, the light of life left her eyes and she was gone.

"Go home, Mother," Micah said, his voice quivering.

"Let peace finally be with you, sister," Rynna whispered.

Chapter 47
Amelia

One month later...

We were in the library, the place that had become our sanctuary since Julia's death. The Hunters still avoided it and Tragar was a fountain of information about what life had been like when Gaea was still revered. We spent a lot of time listening not only to him, but anyone who wanted to share with us. Every memory taught us something new about who we were—to each other and the earth.

Aidan and I sat across from Cole and Bethany. She had done her duty taking him back to the cabin after Joran got them to Tragar. We sent Joran for them as soon as we could and they've both stayed at Cresthaven with us since. They were somewhat inseparable, actually, which I found strange considering Cole had always referred to Bethany as a princess and she seemed to annoy him to no end. Even now, he was rolling his eyes as she chattered on about requesting some southern food from the Hunters who chose to remain cooks.

Cole and I had many conversations prior to today about me trying to give him his Mage power back. I was certain I could do it, but he continued to hesitate. I thought we were here to finally get on with it.

My knee bounced up and down, the anxiety and excitement of the possibility churning through me. Aidan reached out and brushed his fingertips over my shoulder. He fed calm energy into me, which was typically unnecessary. But this was my brother we were talking about. As my knee stilled, he shot me a wink, and I jabbed him in the side to remind him he shouldn't be so cocky all the time.

If cocky is code for right, then fine, he whispered in my mind.

I rolled my eyes and refocused on Cole, but he was watching Bethany, a small smile playing at his lips. She stopped talking and I watched her take in the full weight of his stare. Her cheeks flushed and I knew what that secretive smile meant before either of them said a word.

"No way!" I exclaimed. Shock and elation hit in equal measures as Aidan laughed at my outburst. Cole lifted his arm and draped it across Bethany's shoulders.

"Way," he responded, smirking as both eyebrows shot up and down.

This time, we all laughed. "Tell me everything," I demanded. Realizing what I'd just asked for, I immediately backtracked. "No, not everything, just how and when this all happened! What happened to princesses and dumb as dirt goobers?"

Cole looked down at Bethany and mouthed "goober" at her. Then, he gave her a modified version of the look he used to reserve for me. The one that said I had better start explaining or apologizing.

He didn't get a chance to speak before she swatted at his chest, and said, "Oh, come off it, Cole. Think of it like recess. I just threw the ball at your head, so clearly I like you." She grinned, and he shook his head.

"I may have lost my damn mind, Ame, that's what happened," he said. That got him a shove, but he dropped his arm down and locked her to his side. "Will you just behave?" he asked.

"Never!" she said, her voice muffled from her face being shoved into his chest.

"Okay, cut it out, you're bordering on gross," I said. "Really, though, when did this happen?" I settled back into the couch and tucked myself next to Aidan.

"You may as well spill," Aidan interjected. "She won't let this go."

I poked him in the ribs, but never took my eyes off my brother and my best friend.

"I think in some ways it's been happening all along, we just didn't realize it," Cole said.

"But, really, it started when we came back from Cresthaven," Bethany continued. "I needed someone and so did he, for different reasons, obviously. The more we talked, the more we realized we already knew a lot about each other and we shared some common interests."

This time, it was Aidan who choked on his surprise. "Like what?" he spat out.

"Well, Mr. Negative Ned, we both care about kids and want to help them. Back in Mississippi, I used to do Big Brothers, Big Sisters and I've always admired what Cole built with his gym. And I already told you about my

Kenpo training, so Cole's MMA obsession is something I get. And we both care about you fools," she said.

"But, most importantly," Cole interjected while Bethany continued to give Aidan the eye, "we realized we both needed a little normalcy. We want calm. We want a chance to really get to know each other. I want to take Bethany on an actual date."

"You do?" she squeaked out, sitting taller in her seat to peck a kiss to his cheek.

"Wait," I said as his words clicked into place. "That means…" I trailed off, not wanting to jinx myself if it weren't true.

"We have to go," Cole confirmed. "We want to go back home to Brighton."

"So you can try out a normal life," I reiterated, internally laughing at the irony. There was a time normalcy was all I wanted. Now, here I was, trying to bring together what was left of an Immortal race that didn't trust me or each other.

Aidan squeezed my shoulder and I looked up at him, already knowing we were on the same page.

"You deserve normal, both of you. But, Cole, are you sure you don't want any of your power back? I know I can do it. I don't want to leave you unprotected." I gnawed at my lip, my worry already shouting "what ifs" in my mind.

"I don't actually," he said. "I want to go back to Brighton. I want to run my gym and give kids a role model they can trust. Bethany helped me see that the power didn't define who I was, and she's right." He smiled at Bethany, and they exchanged knowing looks. "I don't need power to be whole, Ame. We don't have to worry about being attacked anymore. You're a badass, and I don't think anyone wants to mess with the badass's big brother." My brother looked utterly at peace with his decision.

"Okay. So you guys are going home, to be together. Wow," I said, still wrapping my mind around it all. I sat up and then stood, gesturing to Bethany. "Get over here," I demanded as tears threatened.

As soon as Bethany was close enough, I grabbed her in a huge hug. "I love you, girl," I whispered in her ear. "I'll miss you."

She smelled like vanilla. It brought back so many memories of days before life got complicated and we were just two girls sharing their first apartment. Bethany pulled away, putting one hand on each of my cheeks. "I will love you forever, Ame, but I have got to get the hell out of here."

We stared at each other for a quick second and then burst into laughter. I would never be able to fill the hole she'd leave, but that's what friends do. You have to let go sometimes.

I felt a hand lightly shoving me out of the way. Aidan pushed through and snagged Bethany in a hug as well. "He doesn't understand how much trouble you can be, Blondie, but he'll know soon enough," he said, pulling her ponytail. She swatted him away and stood next to Cole. It already looked right as he wrapped an arm around her waist.

"Will you talk to Micah?" I had to ask. I thought his absence lately had to do with everything we had in motion, but realized now he knew what I had been oblivious to.

Bethany and Cole looked at each other. "I did," Cole said quietly. "He understands as much as he can. We don't know where this will go, but we want to try."

I struggled to know one heart had to break in order to make another whole, but Bethany had been through too much to be tied to an Immortal. I saw that clearly. I only hoped Micah was okay.

"Then you should go, and know that we're happy for you," I said, meaning every word.

Aidan reached out and pulled Cole in for one of their bro hugs before I was enveloped in a traditional Cole bear hug. It was decided they would leave in the next few days.

I was becoming more and more accustomed to the fact that nothing ever stayed the same. We were all in a state of motion that made standing still impossible. Life just didn't allow for that kind of complacency, even when you wished like hell it would.

It had been hours. A parade of people came in and out of Cresthaven wanting to meet Micah, Aidan, and me. They wanted to confirm what had spread like wildfire through the Immortal world. Queen Julia was dead. Rhi was dead. We hadn't decided the best way to broach the topic of Gaea, and it didn't feel right to sporadically do it with those in attendance, so we sat and we listened.

A dull throb started at my temples. I didn't mind people, but only for so long. I wasn't built for this. Aidan's hands came to my shoulders and I relaxed into his slow massage, appreciating that he instinctively understood what I needed. There were still days I wanted to throttle him for anticipating my arguments and jumping ahead of our conversations before I had the chance to say the things in my head, but every relationship was a constant work in progress.

I was fairly certain he didn't appreciate my constant second-guessing of our plans and my strings of questions with no answers. I also knew he struggled with being here. He wanted the freedom of the forest. He wanted to be out with the AniMages, finding those who were still hiding and unaware they could return. That's where I wanted him to be, but right now, we had to win over the more influential Immortals and ensure they understood what we were trying to build.

I looked across the table at Micah.

Is it over yet? I asked.

Be patient, Amelia, Micah scolded, not for the first time. *These people have waited a long time for this.*

He was right. I knew he was. And he played the part of the royal perfectly. Smiling and nodding, complimenting when I would have said something snarky.

I need a break. Like now. He gave me a quick glare, but then nodded, making some announcement that Aidan and I were needed in another part of the house.

I smiled, truly grateful for the reprieve. As soon as we closed the side door behind us, we ran, laughing and gloating over our quick bit of freedom.

We slowed to a walk and Aidan pulled me into a dark room. I leaned against the door, his hands in my hair and his mouth on mine. Over the last month, so much had changed. We finally had quiet time together. We finally had late nights in the same bed. We shared dreams and made memories. We gave and took from each other, finding connections in ways I had only dreamed about. I hadn't known what to expect, but as he generally was, Aidan was patient and tender. Every day with him stirred new feelings and intense emotions. I couldn't imagine a life without him.

As Aidan kissed his way up my neck, it dawned on me. He gave to me all the time, but too often, I took. We were here, inside Cresthaven, because I believed this was where I was supposed to be. But it wasn't.

I gently nudged Aidan's chest and as we separated, my will wavered against his smoky stare. His eyes devoured me in a way that made me melt, but I shook my head slightly. "Aidan, we have to get back. There's something I have to do."

He glowered down at me. "We're in the middle of doing something," he said, his tone seductive and sulking all at once.

"You're going to like this," I said, lifting to my tiptoes to press a kiss to his scowling mouth. "Trust me."

"I sincerely doubt anything taking me out of this room is going to be better than what was about to happen in it," he said, grumbling.

I rolled my eyes and pulled him by both hands out into the hall back toward Micah. I got lucky. He came out of the main room as we approached and I directed him to a small table in the hall.

Aidan stood next to me, pelting me with silent questions I refused to answer. We had been able to develop some small shields against sharing every one of our thoughts, and these I kept to myself.

"Amelia, there are so many things that need done. You wanted out and I let you out. What do you need now?" I let Micah's frustration roll off me.

"You hit it on the head, Micah. You're great at all of this," I waved my hand around, "pomp and circumstance. You know how to deal with everything they need, even when they don't know they need it. I'm terrible at it. But, you're the royal. I'm the Elder. He's the AniMage King. We don't belong here. This is your kingdom, not mine."

Micah stared at me curiously. "You aren't making any sense, Amelia."

I laughed, the giddiness I felt bubbling up. "Gaea said I was no longer bound by the prophecy. So, what I'm saying is, I will not rule them all. You will." I paused, letting that sink in. He leaned in like he hadn't heard me correctly.

"Elders were never meant to rule," I said, trying a different angle. "I have a role, but this isn't it. And Aidan needs to be with his people. You and I are connected. You don't need me here. Maybe for a little while so we can get people to understand what we're doing, but we won't stay here long term. These are your people, Micah. This is your house. You are the King of the Immortals."

Aidan's shock was just as palpable as Micah's. Even more so when Micah yanked me in for a hug. "Thank you," he whispered.

"You have no idea how happy I am to do it." I laughed as he released me.

I turned to look at Aidan.

You amaze me, he said.

A girl's got to keep you on your toes, Montgomery, I returned with a grin.

Epilogue
Micah

We were in the grand ballroom. I stood at the center of a raised platform built by the Hunters. Amelia and Aidan were on my left and my Aunt Ryannon and Derreck on my right. We faced a crowd of a few hundred. Immortals of all races stared back at me, all in one room. They looked slightly wary of each other, and yet, they were here.

I searched the crowd and found Elias, Nell, and their children, who had awoken one day as babies instead of kittens. Amelia insisted magic lived within them, we just hadn't found a way to activate it yet. She was on a mission to solve the puzzle my mother couldn't. She and Aidan wanted to go out and search for the Immortals still in hiding. She believed there were more out there than we thought.

Joran was there as well, his head held high as he stood among the Hunters who had re-pledged themselves to the Clair line. No one would be forced into servitude again, and each Hunter had been given the choice to stay or go. Some chose to go, and I wished them well. Joran stayed, as did many others. Baleon stood close to the stage, always my second and never far from me. He was ever vigilant. Tragar stood close to Bale, as far from the rest of the Hunters as he could get. He had ink on his cheek, and was wearing a big grin.

My eyes continued, landing on Willow, the lovely blond healer who helped me after we escaped Cresthaven. She smiled as my gaze lingered and I forced myself to leave my eyes on her for a moment longer, bringing a small smile to my lips. The hole Bethany left was still there and gaping, but my head understood why she hadn't chosen me. My heart just needed to get with the program.

Bethany had come to me. It was the first time I'd seen her where she hadn't run in the other direction. Cole had already told me they were leaving and as I watched her walk toward me, I could see her debate between a fake smile and the truth. It actually made me feel better when she let the sadness in her eyes remain. It told me what we'd had was real. Before she could speak, I did.

"I don't blame you for leaving, Bethany," I said, relishing in her surprised expression. "This isn't your world and it isn't your fight. But know I would have fought for you. I would have made a place for you. I would have loved you had you stayed."

Without thinking, I reached a hand toward her, but Bethany sidestepped it, and with a small shake of her head, reminded me she was no longer mine to touch.

"I know this probably felt like it came out of nowhere for you, but I hope you understand I never saw it coming either. Things changed when I left Derreck's and I realized, just like all of you, I have choices of my own," she spoke quickly, but firmly. "I'm not the girl you met at

Brighton Community College, and I understand what we could have been doesn't matter anymore. You made choices and now, so have I."

I swallowed down words that no longer mattered and nodded. When I didn't speak, Bethany turned to walk away, but then stopped. She looked at me from over one shoulder, a small smile playing at her lips. "You chose them and you will be the best King these people have ever had, Prince Mikail. There are a lot of things I don't understand about what's happened here, but I know that." I could only stare after her as she walked away.

"Mikail," Aunt Ryannon whispered, cutting off a memory I couldn't decide whether I wanted to keep, "it is time."

I turned to her, grasped her hand, and brought it to my lips. "Thank you. Thank you for making me a part of this and being here today," I said. Her dark eyes filled with tears.

"Don't cry, Aunt," I said, feeling guilty.

She shook her head. "Mikail, these are tears of pride. I am proud of you. You are a good man and you will make a great King." Her words caused a lump in my throat. It was the first time I'd heard someone say they were proud of me.

Amelia stepped up, her hands in the air as she quieted the crowd. She was truly a vision in a deep purple dress fit for an Elder. She allowed her power to flow freely and her eyes had the white starburst in the center. Aidan stood just behind her, in a tailored black suit similar to mine.

"Hello, everyone," she said. Her voice caught as her nerves showed through. Amelia truly hated being this visible. I held back a chuckle.

"We are going to get right to the heart of things. We've spoken to most of you in person and explained our goals. We want all of our people to be free. Free to live, free to marry, free to do as they want. We hope to re-establish the original castle and lands to their former glory, and to understand more about our history and purpose on this planet. We are obviously different from humans, and we have an obligation to use our gifts for good."

Various groups in the audience started clapping, especially those who already regained their memories and fully understood our path. None of us could stop from looking at each other, grins breaking out all over the stage.

Amelia held up a hand again and they quieted.

"Many of you believed this day would come. You knew of the prophecy and you believed in it—in me. I'm not going anywhere. I will be a part of the rebuilding of our people and our culture, but I am no Queen," she said.

The room broke out in hushed murmurs, and my heart rate increased.

"When we began," Amelia continued, acting oblivious, "there was a purpose to the royal family and the Elders being separate. That purpose was to keep those who were tied to the lifeblood of our people separate from those who needed to make decisions about politics and how we sustained our day-to-day lives. I believe that the balance is still needed. I am your heart, but Prince Mikail is your mind. He is rational, he is trained in how to run a kingdom and rule a people. He sees your needs where I see your wants. We are two halves of a whole, and because of that, I rescind my prophesied right to the crown and put it in the rightful hands of Prince Mikail."

Aunt Ryannon stepped between Amelia and me, holding a pillow with a thin, silver crown sitting upon it. As Amelia took the crown, I crouched so she could put it on my head. A voice rang out from the back of the room.

"At last, decisions are made for the right reasons. It took children to bring peace, and it will take children to bring life." The old woman with long silver hair and a one-shouldered gown of deep green stood just inside the door. A white light glowed around her and two tall men stood on either side of her. Both with bright white hair, one with dark eyes, and the other light.

"Gaea," Aidan said quietly as Amelia moved to his side.

The crowd parted and she walked through, the two men just a step behind her. She looked up at the stage and then floated to land in front of me.

"Prince Mikail, I am Gaea. They often call me Mother Earth." She winked at Amelia and Aidan, who held conspiratorial smirks.

"Welcome to Cresthaven, Gaea," I said, trying to keep the shake from my voice.

She smiled. "I have been here before, many times, but thank you, Mikail."

Aunt Ryannon still held the crown and with a nod from Gaea, she used her shaking hands to put it on my head.

Gaea turned to face the crowd. Making a few hand motions, she brought her two fists together and then burst them apart, her arms flying wide as her head dropped back. It looked and sounded like lightning struck the center of the room as a bright flash blinded us all momentarily and the ground shook. She turned to me and winked again. "This will make it easier," she whispered.

"Now," she said loudly, quieting the crowd with a clap of her hands. "Over the next few minutes, your minds will clear. You will have access to memories you never knew you lost. You are likely older than you thought. You may have done things you don't remember. But, it is time to know who you are and who you can be. I put you on this earth to protect it. You are the guardians of everything I hold dear. I made this sanctuary as a haven for animals and humans alike.

"Mages, you are here to influence and shape the humans. To guide them to the right choices. You could say you are their guardian angels, because you are meant to act without your interference being known. AniMages, you are to do the same for the animals. You work with the Mages to ensure the humans do not overtake this world and destroy the beauty I've created. Hunters, your place has always been the protector of the rest. You keep the peace, you interfere when our presence is known, and you keep those who would harm the Immortals under control.

"No one of you is more or less important than the others," she continued. "That is the truth you forgot once. You are all necessary if you are to succeed. But, you are individuals and require guidance. The choices made today were the right ones.

"Mikail is your rightful King," Gaea said. "He leads the Mages and oversees you on all. His job is to keep you on track and to deal with the day-to-day necessities. He will also appoint the next Hunter leader."

"Amelia is your Elder, the keeper of my power and will." Gaea paused to give Amelia a fond smile. "Eventually, she will be joined by others, but for now, she is as close to me as you will get. Aidan will take his place as the head of AniMages. He will rebuild a race that needs attention after the devastation wrought upon it."

Aidan stood tall and was rewarded with a smile from Gaea before she turned back to the silent audience.

"These three have done what I failed to do when I created you. They are tied together and their futures depend on each other. Their choices, their lives—and for two—their hearts. Hear me when I tell you that you will not get another chance. I created you and I will destroy you. I am a Goddess and that is within my rights."

As the crowd stared, clearly processing her words and their own memories, Gaea focused on Amelia. "I gave you the power you needed to bring us to this place and you made every right decision, Amelia. But, for you to truly be an Elder, and to walk among your people as one of them, you cannot keep my gift," she said. A look of panic crossed Amelia's face.

"Don't fear, child," Gaea reassured her. "As an Elder, you will always be connected to me. The strings that tie you to my heart will never be undone. I will take the Goddess power from you now and leave you the strongest Elder my children have ever known. You are formidable, but you are still one of them. Do you understand?"

Amelia's features relaxed and she nodded. Gaea reached out, laying a hand on Amelia's cheek. With a graze of her thumb, Amelia's power flared and sent a bright white streak into the air. Gaea waved a hand absently and it disintegrated.

"There, it is done," she said.

"And you, Aidan," she continued. "You are the rightful King of AniMages. Your father was a great man and your mother a strong-willed, yet gentle woman. You will honor their memory and you will bring your people together. Trust your wolf and your mate. They will not steer you wrong."

Aidan tipped his head to her in thanks.

"Mikail, never forget where you came from," she said, coming back to me. "But know you are phoenix rising from the ashes of your parents. They are gone and have left you to flourish on your own. Burn bright and call our people home." I was speechless, unable to even acknowledge the words that had struck my soul.

"Your power is my gift, but your obligations have been your choice," Gaea said to all of us, her voice carrying across the room. "You will be tempted by so many things. Others will come for what is yours. It is bound to happen. But you are strong. Focus on the children and use what I have given you. When the time comes, go back to our homelands and start anew. It is where you began and where you belong."

We nodded, solemn in our commitment.

Gaea let her eyes linger on each one of us for a second longer, and then she was gone—no flash of light and without a sound.

As we looked out over our people, we knew our story was only beginning.

We hadn't started this. We hadn't been the ones to make the choices that led to where we were. But we had the ability to change every day going forward.

We were bound by nothing but the promises we made to Gaea, and ourselves.

A note from the author

Amelia and Aidan's story arc is complete and I hope you feel fulfilled with the ending of this segment of the series. But, as you've likely noticed, I left doors open and questions unanswered at the end of Bound by Prophecy.

When I wrote Bound by Duty, I intended for this to be a trilogy. It was never supposed to go past three books. But, as is typical with the Muse, she knew what I didn't (along with quite a few of my friends). This world needs to continue. These characters must carry on. And so, the Bound Series will not end with Bound by Prophecy.

I can't tell you how many books there will be. All I know is this story isn't finished, and I'm looking forward to continue exploring this world. Buckle up, this will be fun!

Acknowledgements

Abe – This one was particularly brutal, wasn't it? But you stuck with me, like you always do. And you pulled me from the creative abyss so many times, reminding me to take care of myself, and remember my life outside the writing cave. Your support means more to me than I can describe. I love you so.

Kristin – You knew how important this book was to me and even in the madness of your own life, gave it so much of your time and attention. As always, you saw through my first draft attempts and asked all the right questions to get me to the heart of the real story. I've said it before and I'll probably never stop saying it, you're so much of the reason I've made it this far. Thank you for everything.

Rachel Higginson – The past six months have been such a huge time of "What am I trying to do here?" introspection for me, and you've been there for every random question, every gut check, every "please talk me off the ledge" moment. I made some big decisions about what I want from this career and your mentorship was invaluable. There aren't enough thank-you's in the universe to tell you what it means to me.

Regan – You are truly the yin to my yang, my friend. I don't know how many brainstorming sessions we had over the time I was writing this book, but you saved me from my own mind more times than I can count. I love every part of your whirling dervish personality.

The Rebel Writers – This was a crazy time for so many of us. So much happened from the time I published Spells until now. One thing stood out to me amongst it all - even when the words were hard to find, and there was no time, and it all seemed to be going to hell, we were all there. We did it together. Let's not stop doing that.

My street teams (both the Rebels and the Storm Troopers) – So much happens behind the scenes. You let me bounce ideas, you celebrate my wins and you share my dreams with your friends and the world at large. You give me a place where I know I am talking to passionate readers, intelligent women and kind souls. Thank you for all of your efforts and know that I deeply appreciate each of you.

And, no acknowledgement would be complete without a massive, humungous, asteroid-sized THANK YOU to every blogger, vlogger, and/or instagrammer out there who has talked about this series. Your passion for books is contagious and without it, authors of all kinds would suffer. Each post, tweet, comment, like or share is an affirmation that I did my job and my story touched you somehow. I couldn't do this without you.

About the Author

Stormy Smith calls Iowa's capital home now, but was raised in a tiny town in the Southeast corner of the state. She grew to love books honestly, having a mom that read voraciously and instilled that same love in her. She knew quickly that stories of fantasy were her favorite, and even as an adult gravitates toward paranormal stories in any form.

Writing a book had never been an aspiration, but suddenly the story was there and couldn't be stopped. When she isn't working on, or thinking about, her books, Stormy's favorite places include bar patios, live music shows, her yoga mat or anywhere she can relax with her husband or girlfriends.

Other titles by Stormy Smith
Bound by Duty (Book one in the Bound series)
Bound by Spells (Book two in the Bound series)

Where you can find me
If you'd like to be alerted when my next book will release, sign up for my mailing list at http://eepurl.com/WLlq1. I promise, you will *only* get new release emails. Pinky swear.

Website: http://www.stormysmith.com
Facebook: http://www.facebook.com/authorstormysmith
Twitter: @stormysmith

Instagram: @stormysmith
Goodreads: http://www.goodreads.com/stormysmith
Email: authorstormysmith@gmail.com

A note about reviews

Whether you loved it, hated it or were completely ambivalent, your review will help others decide if they would like to read my book. Please consider leaving just a few words on the site you purchased from and/or Goodreads. Every review matters and I read them all.

www.ingramcontent.com/pod-product-compliance
Lightning Source LLC
Chambersburg PA
CBHW030658120726
47905CB00001B/264